Louis K. Lowy is a former firefighter with the City of Hialeah, Florida. He is the author of three novels, *Die Laughing*, a humorously dark science fiction adventure set in the 1950s, *Pedal*, an inspirational tale of a laid-off 49-year-old music teacher fighting to reclaim her life back through bicycle racing, and the award winning *To Dream: Anatomy of a Humachine I*, the story of an artificial intelligence struggling to find his humanity.

Lowy is the recipient of a State of Florida Individual Artist Fellowship and an alumnus of Florida International University's creative writing program. He lives in South Florida with his wife, Carol, and their spoiled Yorkie, KC. Their son and daughter reside on the west coast.

Visit Louis on his website: www.louisklowy.com and on Facebook, Twitter, and Instagram.

D1191055

Other Louis K Lowy titles published by IFWG Publishing International

Die Laughing
Pedal
To Dream (Book 1, Diary of a Humachine)

THE SECOND LIFE OF EDDIE COYNE

by
Louis K Lowy

The Second Life of Eddie Coyne

All Rights Reserved

ISBN-13: 978-1-925759-80-8

Copyright ©2019 Louis K Lowy

V1.0

Printed in Palatino Linotype and Arno Pro.

IFWG Publishing International
Melbourne

www.ifwgpublishing.com

Acknowledgements

Writing is rarely an individual effort. Many thanks to John Dufresne, and the Friday Night Writers for their unwavering critiques; Michael Gavaghen, for his gambling acumen; Garry Kravit, for all things aerial; Corey Ginsberg, Fabienne Josaphat-Merritt, Karen Kravit, Kathy Curtin, and Jan Becker for their insights; Aralis Bloise, Marjory Hamilton and Katherine Lowy for their artistic eyes; and Chris Lowy for his counsel. Extra thanks to IFWG Publishing; particularly Gerry Huntman, Elizabeth Lang, and my editor, Maria Kelly.

To Carol, Chris, and Katie, for giving me a wonderful first life.

Chapter One

Eddie Coyne clicked the racing website's *Information & Stats* dropdown menu. As he had done a thousand times, he squeezed his chin twice for luck, then clicked on the *Results* tab. He scrolled past the two local racetracks closed for the season, *Calder* and *Gulfstream Park,* and clicked on *Hialeah Park.* Outside his cramped study, he heard Carly scolding their six-year-old, Ben.

"Let's go, Bennie. Your game starts in half an hour!"

The *Hialeah Park* page opened. Though Eddie had been there the day before, he studied the results. Reliving losses was his personal form of penance — or torture — he never could tell.

"I'm not kidding, Ben. Get off the video game and let's go."

"Almost done, Mom."

Eddie's jaw tightened. He glanced at the picture hanging above his computer: Carly and Ben and himself at Christmas three-years ago, happy and shiny. Before the arguments, the money pressure, the string of rotten luck and the whiskey pick-me-ups. Before he was fired from his job over a lousy misunderstanding. Of course, that was after his last big win, when he didn't give a shit about losing a crummy accountant's position. He scratched his two-day-old whiskers, glanced around his grubby office and once again at the family portrait. Little was happy and nothing was shiny anymore.

"Is your athletic cup on?" Eddie heard Carly say.

"I'm not wearing that thing!"

"Yes you are, mister."

Eddie clicked on the *Today's Races* page. He studied the line-up and compared them to the check-marked, starred, and circled *Daily Racing Form* lying open-faced on his desktop. Eddie compared that with his printouts of the AQHA speed index and his Excel charts of past performances. He scribbled an entry in a notepad that was lying next to the *Daily Racing Form*. He slipped the notepad into his shirt pocket.

"Turn the video game off and put on the cup!"

"I'm not putting that thing on!"

Eddie narrowed his eyes at the closed office door as if it were Carly and Ben. *Shut up and let me concentrate...please?* He clicked on weather.com and eyed the forecast for Hialeah, FL, USA. 82° F, wind SE 12 mph, humidity 75%, Afternoon Thundershowers. He checked the *Daily Racing Form's* Tomlinson ratings—previous results for each horse under various weather conditions. He smiled and starred and circled the name of a horse that was scheduled to race at Hialeah Park. His cell phone struck up the Rolling Stones' "Wild Horses." He glanced at the number. His smile dampened. The caller I.D. read *Jonah the Whale*. He started to press the answer icon, stopped, took two breaths for courage and tapped it. "Whale, before you say a word, I swear I'm good for the vig...Yeah, all four thousand. Absolutely...Tomorrow."

"That's good, because my boss hates tardiness," Jonah answered almost pleasantly. He was seated in a booth at Lester's Diner, the last of Fort Lauderdale's architectural tribute to 1963. Jonah was a tall, slim man with sandy, bottom-of-the-neck-length hair. It was gel-combed straight back. He eyed the waitress as she refilled his coffee. Jonah had long, sinewy arms and a long neck. His left brow was pierced. His arms were sleeved in tattoos of devils and angels. Though he was a regular, the waitress understood that he wasn't anyone to mess with. She avoided eye contact and quickly left.

"It's all taken care of, Jonah. Believe me," Eddie said.

"I hate liars nearly as much as the boss hates tardiness." Jonah picked up a butter knife and unsuccessfully tried to quarter the half-sliced orange next to his bagel. "Don't make me pay a visit to you or your family." Any pleasantness that had been in his voice had evaporated.

"You stay away from them! You'll get your money."

"I hope so, Ed, because if you don't..." Jonah thrust his butter knife into the orange and ripped the flesh from its rind, "I'll tear your intestines out and then I'll come after your wife and kid." He hung up.

E ddie took several breaths to prevent himself from vomiting. He removed a flask from his bottom desk drawer, unscrewed the lid and swallowed hard.

"Put your cup on and turn that thing off!"

"I'm not putting it on!"

Eddie pliered his hands against his ears. *Stop it!*

"Oh, yes you are!"

"I'm not!"

Damn it, damn it, *damn it.* Eddie sprang from the desk chair, flung the door open and stormed into the living room. "I've had enough of this crap!" he screamed at Carly, who was standing over Ben, holding his baseball gear. He glared at Ben, who was cross-legged in front of the TV with his Xbox controller, staring at Eddie. "Put the goddamn cup on before I—" Eddie rushed to Ben and raised the back of his right hand over his left shoulder. Ben crouched and covered his head. Eddie went ashen. His hand shook. He lowered and covered it with his other hand as if to hide it. Eddie reached out to hug Ben, but Carly grabbed Ben away.

She gently said to their son, "Get in the car, bub."

Ben looked at Eddie. "What about my cup?"

"Get in the car, sweetie." Carly handed him his gear. He walked to the front door and turned around. His eyes were moist. "I'm sorry, Dad."

Eddie's throat clutched. All he could do was nod. Pinching back tears, Eddie wanted to embrace his son and tell him how sorry he was for raising his hand, but Ben had walked outside and closed the door. Carly reacted immediately. "Don't you ever lift your hand to him!"

"I was wrong. I'm sorry." Eddie passed his fingers nervously through his hair. "Look, I'm under a lot of pressure."

"You're under pressure? How about Ben and I?"

Eddie lifted his palms in surrender. "You're right, I get it. Forgive me."

"You're a bastard, Eddie."

"I know. I've been on a losing streak, but I've been working on something new. Our luck's about to change." He hugged her. "I mean it, Carly. Statistics don't lie. Look." Eddie opened up his notepad of stats.

"Oh, God, here we go again." She stepped away from him. "Eddie, necesitas ayuda."

"I *don't* need help because I don't have a gambling problem." He took a breath to calm down. "Gambling's for suckers. What I do is manipulate odds. I use them to my benefit." He turned to one of the pages and tapped it. "Look at this. According to my figures, when it rains and the track at Hialeah gets muddy, there's this quarter horse, Heavenly Hiccup, whose sire—"

"Stop it. Just stop it!" Carly grabbed a stack of bills lying on the kitchen counter and brought them to him. "If you want to look at figures, look at these."

Eddie winced. "Where did you get those?"

"Shouldn't the question be how and when did I find them?"

Eddie made a swipe for the papers, but Carly yanked them back. "I was looking for Ben's cup and there they were, in the back of his closet where you hid them."

"I was going to take care of it," Eddie said.

"How? Through odds manipulation?" She shuffled through them one at a time. "Phone, gas, electric, TV, car insurance, Visa, MasterCard. *Aquí está uno bueno*: mortgage payment two months overdue. Maybe you can flip the bank double or nothing." She shoved the stack in his hand.

"I love you and Ben. You know that, Car. I'll make things right. I promise." Eddie placed a hand on her shoulder. She shoved it away. Outside, the car horn honked.

"What's today?" Carly asked.

"What d'ya mean what's today?"

Carly crossed her arms.

Eddie shrugged. "Saturday?"

"It's your son's birthday. He turned six."

"I knew that." Eddie lowered his eyes. "Of course."

"There's a five-thirty reservation at Chuck E. Cheese's. Don't let him down." Before leaving, she added, "I mean it or we're through. I've had enough."

"Of course I know it's Ben's birthday," Eddie said after she left. "What do you think, I'm a fucking idiot?" He threw the house bills on the couch. *"Shit."*

Carly pulled into Miami Springs Middle School parking lot. Ben hopped out of the car with his glove and bat. She tucked in his black with gold lettered *Good Buy! Realty* sponsored jersey and grabbed his catcher's gear from the trunk of their six-year-old Camry. They headed to the baseball field, where the teams were warming up.

"When does the catcher throw to second?" Carly asked.

"When the fat kids are running to it."

"Heavy. It's not nice to say fat," Carly replied.

Ben nodded. They walked a little more. He asked, "Is Daddy okay?"

"Niño, I...I don't know."

"Should I pray for him?"

"Yes." Her eyes welled up. "We both should."

He stopped walking. "He knows it's my birthday?"

"Of course he does!" She hugged him and whispered to herself, "Eddie, you fathead, for Christ's sake don't blow it."

From home plate, Vernon Batton, the *Good Buy! Realty* team's coach, waved and shouted at them, "Coyne, get that gear on. We've got a game today, son. Move!"

Carly smiled at Ben. "Go on, champ. You're late."

He took a few steps and stopped. "Mom?"

"What now?"

"The word is heavy, not fat. He's a heavy head."

Carly smiled sadly. Ben ran to Coach Batton.

Eddie drove his Corolla into the parking lot of Hialeah Fire Station Two, braked and studied the sky. He grinned—gray clouds were rolling in from the east. He slipped from his sport coat interior breast pocket a pen and the birthday card that he had bought for Ben. He opened the card and thought hard about the rotten way they'd parted this morning, and about the last couple of years and what a lousy dad he'd been. He wanted to tell Ben—and by extension, Carly—how much they meant to him. How he knew he had let them down and how much he ached to make it good. It took him a while, but he figured out what he wanted to say to his son and wrote it in the card. He slipped it into its envelope and tucked everything back inside his coat pocket.

Eddie left the car, inhaled deeply and again smiled broadly—rain was in the air. He practically skipped to the front entrance of the building. The fire station was fifteen minutes from his home, and another ten minutes from the racetrack. He and his brother Frank had grown up three blocks south of here. Of course, Eddie thought, that was another time and another place. Before Hialeah was one long snarl of traffic, condos, and storefronts, and before every vendor greeted you with *Hola*.

As he approached the front door, he thought about how his childhood friends had long ago abandoned Hialeah for central Florida and beyond. He recognized their resentment. They felt as if their city had been stolen from them after the tsunami of Cuban refugees arrived in the 1980s. Eddie disagreed. He had no beef with anyone trying to better him or herself. After all, wasn't that what he was trying to do? Besides, he loved the bright colored, fast-talking, multi-cultured nature of South Florida. That's why he settled in Miami Springs, a stone's throw from Hialeah. South

Florida was pulse pounding. It was exciting. It was a perpetual racetrack.

Eddie squeezed his chin twice and pressed the doorbell. He thought about his parents and the modest little house he'd grown up in. Of the green palms in their backyard and the iced tea colored canal water that flowed lazily behind them. Of the high hopes his mother and father had had for him and Frank. Of how proud they would have been of Frank had they still been alive, and how disappointed they'd have been in him.

The door opened. It was Anto Pena, Frank's driver/engineer. Anto nodded at Eddie and motioned him into the small outer office. Eddie made himself comfortable on the chair next to the blood pressure station. Anto walked into the TV room and said, "Lieutenant, your brother's here."

Frank, thirty-two, and two years younger than Eddie, entered. Eddie was always struck by how Frank resembled the best features of their parents. He had their father's thick arms and wide hands; and his mother's dense brunette hair, straight, firm nose and full lips. Most importantly, he had his mother's compassion. Something Eddie had taken advantage of since they were kids.

On the other hand, Eddie knew that he had inherited his father's head for math and his love of horse racing. As far as looks went, he was an amalgam of his parents, but his parts didn't have the grace or symmetry of his brother's. Eddie's dirt-black hair tended to curl, his nose was uninspiring and his mouth was a little large and unremarkable. It didn't help that Frank was in shape and Eddie could stand to lose a few pounds. The only thing he had over Frank were his eyes. They were deep, deep brown and charismatic like their mother's. Carly had told him that they were what had initially attracted her to him. Eddie thought on his best days they gave him a certain striking appearance, but mostly he believed he looked mundane.

"Ed, what's up?" Frank smiled, but Eddie could hear the suspicion in his voice.

"Listen, Frank, I know you're busy so I'll keep it brief." That and the fact that post time was at 1:35, twenty-five minutes from now. "I need to borrow five-hundred dollars."

Frank's smile flatlined. "Goddamn it, Ed. Are you in trouble again?"

"No. I swear. My car has a vacuum leak. Mechanic says I need to take care of it before it gets worse."

"Sorry, but not this time. No can do."

Eddie put on a puzzled, wounded look. "I'll pay you back on Friday, when my paycheck comes in."

Frank tapped the top of his left hand with his right index and middle fingers. Eddie knew the action from when they were kids. It was Frank's way of wrestling with his conscience. "When are you gonna quit Publix and get a real job?"

"The economy's bad. Besides, there's no shame in bagging groceries."

"I wasn't implying that, but you've got a goddamn MBA and a family to support."

"And an ex-boss who's the president of the Accounting & Book-keeper Alliance."

"So what—get over it."

"Don't you get it? I'm blacklisted." He snuck a peek at Frank to see if he was having any effect on his brother. "Over a lousy six-hundred dollars."

Frank sighed. "You took the money to gamble, Ed."

"I admit it was stupid, but I replaced it the very next day."

"You're lucky he didn't throw your ass in jail."

"You're right." Eddie said it with as much remorse as he could muster.

Frank again tapped the top of his hand. "Why don't you get the hell out of Miami? Start over again."

"How many times do I have to go through this? If we leave, Carly loses her position at the bank. We can't afford another financial blow." Before slumping in despair, Eddie glanced at his watch: fifteen minutes to post. "If I don't get my car fixed I can't get to work. I'll lose my job and then…" He lowered his head.

Frank reached in his rear pocket for his checkbook, but pulled his hand back. "No. You're gonna blow it on the horses."

Eddie thought about telling him that it was Ben's birthday,

and he needed the money to buy Ben a computer, but forced himself not to. Doing that would be to cross a line of dishonesty that he could never return from. Instead, he took a deep breath and said, "The truth is I'm in debt to a loan shark for a grand. I have half the money, and I was hoping to borrow the other half from you. He's a son-of-a-bitch who's threatened me."

"I know plenty of cops." Frank reached for the office phone. "I'll call them."

"No! He'll go after Carly and Ben. All I need is the money, and he'll get off my back."

Frank again scrutinized him, but released the phone.

"I didn't want to say anything to you because I'm embarrassed and ashamed." Eddie again thought about his parents and how he had let them down. To his surprise, he welled up. "You're my last chance, but if you refuse, I understand."

Frank took a big breath and slowly let it out. "You need help, Eddie. I'm contacting Gamblers Anonymous." He took a seat at the desk, jogged the computer mouse and awoke the screen.

"I've already done that. I'm attending a meeting on Tuesday."

Frank studied him. "Where at?" he asked skeptically.

"Fulford Methodist Church in North Miami. 7:30 p.m."

"You mind if I confirm that?"

Eddie smiled wanly. "I deserved that."

Frank navigated to the Gambler's Anonymous website.

Eddie watched Frank type in their local zip code under *U.S. Meetings.* Frank studied the listings. Eddie took a quick look at his watch. He was going to miss the first race, but that was no big deal. The fourth one was the one he was interested in. Frank scrolled down until he found the date, location and time mentioned. He turned to Eddie. "Sorry for doubting you."

Eddie shrugged.

Frank stood and gripped Eddie's shoulder. "I'm proud of you for taking this step."

For the second time today Eddie felt like shit. In his doubtful moments, he had gone to the G.A. site and checked out information on local meetings. He had even entertained once or twice the idea of attending. Eddie stood. "This'll be the last time

I'll ask for help, Frank. I mean it."

A deep drone filled the station: the fire alarm.

"It better be." Frank's brows bunched and his mouth tightened. It was another look Eddie had known since childhood—he was dead serious. Frank handed the check over, quickly opened the office door, ushered Eddie out and then rushed to the engine bay. As the pumper roared from the station, Eddie glanced at the sky. The clouds had darkened and were nearly overhead. He hopped in his car and headed to the bank to cash the check.

Carly leaned against the tall chain-link fence separating the playing field from the spectators. Ben was up to bat. She stood near third base. She wanted to stand closer to home plate, but she knew that made him nervous. Ben took his first swing and missed. Carly winced.

"That's okay, Ben," Vernon Batton shouted from his perch behind third base. "Square up. Keep your feet shoulder width apart and lower your right elbow." Ben nodded at him, repositioned himself. The pitcher threw. Ben took another swipe. The ball flew past second base.

Carly jumped up and down. "Go, Bennie!"

Ben raced to first base.

Vernon walked up to her and from the playing field side of the fence said, "No Ed, today?"

"Uh, no, he's…tied up."

"Too bad." He stroked his cheek a few times before adding, "You going to our high school reunion?"

"I haven't even thought about it." She kept her eyes on Ben because she was afraid to look at Vernon.

"It's at the Hard Rock, a fifties sock hop theme. It'll be a lot of fun."

Despite herself, she glanced at him. He was smiling at her. She blushed.

"Over ten years. Can you believe it?" Vernon said.

Before she could answer, the next batter swung. The ball flew into center field. Ben and the batter took off. Carly yelled, "Way to go, Tigers! Woo! All the way."

Vernon yelled to them, "Keep running, boys! Don't stop... Yeah!"

Ben and the other boy touched home plate. As they headed to the dugout, Vernon ran over, high-fived them and returned to Carly. "Just like old times, huh? The athlete and the cheerleader. Remember what they called us?"

Of course she did. "That was a long time ago."

"And hokey, too." Vernon laughed. "But there're fates a lot worse than being referred to as the Platinum Pair."

Carly smiled at Vernon. A lock of his blonde hair hung in front of his forehead below his baseball cap, like it did when they were going together. In that lock of hair she felt herself leaping upward in her cheerleading outfit, winging toward a platinum future unencumbered by the drudgery of work, child rearing, and the heavy, heavy chains of a man who worshiped gambling. Though she was under no illusions that she should splinter those chains, she also knew, God help her, that she loved Eddie. Not the Eddie of today, but the kind, humorous man she had fallen in love with and married. The father of their child. That man was dimming and Carly didn't know if she could get him back, but she owed it to herself and Ben to try.

As if glimpsing her thoughts, Vernon said, "It's none of my business, and you can stop me if you want, but Ben's a great kid and you deserve better than..."

"Vernon, I—"

"I'm just saying my marriage didn't exactly end on a high note so I may not be the best person to talk to, but if you need an ear, I'm around. Okay?" He said it with kindness and a comforting nod.

Carly's eyes glistened. She quickly lowered them so he wouldn't see.

"Come on, blue!" Vernon yelled to the umpire. "My runner was safe by a mile." Vernon dipped his head to catch Carly's line of sight and winked at her before scooting off to argue with the official.

Eddie parked his car in the half-empty south end of Hialeah Park. It was the side where the horse track was located. At the clubhouse entrance he purchased a racing program and walked a few hundred feet west toward the saddling paddocks. On the far north side of Hialeah Park, the side he detested, was the gambling casino. He disliked the casino for two reasons. First, in his opinion, it was nothing but a two-acre indoor flea market saturated with cheap lights and heart-rousing buzzers and bells. Other than cards, which weren't his thing, the rest was a sucker's game: slots, slots, slots—no skill required and no odds manipulation. Deposit your coins: wham, bam, and spank you ma'am. But his second and biggest reason for loathing casinos had to do with how they affected racing.

Florida law stipulated that in order to have casinos, track owners had to have an operating horse track. The owners complied. Barely. Racing was funded only enough to keep it on life-support. That meant Hialeah's once spectacular mile-round track had been reduced to a quarter-mile dirt straightaway. The racetrack's trademark pink flamingoes remained, but their number was reduced. They were thin and weary and were no longer prompted to circle the infield lake, where they resided.

The clubhouse's sweeping staircases and Monte Carlo-influenced balustrades needed pressure cleaning. Its once opulent terraces were bare and dotted with shuttered concession stands. Outside, the trellis-clinging bougainvillea that once blanketed the three-story building were long gone. The ten thousand palm trees and one hundred thousand small shrubs and plants that used to decorate the grounds were now only sparse, limp shadows of themselves. And most of what was left required pruning.

Half the stables had been torn down. The remainder had leaky roofs and needed paint. The legendary thoroughbreds that had lain tread on this sacred ground—Seabiscuit, Forego, Bold Ruler, Whole Lot A Hooey, Northern Racer—were forgotten ghosts of a better time. The only survivor was Citation—or rather, the bronze statue of Citation.

As he approached the paddocks, Eddie glanced at the six thousand pound horse. Citation was perched proudly upon a marble pedestal in the middle of a concrete pond that was once dotted with lily pads. He wished he could travel back in time just once and be sucked up in the glamour and buzz of the racetrack when she was in her prime. He stopped.

Eddie took a long breath and tried to conjure the perfumes of the society women and the Cuban cigar smoke from their husbands and lovers. Instead of being swept up in the imaginative essence that he wanted to be a part of, emptiness passed through him like a descending beach wave. It dragged him down, and in its wake he was left with remorse for his miserable treatment of Carly and Ben. He was a shitty husband and father and he knew it. He studied Citation one more time. There was a champion. A winner. Eddie forced his eyes from the bronze stallion and again headed to the paddocks. He squeezed his chin twice. This was his chance to finally make amends. To be a winner.

Chapter Two

Eddie leaned against the wooden railing that separated him from the horses and their handlers. He studied Heavenly Hiccup. The paddock was little more than a wide, wooden stable with an opening facing the railing. A purple and green clad jockey—a Dominican named Andres Mendoza—petted the four-year-old sorrel mare as his aide strapped an overgirth on her. The paddock was divided into ten small adjoining stalls separated by side partitions. Inside each stall were the other nine horses running in the upcoming race: a 350-yard allowance race for fillies and mares 3-and-up. Heavenly Hiccup was number nine and therefore in the ninth corral. Eddie felt a drop of rain. He looked up and thought, *Here we go!*

Eddie glanced at the thirty or so other people mulling around the paddocks. Most were gathered near the two favorites: Kastle King in stall two, and a filly named Asian Allowance in stall seven.

Asian Allowance was calm as she was being saddled up, but Kastle King was jumpy. Eddie made notations of this in his program book. More raindrops fell. The paddock dirt unprotected by the roof dotted up with wet splotches. Eddie drew his attention back to Heavenly Hiccup in time to catch her front left hoof scratching toward one of the wet spots.

Eddie glanced around to see if anyone else had caught the long shot's movement. No one had. *And why should they?* he thought. No one would make the connection between the rain and Heavenly Hiccup unless they had seen her father—Cranky—

race under the same conditions. In his day Cranky hadn't been that hot, but five years ago Eddie cashed in big on two of his races. Both times Cranky had beaten his best times and both times it had rained. Eddie didn't know what it was about a wet track, but it inspired Cranky to do his best running. From all indications, it appeared that Heavenly Hiccup had inherited her father's love of wet weather.

A light shower came. Eddie removed a dollar store plastic poncho from his pants pocket. He unfolded and placed it over him. He glanced at the surrounding dirt. Wet spots supplanted the dry ground. He again eyed the two favorites.

Kastle King's jockey stood next to him, holding fast to the thoroughbred's reins as he pranced in a half-circle. He was the public's odds-on favorite to win because he was racing in a lower class, but Eddie wasn't buying it. He had studied Kastle King's last nine races and concluded that he was on the decline. That his trainer had placed him in this lower class today only confirmed his opinion.

In stall four, the jockey mounted a long shot named Itchyboo Park. The ebony mare snorted and waggled her head. She wants to race, Eddie thought, and that was the problem. Itchyboo Park was an early starter. She had to be in the lead and stay in the lead. She fought other early starters for that position. It caused her to crash and burn before the race ended. He scratched her name off in the program.

He turned his attention back to the other favorite, Asian Allowance. He still couldn't read her. The more it rained the more serene she became. Was she shutting down or gearing up? His future depended on the correct answer, and it scared the bejeezus out of him. Her past performance record indicated that she performed better in good weather, but still, he wasn't getting a clear reading. Eddie nervously studied the horse for several moments. The jockey's assistant turned the horse for the jockey to mount. Eddie smiled. Asian Allowance had kidney sweat—lather between her hind legs caused by perspiration that had rubbed up against itself. He had his answer; kidney sweat was an indicator of anxiety. She was closing down. He scratched

Asian Allowance out in his program.

Eddie studied a black and white piebald mare in stall eight. She was a long shot named Spotless. Only she wasn't a long shot. Her trainer was a guy named Gerry McCracken. He mainly raced Spotless out of a Podunk track in West Virginia called Mountainside Park.

The program indicated that in her last half-dozen races there she had finished in the bottom half. But Eddie had studied the trainer's pattern, and gone deeper into the horse's past performances. About eight times a year McCracken entered her in larger out-of-state tracks, like Hialeah. Because of her immediate record, her odds were low on winning. As a long shot, McCracken would dump cash on Spotless. She would nearly always finish in the money and haul in enough winnings for McCracken to make a nice living. In other words, he was holding her back in West Virginia to up the odds for the bigger races.

He turned back to Heavenly Hiccup. Though he worried about Spotless, Eddie was convinced Hiccup would run better in the rain. He caught the eyes of Andres Mendoza, who had just mounted the horse. Eddie thought the jockey had sensed how much was at stake for him, because Mendoza rode the horse out of the stall and stopped her a few feet in front of Eddie. When the first raindrops hit Heavenly Hiccup, she lifted her nose high as if soaking in the glory of the drizzle, then settled her gaze on Eddie. He smiled in return and spoke to her in his mind. *You and me have something in common, don't we? You've been winless in your last eight starts and I've been losing for nearly the same amount of time. Oddsmakers say you haven't got a prayer of finishing in the top three. Talk is you can't cut it. Another thing we have in common.* He studied Heavenly Hiccup's round, sable eyes and swore that she was studying his. *You love to run in the rain like your father, don't you, girl?* He stretched out a hand to pet her, but she was beyond his reach. *My wife and kid, they think their old man ain't up to snuff and they're probably right.* Eddie gripped the hand railing and squeezed it. *But if we pull this off, I can get us out of debt and show them that they didn't get stuck with a loser. What d'ya say, Hiccup, can we do that?*

Heavenly Hiccup dug her hoof into the wet ground and shook her head. Eddie didn't know if that was a yes or no. Before he could come to a conclusion, the bugler's reveille "Call to the Post" sounded. Mendoza rode the mare, alongside the other horses, down the crossover and through the clubhouse tunnel leading to the track. The rain intensified. Eddie tightened his poncho. He made his way to the clubhouse to place his bet and to watch the race.

Raul Carbonell, dressed in black slacks and a tan guayabera shirt, entered the second floor clubhouse Men's Room. The bathroom was much like the rest of the clubhouse: large, stony, and austere. The door was always open, but a short L-shaped hallway obscured the urinals and stalls. Raul walked to the first urinal. He ran a hand through his thinning salt and pepper hair, and unzipped. He was alone and so decided to whistle, "Bésame Mucho," a favorite of his elderly mother, who was still in Nicaragua. Two bars into it he cut himself off. Someone else was entering. The door closed. The lock clicked. Raul looked toward the sound — at the long-limbed man who was approaching him — and swallowed hard. "Look, Whale," he said. "I'll get the money. I swear. Don't hurt me."

Jonah the Whale casually approached him. Jonah's hand was tucked into the inside of his sport coat. He smiled. "The boss hates tardiness. ¿Tú comprendes, Raul?"

"Yes, I understand, but I've never been late before. You know that. I'll have every cent tomorrow." Raul glanced at the bulge on the side of Jonah's sport coat and again swallowed hard. He knew exactly what Jonah was hiding there. He jerked his zipper up and headed toward the exit.

"Hey, mi amigo." Jonah clamped the back of Raul's neck and dragged him back. "You forgot to wash up." He rammed Raul's head in the urinal and flushed it several times. Jonah reached into Raul's rear pocket and removed his wallet.

There was a bang on the door. "What's the deal? I gotta pee

worse than Seattle Slew. Come on," a man said from the other side.

Jonah slammed Raul's face against the urinal. He slumped to the floor, hacking.

There were two more door bangs.

Jonah removed the cash in Raul's wallet. "Have the rest by noon tomorrow with a three percent late fee." He tossed the wallet to Raul, who was trembling. "If you don't," Jonah patted the bulge on the side of his sport coat. "I won't be as nice as I am now."

There were more thumps on the door. "Goddamn it, if you don't unlock the door I'm calling management. I have to piss!"

Jonah tucked the money in his pocket and helped Raul up. "Wipe the blood from your nose, you look a mess." He walked to the bathroom door and before unlocking it, added, "Have a great day." As Jonah exited a heavy-set man in a Hawaiian shirt sniffed his nose at him, rushed past and beelined to the nearest toilet.

Eddie entered the clubhouse and trashed his poncho. He studied one of the numerous electronic tote board monitors dotting the three-story building. With twelve minutes to post, Kastle King remained the favorite at 2 to 1. Asian Allowance was a close second at 3 to 1. Heavenly Hiccup, who was clearly a long shot, was at 53 to 1 odds. The other long shots, Itchyboo Park and Spotless, hovered in the 50 to 1 range, too.

Eddie hadn't placed his wager yet because he was having second thoughts about his strategy. His plan was to bet on Hiccup to place, which meant that if she finished first or second he would get a payout, not a particularly large one, but enough to get that maniac Jonah the Whale off his back and a few bucks left over to pay some household bills. He opened his program and studied the line-up one final time to calm his nerves. When he got to Itchyboo Park, who was an early starter, something struck him. He had been so consumed with Heavenly Hiccup that he had missed the obvious: *There were no other early starters in the race. No one who would try to pull past her early on. That meant Itchyboo Park wouldn't waste energy trying to maintain the lead. She could finish in the money.* Eddie began to think that he could do better—much better.

Eddie scrutinized the odds board again. Heavenly Hiccup was still at 53 to 1. Itchyboo Park was at 48 to 1, and Spotless remained at 50 to 1. Eddie wrung his hands for several seconds. He took a deep breath and approached the betting window.

"Ed, everything good, brother?" This was Nelson speaking. He was behind the betting window. Nelson was old, and completely bald. He had been around since before the days when Eddie and his dad spent time together at the track. Eddie liked Nelson. He was lucky.

Eddie flashed thumbs up. He pulled out his wallet and removed all five hundred dollar bills. His hand trembled. "Ten dollar wheel, Nelson. Four, Nine, Eight; with Four, Nine, Eight; with all." He handed the money to Nelson, then squeezed his chin twice.

"Four, Nine, Eight; with Four, Nine, Eight?" Nelson lowered his glasses. "Are you sure you don't want to rethink that?"

The cold sweat of doubt chilled Eddie. Nelson had given him a break. Eddie had wheeled the bet—that is, placed multiple, ten dollar bets. Each bet was that two of the three long shots— Heavenly Hiccup, Itchyboo Park, and/or Spotless—would finish first and second, and that one of the remaining horses would finish in third. That came to forty-eight separate wagers. Each wager cost ten dollars, for a total of four hundred and eighty dollars. Of course, everything depended on two of his long shots coming in first and second. Nelson was right, he thought. The bet was foolish. It went against every principle Eddie had ever learned. He was about to cancel the wagers, but stopped. *No. Nelson means well, but this is the right choice.* His stats and gut told him so. He smiled cockily to hide his uncertainty. "I'm a pro, remember? Place the bet."

"Eddie..."

"Place the bet, Nelson."

Nelson shrugged. "It's your dime." He counted Eddie's

hundreds, printed out the ticket and handed it to him along with his twenty dollar change. As Eddie departed, Nelson said, "Hey wise guy, you're only a pro if you get paid."

Eddie waved once without turning around. He headed up the escalator to watch the race from the second floor roofed, open-air grandstand seats.

Eddie took a seat facing the finish line. He held a plastic cup of beer in one hand and his rolled up racing program in the other. He looked downfield, to his left. Three hundred and fifty yards away the horses entered their starting gate cages. The rain continued to fall. It was steady, but not heavy. With less than two minutes to post, the outdoor tote board showed the favorite, Kastle King, at 6 to 5, and the other favorite, Asian Alliance, at 1 to 2 odds of winning. Itchyboo Park had fallen slightly to 38 to 1. Heavenly Hiccup still swept the basement at 46 to 1. The odds on Spotless winning had risen to 19 to 1. Eddie knew why. The horse's trainer, Gerry McCracken, had dumped his cash on the horse and the influx of money had upped the odds.

Eddie did a rough calculation in his head—even with the higher odds on Spotless to win, the payoff would still be plenty big.

Slipping the program into his coat pocket, he felt the envelope housing Ben's birthday card. It reminded him that he had made a mess of it with the two people he loved most in the world. He would make it up to them by proving that he had been right all along.

He would use his earnings to start his own accounting firm. It would be small at first, but he didn't give a shit because he'd work hard to build it up. He'd treat Carly and Ben the way they deserved. Eddie removed his wager ticket from his chest pocket and studied it. *Now that Ben is old enough, we'll take that trip to Disney World and Universal Studios that we've always talked about. We'll be a real family again.*

He thought about the time when he and Carly met. It was nine years ago at First Coast Bank's New Year's Eve party. First Coast Bank was a client of Miami Springs Accounting & Bookkeeping, the firm where he worked. Carly was twenty-one and a teller back then. He was twenty-five, a bookkeeper working his way to accountant. Most of all, he remembered what he always remembered—their first kiss when the clock struck twelve. It was meant to be a brief *Hurray!* thing, but it lingered beyond that. The sweet taste of her soft, moist lips pressed against his were beyond intoxicating. His eyes had been closed, but behind them he had been swept up in the vanilla-honey scent of her flesh and the image of her whispery brown eyes. He knew in that moment that he would never love any woman as much as he would her.

"Heavenly Hiccup, Itchyboo Park, and Spotless? I wouldn't give you a nun's ass for any trifecta that had them in it."

Eddie shuddered and nearly dropped his beer. He drew back and tucked the ticket back in his chest pocket. "Christ, Whale. Leave me alone. I told you I'd have the money."

Jonah took a seat beside him. "Relax, big man. You have until tomorrow."

A bugle recording of the final call played over the P.A. Eddie glanced at the jockeys and their horses. They were poised at the starting gate. He glanced at Jonah. "Haven't you got somewhere else to be?"

"Nah," Jonah said indifferently. "Had a little work earlier, but it's taken care of." He locked eyes with Eddie. "I'm all clear until tomorrow."

The starter's pistol fired. Both men's gazes snapped to the starting gate. The horses clamored down the muddy track. Through the P.A. the announcer said, "And they're off! It's Kastle King followed by Asian Allowance, Itchyboo Park, and Four Legged Kraziness." Eddie squeezed his rolled program. "It's Kastle King, Four Legged Kraziness, Itchyboo Park and Asian Allowance."

Eddie glanced at the mud flying from Heavenly Hiccup's hooves. "Come on, baby," he mumbled. "Come on, baby, come on."

"At the half it's Kastle King, Itchyboo Park, Asian Allowance, and Heavenly Hiccup."

Eddie stood and smacked the program against his thigh. "Bring it home. Hiccup, remember what we talked about."

"It's Itchyboo Park, Kastle King, and Heavenly Hiccup."

"Come on!" Eddie shouted. "Go, Hiccup, go! Squeeze yourself between Itchy and Kastle. Do it!"

Jonah inclined his head as he focused his attention on both the race and Eddie.

"Coming up to the finish line, it's Itchyboo Park, with Kastle King running neck-and-neck with Heavenly Hiccup." Whoops and howls filled the grandstand. Pleadings in English and Spanish erupted. Blood pounded in Eddie's eardrums. It muffled everything except the voice inside his head, which repeated, "Kastle King and Heavenly Hiccup neck-and-neck...Kastle King and Heavenly Hiccup neck-and-neck." Eddie's stomach clenched. His breaths came in quick, hot spurts. "...Kastle King, Heavenly Hiccup, Kastle King, Heavenly Hiccup, Kastle King." *You love the rain, Hiccup*, Eddie pleaded. *You love the rain.*

Eddie whipped the racing form against his hip as the two horses jockeyed for second and third. He stopped breathing. Everything went silent. The bellowing crowd faded. Eddie watched the horses approach the finish line and one thought dominated: *You love the rain. You love the rain. You love the rain. You love the—* "Hallelujah!" He flung his hands in the air and hopped in a circle as his beer spewed over him. "I'm a genius. A goddamn genius! I'm a—" He stopped, realizing that Jonah was eyeing him.

"Unofficial results show the winner is Itchyboo Park, followed by Heavenly Hiccup, Kastle King, and Spotless." The announcer repeated the message in Spanish.

"What's the take?" Jonah asked.

"Enough to get you off my back." More importantly, Eddie thought, it was more than plenty to make a wife and a little boy happy and to get their old man out of the doghouse.

Jonah stood. "Let's go get my vig."

Eddie shook his head. "You'll get it *and* the principle tomorrow when it's due." With his newfound winning, he felt emboldened enough to stick it—at least a little—to Jonah. "Today I'm going to my son's birthday."

"Sure, Ed, sure." Jonah crossed his arms and smiled. "Call me tomorrow before noon. You know my number, right?"

Unfortunately like the back of my hand, Eddie thought. He walked away. Jonah remained in place but watched him through the corners of his eyes. When Eddie had traveled several feet, Jonah followed him.

The Mediterranean Lounge was a breezy bar. It was half-deserted. Eddie ordered an Amstel and took a table facing away from the panoramic windows looking down on the track. He wanted to concentrate. Even though the payouts were already posted, Eddie scribbled the calculations down on a napkin for the pure joy of it.

The rough formula for figuring out a trifecta payout per $1.00 bet was easy: take the three horses, figure out the payout of their odds as if each one had been the winner, and multiply each payout in the order in which they finished. Itchyboo Park's first place winning odds were 38-to-1. Using another quick formula—multiply the first odds number by 2, divide it by the second number and add the $2.00 amount of the bet—Eddie calculated Itchyboo Park's payout at $78.00 per each dollar waged. Heavenly Hiccup paid 46 to 1, which came out to $94.00, and third place Kastle King paid at 6 to 5, or $4.40 for each dollar.

Eddie took a slug of beer and grinned as it tickled his throat. He knew the bottom line and wrote it out.

$78.00 x $94.00 x $4.40 = $32,260.00 for every dollar bet.

$32,260.00 x his total $10.00 wager = $322,600.00

Eddie laughed. He couldn't help himself. He was giddy. Uncle Sam was going to hit him for twenty-eight percent, but who cared? He'd still be left with over two hundred and thirty thousand tax-free dollars. The first thing he was going to do was buy the sweetest, most goddamn expensive video game system he could find and give it to Ben for his birthday. That, and two-dozen roses for Carly. He checked his watch. He had two hours before the party started.

Then, Eddie thought, I'll take them all—Carly, Ben, Frank and Natalie and their kids to Joe's to stuff ourselves silly with crab claws and champagne. He finished his beer and belched contentedly. Eddie tucked the napkin into his pocket and left to cash in his ticket with Nelson, whom he planned to tip handsomely.

Lost in a cloud of elation, Eddie made his way to the escalator. As he did, he held an imaginary conversation with Nelson: *Is this professional enough for you? Do I know my stuff or what? Odds manipulation, brother! Next time, check with Eddie boy, he'll lead you straight to the promised—*

Eddie smacked into a pair of elderly women. One gripped a soda cup and an empanada, the other a tip sheet. The woman with the empanada dropped it. The other woman dropped her tip sheet. "Crap," Eddie said. "I'm terribly sorry, ladies. Lo siento." Flustered, Eddie pulled the napkin with his calculations from his pocket, bent down and tried to scoop up the food and the tip sheet with it.

"No quiero con eso," the woman who had been holding the empanada said. She scrunched her nose at her friend and added, "Está sucio!" Her friend crinkled her lips and nodded.

Leaning against a dark corner not far from the escalator, Jonah stepped from the shadows and watched with amusement.

Eddie was knowledgeable enough in Spanish to know what the woman had said to her friend: *I don't want it. It's dirty!* He replied to them in English, "I was only trying to get it off the floor before someone slipped on it." Eddie stood. Doing so, he knocked the woman's soda from her hand.

The woman yelped and said to her friend, "Llama al guardia de seguridad, Rosa!"

"No, no! Security no es necesario." Eddie wiped his hands with what was left of the napkin and tossed it with the rest of the mess. He removed his wallet and slipped out two twenties. "Sorry, sorry. My mind's elsewhere. I just won big, over three-hundred thous—" He cut himself off. *Christ, am I that stupid?* He looked around. Jonah slipped back into the shadows. He glanced down at the food-smeared napkin. It was unreadable. Satisfied that no one had been paying attention, Eddie turned back to the ladies and handed them each a twenty. "My treat. Okay?"

The women frowned at each other, but accepted the money.

"Have a nice day," Eddie said. "Un buen dia." He back-pedaled and left.

Rosa tapped her temple and said to the woman whose food had fallen. "Ese hombre está loco, Maria."

"Muy," Maria replied.

Yeah, Jonah thought. He's loco, all right. Three hundred and twenty grand loco. He trailed Eddie, who was a few yards in front of him.

Calm down, Eddie thought as he approached the escalator. *Think straight. First things first. Go to Nelson and give him my ticket.* He removed the ticket from his upper coat pocket. *After it's cashed in, give him five hundred as a tip. He'll have a tax form for me to sign. Sign it, then get the hell to the bank and deposit the winnings. No—have a security guard escort me to my car first—then get the hell to the bank. Afterwards, get Ben and Carly's gifts and haul ass to Chuck E. Cheese's. Tomorrow pay off Jonah, and finally on Monday morning call my taxman.* He kissed the ticket and stepped on the down escalator.

Jonah reduced his distance behind Eddie to within two steps. He rushed forward, grabbed for the ticket and pushed Eddie hard from behind. Eddie instinctively shoved the ticket back in his coat pocket as he tumbled ferociously. Jonah bounded up the escalator as Eddie's skull slammed once, twice, three and four times against the moving steps. He smacked into another man who was riding it. Something snapped in his chest and thigh. Blood. He was dizzy, nauseated, woozy and then nothing. Eddie landed in a twisted, gory heap on the first floor.

A woman screamed. A crowd of people gathered.

"Oh, my god. Is he...?" the woman asked.

A man wearing a Miami Heat ball cap felt Eddie's wrist.

Another man brought his ear to Eddie's mouth and nose and listened for breathing. The men exchanged grave looks.

"Call the paramedics!" Jonah yelled from the second floor. "Hurry!" He thought about going down to retrieve the ticket, but it was too late. "Damn it," he muttered. Too many people had crowded around Eddie. Amid the growing chaos Jonah strolled away.

Chapter Three

Eddie opened his eyes. He was seated on a worn couch in an untidy office. He faced a pale, prissy woman who looked to be around fifty. She was seated behind a desk, furiously typing on a computer keyboard. There was a marble nameplate near her, but it was partially hidden by a telephone so Eddie couldn't read it. The woman's hair was pulled back in a tight bun. Behind her, a dozen printers clacked and buzzed out a continuous pile of what looked to be data sheets.

Eddie figured he had passed out and ended up in Hialeah Hospital's ER, where he had been examined, deemed okay, and was now awaiting his discharge papers. He stretched his arms and flexed his back. No pain. He touched his head; it wasn't bandaged or even swollen. He was surprised. He figured he had sustained serious injuries. Eddie cleared his throat to draw the woman's attention.

The woman glanced up without stopping her typing.

Eddie stared at her impatiently and tapped the top of his hand with the bottom of his other hand several times. She never looked up again. Finally, he said, "Excuse me. Perdón." He leaned sideways to read the nameplate and winced: *Ms. Place. Really?* "If you'll just give me whatever papers I need to sign, I'll get out of here."

Frowning, Ms. Place stopped typing and said, "Oh, cripes, not another uninformed. Doesn't anyone do their job anymore?"

"Excuse me?"

"Look, I'm not the one who's supposed to break the news to

you, but you're not on Earth anymore. Okay?" Ms. Place resumed typing.

"Whoa, whoa." Eddie pushed his palms forward as if shoving her words back to her. "What was that?"

Ms. Place's mouth tightened. Her fingers continued to skate across the keyboard.

Eddie watched her for a second, then stood. "I've had enough. Either give me my discharge papers or I'm leaving without signing." He snorted. "And for the record, you're highly unprofessional."

Ms. Place stopped typing and narrowed her eyes. "You want professional? Here it is. This is where people like you go before their final destination."

"People like me?"

She smiled smugly. "The dead and the dying."

Eddie stared at her, wide-eyed. He decided she was on something. "Okay, then. I'll just leave you to your work." He rose to his feet.

She picked up the marble nameplate, raised it over her head and aimed it at him. "Sit down!"

Unnerved, Eddie dropped back on the sofa.

Ms. Place continued typing.

Not sure what to do next, Eddie thought it best to play along until he figured it out. He cleared his throat. "You said this was where the dead and the dying go. Which am I?"

"Don't know, don't care. They're all the same to me around here." Ms. Place stopped typing. "Look, by the time you get here, your scheduled demise has already been arranged, therefore it really doesn't matter. Capisce?"

"But if I'm dying and not dead, then I'd like to be unscheduled."

"From your mouth to His ears." Ms. Place's fingers once again skirted across the keyboard.

He gaped at her for a long second, then grinned. He had figured it out. "I'm under anesthesia, aren't I? Sure, that's what it is. I'll wake up soon, and all this madness about dying people and final destinations will have vanished."

Ms. Place shook her head. "I'm afraid not. You're here. Period."

Eddie laughed. "Here? Here, like in purgatory?"

She stopped typing. "No, smarty. Purgatory's for those working through their wretchedness. This is more like limbo—the neutral ground. Now, if you'll excuse me, I have a ton of work to do." She went to one of the printers and sorted through a stack of papers it was spitting out.

"You're crazy." Nameplate or no nameplate, Eddie rose to his feet and turned to leave. A flutter ran down his spine. He turned again, and again, and again. There was no door. No windows, only four beige walls. He went to the walls and tapped against them.

They were solid.

He pinched the skin separating his thumb and pointer finger and flinched from the pain. He didn't wake up, which meant he wasn't dreaming or drugged out. *If it's not a dream, then what?*

He pressed his hand against his heart. It was beating, but…but he didn't know what to think. He remembered stumbling and somersaulting down the escalator and his head striking the edge of one of the steps, and then blood, but that was it. He rubbed his fingers along his head. No bumps, no pain and no bandages. *How can that be?* He looked at Ms. Place. She was smirking at him. "Lady, what the hell is going on?"

"We don't use the 'h' word around here." Ms. Place toted the papers back to her desk, plopped them next to the computer, sat, and resumed typing. Her desk phone rang. She picked up the receiver, cradled it between her ear and shoulder, and once more plucked on the keyboard. Behind her, more printouts piled up. "Yes, sir…I know it's messy," Ms. Place said into the phone. "No, sir, no replacements…I'm doing my best, but I'm swamped with my own work." She frowned at Eddie. "Yes, sir, he's here…I'll do it immediately."

Eddie listened incredulously. This whole thing was absurd, yet something in his gut told him it was real. Just as unbelievable, he didn't feel as panicky as he thought he should. He felt out-of-kilter for sure, but at the same time he felt as if he were walking a path that was oddly meant to be.

Ms. Place hung up the receiver and stopped typing. "You may enter."

Eddie scoured the four walls. "Enter where?"

Ms. Place chin-pointed to the wall on her right. Eddie's lower-lip dropped. At the center of the wall a plain, gray door had appeared. He took a half-step back.

"They don't like to be kept waiting."

"Who doesn't like to be kept waiting?"

"Ms. Place raised an eyebrow, directed her nose toward the door and went back to typing.

Eddie studied the door, swallowed, and stepped toward the entranceway. He grabbed the knob, slowly twisted it, stuck his head inside and entered.

Eddie faced six gray-hooded figures. They were seated at a long rectangular table about ten feet in front of him: three men to his right and three women to his left. There was an unoccupied chair at the right end of the table. The women resembled each other just as each man resembled the other men. All six looked oddly identical—much as male and female twins from the same family might. Eddie couldn't get a grip on their age or ethnicity.

They looked to be in their twenties or their eighties. Their skin was neither smooth nor wrinkled and the color seemed to change in complexity. Their faces were thin and hollow. Their eyes—sometimes almond shaped and sometimes oval—had a youthful twinkle behind them, but also a look of age-old wisdom. Each sat identically, with their hands clasped together on the tabletop. Other than a gangly, unassuming young man who stood to Eddie's right of the group near an overflowing trashcan, the room was nothing but four gray walls and a few more overflowing trashcans.

Eddie looked around gape-mouthed, not sure if what he was seeing was real.

"Mr. Coyne. Eddie. Allow us to introduce ourselves. We're the Jesses and we have a problem." Dumbstruck, Eddie poked his pinky into his ear and wiggled it. Only the man and woman seated in the middle of the group had moved their mouths, but Eddie heard all six voices in unison. The young man standing on the side near the trashcan removed a ballpoint pen and notepad from his pants pocket and began to take notes.

Eddie studied him. He was probably in his early twenties. He looked boyish and very nerdy. He wore half-rim glasses and had large teeth. His auburn hair was long and curly on top and short on the sides. Though Eddie was positive he didn't know the young man, he looked vaguely familiar.

"Mr. Coyne, I suggest you pay attention. A lot is at stake."

Eddie turned back to the Jesses. "Sorry."

"We've studied your case and have concluded that while you're not exactly a dreadful individual, you're not a man of exemplary character, either. Do you understand?"

Eddie shook his head.

The Jesses stared at him. They squeezed their clutched hands. Something blew into Eddie's head like a hot breeze. Key moments of his life came with the gust—how he manipulated Frank when they were youngsters, sticking up for the mentally challenged boy in elementary school when no one else would, fifteen and grabbing Marlene's breasts in the schoolyard when she wasn't looking, cheating on his English Lit exams, strong-arming Boyer's grocery store after he and some high school buddies smoked pot, pilfering the family fund account to gamble and lying to Carly about it, stealing from Miami Springs Accounting, lying about it, giving his last twenty bucks to the homeless girl on the corner with the toddler, and most recently losing his temper at Ben in front of Carly.

Eddie understood. The Jesses were his judges. They were to decide if he went on to a higher plane or wallowed in an eternal muck.

"You see," the Jesses said. "You're one of those extremely rare people who is teetering on the edge."

"The edge of what?"

They again squeezed their hands. Eddie once more understood. His physical life was draining away. What remained, balanced between the upper and lower levels of afterlife. He was smack dab in the middle and a featherweight on either side of the scale would determine where he'd end up. He was afraid to ask the next question, but he did. "What's the difference between the two places?"

"There is no clear cut answer. There are many levels to the higher regions and many depths to the lowlands," the Jesses said. "They are eternal and individually tailored for each recipient. The only constant is that the upper levels are more pleasing and the lower ones not so much. Would you care for a sample of each?"

"I don't think so."

The Jesses smiled. "It wasn't really a question." The half-dozen hooded group again clenched their hands. Eddie felt himself rise one level from the midpoint where he was. He smelled fresh popcorn. He was seated between Carly and Ben at a movie theater, sharing a popcorn tub and watching a Pixar film. The theater was the nicest one he'd ever been to. It had ornate, overhead balconies and large, padded reclining seats. He leaned back, closed his eyes and drifted away in a stream of contentment.

The Jesses loosened their hands and once more squeezed them together.

Eddie felt himself sink to one stage below the midpoint. He was at home watching the news. The phone rang. He picked it up. A voice said, "Mr. Coyne, I'm sorry to have to tell you this." The Highway Patrol trooper went on to say that Eddie's parents had been killed in an auto accident.

The damp, depressing nausea of that moment ten years ago knocked the wind out of him. His throat watered and he nearly retched. Eddie was at home watching the news again. The phone rang. He picked it up and the whole scene played out again... again...and again.

The Jesses loosened their hands.

Eddie snapped out of the loop and was stunned to feel tears in his eyes. While he could never put his parents' death behind him, Eddie had managed to make peace with it. If he were forced to face this personal hell over and over, the pain would be unbearable. "But I'm not dead yet, right?"

"No, but you're scheduled to be," the Jesses said. "And that's practically the same thing."

"I don't care. I want it postponed to a later—much later— date."

"It doesn't work that way."

"Says who? It's my life."

The Jesses clenched their hands.

Eddie's throat tightened, soured. His heart pumped savagely. His knees blazed and his face chilled. He tried to suck air, but nothing came. Eddie held a palm up to indicate he got the message. The Jesses loosened their grips. Eddie's breathing resumed. His body returned to normal. With his recovery came the understanding that the Jesses were not only his judges, but also that they were more powerful than he could comprehend.

Eddie thought about a thousand incidents in his life. What if he had handled one of them differently, would he be in this predicament? He tugged the flask from his back pocket and un-screwed it.

The note-taking young man cleared his throat. He shook his finger at Eddie. Eddie grimaced, tightened the cap and tucked the flask away.

The Jesses tapped their thumbs together several moments and said, "So, Eddie, the real question—as it always was—is what we should do about you." The three men and three women turned to each other. Though Eddie heard no sound and their mouths were closed, he knew by their head movements that they were communicating with each other. He glanced at the note-taking young man, who was dressed in a long-sleeve tan pullover sweater and jeans. Evidently, he didn't hear anything either, because he had stopped writing.

The Jesses turned back to Eddie. "Well, the solution isn't as difficult as we first anticipated. We've concluded that the only fair thing to do is to summon Lizzie Borden and have her whack you straight down the middle. One half of you will," they pointed their thumbs up "and the other half will," they turned their thumbs down.

Eddie went numb. His pulse raced. The note-taking man furiously scribbled. Eddie pictured the axe splitting him down the middle. "There's gotta be a better way. Please!"

The Jesses chuckled. "Relax, it was a joke. This is such a serious job, you know, that occasionally we have to let off steam." They turned to the young man taking notes. "Charles, expunge that last sentence."

Charles scratched it out. As he did, Eddie wondered if he was already in hell. These people, or whatever they were, were out of their minds.

"Kidding aside," the Jesses said. "We have to make a decision. We could let you hang out here, assisting Ms. Place. She's set to retire in nine or ten centuries, and there might be an opening for you. How's your typing?"

Eddie cringed. The last thing he wanted was to spend another minute with that woman. "With all due respect, that's not for me and I'm a lousy typist."

"Well...there is another way." The twinkle Eddie had earlier seen in their eyes, sparked. "That is, if you're a gambling man."

"You know damn well I am."

The twinkle darkened. "This is the second time you've been told to mind your language." They clutched their hands.

"Don't squeeze!" Eddie blurted. "It won't happen again."

The Jesses eyed him for a second, then loosened their grip. "What we propose is a wager. Suicide is normally a big no-no around here. For the most part it's considered the wrong thing to do. Those who take their own lives don't usually, shall we say, reach their potential. Does this make sense?"

Eddie thought about it. He nodded.

"Excellent. Here's our proposal. We will send you back to Earth. We will then choose two or three people who are going to take their lives. Should you accept our bet, it will be your job to convince any one of them not to commit suicide. If you succeed in persuading just one you will be given the green light to advance upward."

"Two *or* three people?" Eddie said. "I need a set number of chances."

The Jesses shrugged. "Okay, two."

"No, I meant three. That's fair."

"We determine what's fair. Not you. Is that understood?"

Eddie frowned. If there was one thing he understood about this nightmare, it was that the Jesses held the power. "OK, but at least let's go back to the original terms. Two or three people."

The Jesses glanced at each other, looked at Eddie and nodded. Eddie felt a surge of relief. "Can I ask how you're going to decide how many shots I get?"

"Our decision will be based upon how well you perform. If we think you're not up to the task, or unable to complete it within your allotted schedule, we cut bait after two attempts."

"My schedule? Do you mean when I'm—" he swallowed hard "—supposed to die?"

They nodded. "Because you're not officially deceased yet is why we can make this wager. It allows us to ingratiate you into the world of the living. Otherwise you would be, for lack of a better term, a ghost, and as a ghost it would be impossible for us to do that."

"How long do I have before my time schedule runs out?"

The Jesses shrugged. "Long enough."

"What does that mean?"

"It means that it's difficult to explain to someone who is used to measuring intervals in years, hours, minutes and seconds, and that by the time we make it clear, your schedule would have run out. If that's what you wish, though, we can do it."

"Forget it," Eddie said. "Explain it to me after I win."

They nodded. "As we were saying, if you convince just one of these people to do the right thing, you will be given the green light to advance upward."

"How far upward?"

They shrugged. "For certain one level, maybe two or three depending on how well you do."

Eddie thought about it. At the very least he wouldn't mind an eternity of eating popcorn and watching a film with Carly and Ben. But still, he wondered what was in it for the Jesses? He asked the question.

"Frankly, it's boring around here," the Jesses responded. "Charles, that last sentence is off the record." Charles crossed it out. "Even we need a change of routine, Eddie, and an opportunity to wager is something that rarely presents itself. Cases like yours just don't come along very often."

Eddie thought about the horses, handicapping and odds manipulation. One-in-two, with a possibility of one-in-three. He'd had worse, though he wished he had past performance stats on the Jesses and others who may have been given similar options, and a definite answer on how much time he had. "What if I say no?"

"Then we make our decision now." Their faces were stoic— unrevealing. That frightened Eddie because he didn't know what to read in them. Were they in a thumbs-up mood or not? He could understand why, if they weren't. He had caused a lot of grief to Frank, and most of all to Carly and Ben. "Suppose I take the deal and lose?"

"Then it's straight down the fecal river."

Eddie thought about his chances. He reached inside his coat pocket. Though he wasn't sure how—other than a suspicion that the Jesses had something to do with it—he knew that the winning ticket wouldn't be there, but that Ben's birthday card would. The card saddened him, but it also gave him courage— sadness and courage. Eddie recalled his promise to Carly that he would attend Ben's celebration. "I'll tell you what." He pulled out the envelope. "I'll take the bet under one condition. I get to deliver this card to my son's birthday."

"No conditions. Take it or leave it."

Eddie nervously scratched the top of his hand as he pondered their offer. *If I accept the bet my odds of winning are one-in-two or one-in-three. If I don't take the wager they shoot up to fifty-fifty, but then I have no say in the matter.* He glanced at the Jesses. They remained poker-faced. He was reminded of the slot machines he abhorred: stick the coin in and hope for the best—no skill involved. *If I take the wager it'll give me one final shot to prove myself and make something good of my gambling skills. To maybe vindicate myself to Carly and Ben.* He smiled slowly and squeezed his chin twice. "If I'm going down, it's not gonna be without a fight. I'll take your offer."

The Jesses' eyes brightened. "Excellent! Here are the rules. One: no mention of your mission or who you really are. Two: you must have the chosen individual touch your hand and utter the phrase, 'I accept life.' Got that?"

"I accept life, got it." Eddie glanced at Charles, who was writing it all down.

"Three: all decisions are final."

"Is that it?" Eddie swept his eyes across all six of them.

The Jesses nodded in unison.

Eddie shrugged. "Seems simple enough. When do I start?"

The Jesses held up a hand. "One other thing. Charles is to accompany you." Charles dropped his pen with a clatter. The Jesses eyed him. "His job is to keep things on the up and up." As Charles scrambled to retrieve the pen, they turned back to Eddie. "He is to observe and record. He will not actively participate." They locked eyes on Charles, who was once again making notations. "Is that perfectly clear? *Observe and record only.*"

Charles said in a slight southern drawl, "I understand perfectly."

"Do this right, and who knows?" the Jesses added. "You may get that promotion after all."

"Hold on," Eddie interjected. "No offense, but I work alone."

"Not here you don't," the Jesses said. "These are non-negotiable house rules."

Charles looked at Eddie and flashed a toothy grin. Eddie rolled his eyes. "Whatever."

"Perfect. Now then, are you ready to begin?" the Jesses asked.

Eddie took a deep breath and again double-squeezed his chin. "Say the word."

"Your can-do spirit is admirable." The Jesses clutched their hands and squeezed.

"I hope that counts in my fav—" Eddie disappeared.

Chapter Four

Eddie reappeared. His mind was foggy and he felt dizzy. Several deep breaths later the feeling receded and Eddie was able to take note of his surroundings. He was stunned. The Jesses and their chamber were gone. He was standing in a room on the second floor of an enormous ashlar stone manor that resembled a castle. He peered out of a partially open door. Below him on the first floor was a main hall. Eddie was dressed in something out of a movie set for *Robin Hood*, a tan, knee-length tunic with matching leg hose. Over his tunic was a brown vest. Crude, leather poulaines adorned his feet. Men and women, dressed in variations of this type of clothing, scrambled about below, lugging large flagons and platters of roasted meat. Huge medieval paintings, mostly of Jesus or hunting scenes hung on the wall. *What the fuck?*

"Edward, is it high enough?" This came from a girl's voice inside the room he was peering out of.

Eddie turned to her. "Are you speaking to me?" The girl had bright, hazel eyes, and long, flaxen hair. She looked to be fifteen or sixteen. Wall-sized tapestries of swans, fairies, and lavishly dressed women in flowing gowns adorned the room. An ornately draped canopy bed lay in the corner. A couple of feet away from the bed rested a carved wooden chest and toiletry table. The girl stood beside the table. Charles stood beside her. He was dressed in his pullover sweater and jeans.

"My halo," the girl said. "Do angels wear it higher?" Above the girl's head was a thin silver halo tethered to a six-inch vertical rod.

The rod was attached to the back of a headband ringed around the girl's forehead.

Eddie nodded to Charles. "Ask him. He'd know better than me."

The girl, who was attired in a white, floor length gown with floor length sleeves, glanced to where Eddie pointed and looked back at him. "You make a poor jester."

"I don't get the joke," Eddie said to Charles.

"She can't see or hear me," Charles replied. "No one can. Only you."

"Your joke was a bad one, Edward," the girl said, thinking Eddie had spoken to her. "If you were a jester, you would have to be more amusing than that to keep your head."

"Oh, right," Eddie replied. "Now I get it." He glanced at Charles, who smiled.

"Now, once more. Is my halo too high or too low?"

"Well, um...my lady?" She nodded. Eddie continued, "My lady, I would say it's a touch too low." He slid her headband an inch up her forehead.

She gazed into a polished tin plate propped on the toiletry table she stood next to. "Do you think Walter will be at the masquerade ball? He is so handsome, don't you think?"

Eddie's eyes widened. "Masquerade ball?"

"We must hurry or Father really will have your head." She walked toward the door. Eddie and Charles followed. The girl turned back. "Did you forget something?" Puzzled, Eddie glimpsed around her room. The girl pointed to a chamber pot below the four-poster bed. "Surely, you don't expect me?"

Eddie grimaced. "Servant's job, right?" He glanced at Charles, who jotted in his notepad.

The girl giggled. "You do make me smile so." She departed.

Eddie looked at Charles, who couldn't quite suppress a smile. "What the hell—"

Charles waggled a finger to cut him off.

"Yeah, right, okay," Eddie said. "What the *heck* is going on?"

"What do you know?" Charles replied.

"That I'm in a manor or castle somewhere in the past. Medieval England?"

"Manor," Charles said. "1485."

"How come the girl acts as if she knows me? And how do we understand each other? I don't know much about Medieval England except that we speak differently than they do."

"The Jesses arranged it."

"But she can't see or hear you. That means you're...?"

"Yes," Charles replied. "A ghost."

Eddie glanced around the girl's room as he tried to take it all in. His eyes locked on the bedpan. "I suppose it also means that they arranged for me to be a servant—a *male* servant—to a giggly teenager."

Charles shrugged.

"Great." Eddie held his breath, grabbed the covered pot and carted it away at arm's length. Charles jotted in his notepad as he followed Eddie from the room.

In a corner of the main hall two viol players, a sackbut player, a man with a recorder, and a tambourine player rehearsed a lively tune. In another corner an acting troupe reviewed lines. Servants dashed about arranging food, platters and utensils. Dressed as a lion, a stout, bearded man in his early forties checked over the servants' actions. A plump woman in her mid-thirties stood beside him, double-checking his checks. She was dressed as a peacock. The man in the lion costume plucked a chunk of meat from one of the platters. He said to the woman, "It was another banner year for the spice market, my dear, as this ball will attest." He popped the meat inside his mouth.

The woman's jaw tightened. "The market is too good, I fear."

"You're a fine woman, Gussalen, but you worry too much. The prince has no use for our trade. It's merely a bauble to him. He has the entire country."

Gussalen grabbed the costumed man's lion tail and wiped his lips and fingers with it. "I hope you're right, Merek."

"Why do you fear when you know I have a contract signed by the King, himself, granting us unlimited rights?" Before she could answer, Merek yelled to a servant, "Not over there! Keep the wine away from the actors."

When his attention turned back to Gussalen, she said, "The prince does not rule as his father, the King, did."

"My peacock, you worry too much." Merek raised his fingers, half-balled them as if they were claws and roared. "No one challenges the king of beasts!" He nuzzled Gussalen's neck.

Two torch-toting young men rounded the bend of a dirt road. They walked toward the manor, which was about a half-mile away. Woods surrounded them. One of the young men was smiling. The other was sullen. Both were in costume.

"Mark my word, Devin," the sullen young man said. "We'll never gain entrance to the ball, not after the row between my uncle and De Bromwell." He was dressed as a monk in sandals, an ankle-length tunic, and hooded scapula.

Devin laughed. A jolly man with bright green eyes, he was dressed as a long-bearded wizard with an ankle-length robe and conical hat. "Where's your faith? Between our costumes and my magical tongue, the party gates will open wide for us."

"More likely the prison gates," the sullen young man replied.

Devin laughed. "Does the entire Falk clan brood so? Or is it just you?"

Falk—the brooding man—dismissed him with a wave of his hand.

Devin patted Falk's shoulder. "I know your sweet Adelaide has abandoned you for another, but still, it's no reason to act as if the grim reaper were on your back."

Two young women walking in the opposite direction, approached. They appeared to be costermongers by their plain attire. Devin bowed ostentatiously as they neared. The women stopped, raised their chins and sniffed. Devin smiled and removed a wineskin slung across his back. "What say you, fair maidens?"

He held it out to them. The two women looked at each other, smiled, and stepped closer. Devin raised the spout over one of their mouths. As the wine was about to spill into the girl's lips he pulled it back. "A kiss for luck, first."

"Hmmph," she replied.

Devin raised a brow at her.

She smiled and pecked him on the jaw. Devin poured the wine into her mouth. He repeated the action with the second girl, but this time, as she reached for his jaw, he kissed her on the mouth. She smacked his face. He laughed as the girls ran off.

"You see? A woman's lips are the cure for all sorrow," Devin said to Falk. "There are plenty of doves in the world. We'll find you another. Trust me."

Falk smiled faintly. "Do you think?"

"Of course!" Devin passed the wineskin to him. "There'll be plenty of women at the ball to lift—"

A four-horse carriage raced around the bend. The driver, a large, stern man with a crooked nose glanced at the two young men as the carriage neared. He whipped the horses faster. The duo leapt to the side of the road. Devin tumbled onto the ground. The lone passenger inside the carriage glanced distantly at them as they passed. His stony countenance was in stark contrast to the yellow, green, and purple jester costume he wore.

Devin shook his fist at the rear of the coach as it rushed toward the manor. "Piss on you and your ancestors!"

Falk laughed and lifted him to his feet.

A large group of bell-legged morris dancers capered in and out of a circle dance inside the main hall of the manor. Many of the participants were robed as hobbyhorses, pigs, and bushy hedges. One hairy man was dressed as a woman. The morris dancers flailed long, white rags and bounced the bells strapped on their legs to match the rhythm of a buoyant jig-like tune the musicians played. Costumed men and women roamed about. They laughed and slugged down tankards of mead and ale.

Servants skirted around the partygoers, replacing empty jugs and salvers with full ones.

Merek the lion and Gussalen the peacock stood near the entrance, smiling and greeting guests as they entered. Gripping a walking stick, the somber man costumed as a jester approached them. His coach driver shadowed him. The man in the jester attire motioned with his stick for the driver to stop a few yards behind him. The costumed jester continued on to the couple. "Lord and Lady De Bromwell, my complements on a most festive evening." He glanced about. "Where is your lovely daughter?"

"Baron Cleves, you know how the young are," Gussalen said. "No doubt she's still primping."

The baron raised his chin. "It's a crime they have no matters more pressing than dress and music."

Gussalen glanced at Merek. She rolled her eyes and said to Baron Cleves, "Where *did* these younger ones go wrong?"

"Lady De Bromwell, even the favorite cousin and most loyal advisor to the prince can't answer that." Before Gussalen could express her derision again, Baron Cleves moved in closer to Merek and said, "Is there any truth to the rumor that you're contemplating wedding bells for your daughter?"

Gussalen laughed. "Yes, and the world is round as a ball!"

Baron Cleves side-eyed her, then half-bowed to Merek. "If you are looking for a suitor. I modestly offer myself."

"Though there's no truth to the rumors," Merek replied, "we are humbled by your offer. Aren't we, sweet?" Merek smiled at Gussalen.

"Indeed, indeed!" This time when she looked at her husband the ridicule in her eyes was replaced with apprehension.

"That's comforting to know." The baron looked around indifferently. "By the bye, I'm sure you have heard that the prince has entered the spice market?"

Merek's mouth tightened. Gussalen's hand went to her neck. Baron Cleves smiled inwardly at their reaction. Merek said, "He knows, after all, that I have a document signed by his father, the King, stating—"

"Alas," Baron Cleves interrupted. "Due to our rising conflict with France, the prince has declared an emergency. He's voided all preceding agreements regarding the spice trade until such time that the King returns from the battlefield." Baron Cleves smiled. "Unless, of course, either of you is related to the royal family. In that case, all previous arrangements remain." He shrugged. "It's a pity. Even an in-law would do."

The De Bromwells exchanged hard looks. "How goes the war?" Merek asked him.

"It's a slow, slow process. Slower than—" Baron Cleves was cut short by a servant girl balancing four pies on a platter. She stumbled on Cleves' walking stick as she attempted to pass. A pie slipped and spilled on his sleeve. "You clumsy oaf!" He raised his cane over her head. The girl cowered. He swung.

Merek clamped the cane before it struck her. Baron Cleves' driver stepped forward. Merek said, "Now, now, my good Baron. We don't want to waste any more of these wonderful pies, do we?"

Cleve studied the pie platters in the frightened girl's hands. His face, which had hardened with rage, relaxed. He yawned and signaled his driver back. Gussalen quickly moved the servant girl along. Baron Cleves smiled at Merek. "Perhaps we may continue our conversation regarding your daughter's wedding plans at a more opportune time?"

Merek bowed. "Certainly, Baron." Cleves motioned to his driver. He trailed Cleves into the crowd. Merek frowned at Gussalen. She gripped his hand. More arriving guests approached. The De Bromwells took big breaths and forced the worry from their faces. They smiled gaily and greeted the invitees.

Eddie and Charles rushed along the castle kitchen. It was separated from the main hall, but connected by an enclosed wooden passageway. The two men shadowed the De Bromwells' daughter as she scurried past cooks, servants, and several fireplaces. Simmering above the flames were spit-roasted pigs and chickens, and large iron vats of stew.

"Hold up, my lady!" Eddie yelled. "I'm not as young as I used to be."

"Hurry." She rushed into the passageway. "Father will flog us—well, rather you—if I'm any later."

Eddie struggled to keep pace. As the girl was about to push the curtain aside separating the passageway from the manor proper she stopped, adjusted her hair and tugged on her robe. She turned back to Eddie, who, along with Charles, had caught up to her. "Tell me, Edward, do I look befitting? Be honest. I want to make Mother and Father proud."

Eddie adjusted her halo. "Angel, may I call you Angel?"

She thought about it. "In private, but always 'my lady' in front of my parents or you truly will be whipped."

"Got it. Now as to how you look." He examined her over and smiled. "Angel, you look…heavenly."

Charles made a notation. Eddie tried to see what he had written, but Charles turned away from him.

"This may sound foolish, Edward," Angel said, "but I've always thought of myself as the ugly duckling in that silly fable. I pray that tonight the world will forget the duckling and welcome the swan."

Eddie bowed ceremoniously and swept the curtain aside. "Go for it, oh swan." Angel walked through the opening and collided head on with Falk, who was stepping across it. Angel fell on her butt. Falk spilt the tankard of ale he was drinking on the both of them. He said, "By God's bones, watch where you're going!" as he adjusted his ale-soaked hood, which had fallen down his face.

"You clumsy moose. You ran me over!" Angel replied.

"If your head wasn't too big for your halo, you might've seen me coming," Falk blurted.

Angel felt the halo. The rod holding it had bent sideways. "The only thing obstructing my vision was a hooded pile of dung!" She stood. Falk threw back his cowl. The two glared at each other. They blushed. From his vantage point behind the curtain, Eddie could see their faces soften and their eyes glow. The vision of kissing Carly an eternity ago on New Year's swept through and filled him with longing for her and Ben.

Angel said to Falk, "Perhaps it was I who was at fault."

"No, it's true," he replied. "I'm a clumsy moose."

Two servants in the kitchen carrying a platter with a roasted pig on it approached the curtain to enter the main hall. Eddie barred his arm to prevent them from interrupting.

"This duckling has spoken most foul. Forgive me," Angel replied.

"Duckling?" Falk straightened the rod holding her halo. "Oh, swan, I'd have you curse me a thousand times to see your face once more."

Angel smiled bashfully, lowered her gaze and got a look at her ale-soaked gown. Mortified, she uttered, "I must leave," and darted back into the kitchen passageway. She swept past Eddie and Charles. They rushed after her.

Falk stuck his head through the curtain. "Wait! I don't even know your name." He tried to follow, but the servants carrying the pig blocked his way. By the time Falk worked his way around them she had disappeared. Falk stepped back into the main hall, took a heavy breath and stared at the curtain that Angel had disappeared behind.

Someone clapped him on the back. "I saw that." It was Devin. He handed Falk another tankard. "Knocking down a maiden and spilling ale on her is a most unorthodox way to win her heart."

"Who was she? Do you know?"

Devin raised a brow. "You jest."

"No. Who is she? I must see her again."

"My dear holy monk," Devin said with a gleam in his eye. "You just soiled the daughter of the man who sent your uncle to debtor's prison."

Falk groaned. "Her father is Merek De Bromwell?"

Devin nodded.

Falk lowered his hood over his face and slumped against the wall.

Outside the kitchen, beneath the moonlight, Angel sat on an overturned vat. She cupped her hands over her eyes and cried. Eddie knelt next to her. Charles stood behind him. "Come on, Angel," Eddie said. "Cheer up." He tried to adjust her halo, but it tumbled to the ground.

Angel kicked the fallen ring. "Why do I even try? Oh, death, carry me away on a cloud."

"Hey," Eddie said. "Don't joke about that."

She looked at him as if she had just noticed he was there. "Leave me be, Edward."

"But the guy likes you. It's obvious."

"Please. I want to be by myself."

"I don't think that's a good idea."

She gave Eddie a tearful look. "Leave."

Eddie glanced back at Charles for advice, but Charles kept a straight face. "Okay," Eddie said to Angel. "But I'm only going over there." He nodded to a tree stump about twenty feet away. "Call me if you need anything."

She nodded. Eddie and Charles walked to the spot. Eddie took a seat on the stump and watched Angel while she stared pensively at the moon. "She looks like she wants to throw herself in a river," he said to Charles. "Do you think she'd actually do it?"

"Sorry, but I can't tell you that."

"Sorry, but I can't tell you that? Listen, Charles, my wife thinks I'm an asshole. I missed my son's sixth birthday — the one I swore I was going to attend, and after losing one bet after another I finally hit the big payoff, and then I find out I'm fighting for my soul. It hasn't been a good day, you know?"

Charles nodded.

Eddie frowned. He continued to watch Angel sob.

Eddie and Charles stood on Angel's veranda as they waited for her two maidservants to wrap up their prepping of her for the night. It had taken Angel a good half-hour to stop crying and leave the kitchen area. Afterwards, she changed and made a token appearance at the party. Eddie looked for Falk.

He suspected Angel did too, by the way her eyes darted around the chaotic room. Neither of them had success. There were no clocks, but Eddie guessed that sometime around nine o'clock Angel whispered to him that she was ready to be escorted back to her chamber.

As he continued to wait for the all-clear signal from Angel's maidservants, Eddie gazed at the garden below. The glow of the moon gave a silver tint to the expanse of herbs, gillyflowers and vine-covered pergola growing beneath Angel's veranda. A sweet-smelling apple tree stood on one side of the veranda. "What now?" he asked Charles.

"I suppose that after you check to make sure she's safely tucked in her bed, then you head off to your quarters."

"No, I mean what happens next? Angel's a kid. Tomorrow she'll be as good as new, right?"

"You know I'm not at liberty to speak about that," Charles said. "My job is to observe and record."

"I was asking the question rhetorically."

"It's still a fine line."

Eddie turned to him. "You're starting to piss me off."

"I'm sorry, but I can't help that." Charles made a notation in his book.

"Fuck you," Eddie said. "And fuck the Jes—"

"No!" Charles grabbed Eddie's wrist. "That'll count against you."

Eddie shook his arm away.

"Edward," Angel called out. "You may enter now."

Eddie heard the sadness in her voice. He didn't need Charles to tell him that her sorrow wasn't going away with the rising of the sun. "Okay, my lady. I'm coming." He took one more look at the garden, took a deep whiff of the sweet scents and turned toward the chamber. Something pinged him in the back of the head.

"Don't go. I must speak with you, lovely one." This came from a voice hidden in the shrubbery below.

Eddie turned back and was pinged again. It was a pebble. "You've got the wrong lovely one," he said as he scoured the garden for whoever it was that had spoken.

Falk emerged from behind a hedge. "A hundred pardons. I was looking for your lady."

"Wait right there. I'll get her." Eddie rushed into Angel's chamber as the two maidservants carted Angel's party clothes and a water urn out the door. Angel was lying in bed, clutching a pair of linen sheets to her chest and staring forlornly at the canopy bed's ceiling.

"Angel, someone wants to speak with you," Eddie said.

She sighed. "Tell Father and Mother I'm sleeping."

"It's not them."

"Whoever it is, tell them to wait until morning." Angel rolled on her side, away from him. "Good night."

Eddie smiled. "It's the hooded pile of dung."

Angel rolled back, clutched the sheet to her chest and sprang upright. "Where?"

"In the garden. Outside your terrace."

"Oh…oh!" She glanced at herself beneath the sheets. "Tell him I'll be but a moment."

Eddie returned to the veranda. He heard Angel bound from the bed, open the wooden chest and shuffle through it. Eddie cupped his hands around his mouth and said to the shrubbery Falk was hiding in, "She'll be here in a minute."

Shortly, Angel walked out in a black velvet gown with a cone-shaped skirt, and a short jacket that did little to hide her plunging neckline.

When Eddie saw her attire he shook his head at Charles and whispered, "The more things change, the more they stay the same."

Charles smiled.

"I'll wait for you inside, my lady," Eddie said to Angel. "Good luck." He motioned for Charles to follow him into the chamber. Inside, Eddie stood at the side of the veranda's entrance to covertly catch what was going on. Charles stood over his shoulder for the same reason.

Falk again emerged from behind the hedge. "Are you still upset with me?"

Angel replied, "I don't know. You spoke harsh words to me."

"Smart," Eddie whispered to Charles. "She's playing hard to get."

"It was my own stupidity. I beg your forgiveness." Falk moved in closer. "Though I've seen you only briefly, my heart has known you forever."

He's not too bad in the courting department, either, Eddie thought.

Angel laughed. "Do you speak such flowery language to all the maidens?"

"Of course not!"

Angel folded her arms across her chest. "Ha!"

"By God's blood, it's true." Falk pushed his hood back and added, "If we were doves, I would pray our love unite this very evening and fly away."

Angel leaned over the balustrade and smirked. "You speak of lust, not of love."

"Yes...no!" He grabbed on to the trunk of the apple tree and launched himself up it. Falk inched out on a thick branch a few feet from the veranda. He looked Angel in the eyes and softly said, "You may call it what you wish, but whatever this feeling is, it is enflamed with love."

"The kid's got game," Eddie said. Charles nodded. Eddie lamented if Ben would, too, when he grew older.

Angel studied Falk for several moments. "If your words are as true in the light of day as they are beneath the moonlight, I would be the happiest maiden in all of England."

Falk's face lit up. "Do you mean it?"

Angel corner-eyed him. "Do *you* mean it?"

"Yes," he replied. "With every hammer of my heart." Falk stretched out as far as he could, while Angel leaned as far over the balustrade as she could. It was barely enough, but their lips met.

"That's sweet," Eddie said to Charles. "They're going steady."

"I don't think so."

He looked back at Charles. "What does that mean?"

Charles raised his eyebrows.

Eddie cocked his head back. "Marriage? You gotta be kidding."

There was a loud ruffling noise outside, followed by, "Oww!"

"Are you hurt?" Angel called out.

Eddie and Charles raced on to the veranda. Angel was leaning over it. Falk was below, rubbing his knee and picking himself off the ground. "A little," he said to her. "But it will vanish." He waved. "Until the sun's light." Falk slipped his cowl over his head and raced away.

Angel turned to Eddie and pressed her hand against her heart. "Oh, Edward, I'm so happy I hope I live a thousand years!" She hugged him and practically floated into the chamber.

For a moment Eddie contemplated warning Angel about the impulses of youth and falling too quickly in love. Then he thought, was that really his business? No. This was another time, another era. She was happy and that was good. Good for her, good for the hooded kid and great for his bet. He shrugged away his concern and entered the room. Charles followed along as he made notations in his writing pad.

Inside the chamber, Angel swayed her arms and glided in circles across the floor.

There was a knock on the door, followed with a "May we enter?"

"Of course, Father." Angel swept to the door and opened it.

Merek and Gussalen entered. Both wore long, heavy, sleeping gowns.

"You didn't stay long at the ball," Gussalen said to her. "We were worried, my dearest. All is well?"

"All is divinely well." Angel kissed them and added, "Oh, most noble parents, with your blessing, I wish to take a husband."

Merek flinched. "Did you fall in a wine casket?"

"No," Angel said. "I truly want to marry." She again coasted across the floor.

Merek and Gussalen looked at each other with brows raised. Gussalen turned back to Angel. "This is what you desire?"

Angel did a gleeful twirl. "As surely as the sun rises."

"Well?" Merek turned to Gussalen. She shrugged and spread her palms. He said to Angel, "Is four eve's hence too soon?"

"They sure move quickly around here," Eddie whispered to Charles.

Angel smiled. "Oh, Father it's a dream come true!"

Merek said to Gussalen, "And you said she would rather face the rack than marry Baron Cleves."

"Who's Cleves?" Eddie whispered to Charles. "Is he the kid in the monk's hood?" Charles held a finger up for Eddie to keep quiet and listen.

"Baron Cleves?" Angel's face went ashen. "I cannot possibly marry—"

"I'm sorry," Merek interrupted, "but it's impossible for us to make the marriage arrangements any sooner. You must have patience."

"No." Angel looked at Gussalen as if she were in a trance. "I won't do this."

Gussalen smiled sympathetically. "You'll have to be patient, but I promise the celebration will be the grandest of affairs."

Merek wrapped his arm around Gussalen's shoulder. "I wouldn't be surprised if the prince, himself, attends."

"No!" Angel pushed him away. "You misread me."

"You will marry Baron Cleves when I say. Not a day before. Is that understood, daughter?"

She crossed her arms—"Never!"—and stomped her foot for emphasis.

Merek's face reddened. "How dare you defy me!"

"She'll come around," Gussalen replied. "Give her time."

"Not in a million winters will I come around!" Angel tossed the empty water basin on the floor. "Now get out. I mean it!"

Merek glanced at Gussalen. "Perhaps a little time in the oubliette will alter her view."

Gussalen gasped. "Surely, you jest?"

Angel crossed her arms and glowered at him. "You wouldn't dare."

Merek narrowed his eyes. "Do not tempt me. I mean it."

Angel looked fearfully at Gussalen.

"What's the oubliette?" Eddie asked Charles

"The forgotten room—a dungeon in the floor with a trapdoor above it," Charles said.

"Now, now, my lord." Gussalen gripped Merek's arm. "I'm sure this is nothing more than a misunderstanding." She turned to Angel. "Tell him, dearest."

Merek eyed Angel. "Speak, daughter. Is this a misunderstanding?"

Gussalen nodded at Angel as if to say, "Please, you must tell him."

"I…" Angel gulped, fell face down on the bed and wept.

Merek said to Gussalen, "Come, we have a wedding to prepare."

Gussalen's eyes remained on Angel as they left the room. Eddie saw the apprehension in them. He said to Charles, "Who is this Baron Cleves?"

Charles frowned and shook his head.

"He's an ogre," Angel blurted out, thinking Eddie had spoken to her. "I wish I were dead."

Eddie watched the girl's shoulders heave from the force of her sobs. He sat next to her and patted her arm. She leaned into him. He cradled her and thought how much he missed Carly and of the misery he had caused her and Ben.

Chapter Five

"We must have new drapery for the wedding now that it's been confirmed the prince will be attending," Gussalen said as her maid placed a bowl of broth and bacon in front of her. Two male servants quietly passed with empty platters from the previous night's ball.

"Mother, I don't want—"

"Nonsense," Gussalen said to Angel, who was seated across from her nursing beef marrow filled pastries. "You are our baby. It's our pleasure to do this."

Angel had lavender semi-circles beneath her eyes. Her face was pallid. She turned to Merek. He was seated at the head of the table. "Father, please." Merek was merrily gulping large chunks of lampreys sprinkled with hot sauce. Before he could answer, a servant approached and whispered something to him. Merek nodded to the servant, who bowed and left.

A short time later, Baron Cleves entered with his chin raised. He was dressed in a red wool houppelande. A bejeweled baldric was strapped diagonally over his right shoulder to the opposite hip. His walking stick was tucked beneath an arm. Cleve's baleful carriage driver remained a few feet away in the shadows. Cleves half-bowed to Merek and kissed Gussalen's hand. He glanced at Angel, who avoided eye contact by trifling with her uneaten pastry.

"I am here but for a moment," Baron Cleves said to Merek. "I bring word from the prince. He wishes to discuss the spice market with you. He seeks your council on how best to disperse the new areas bequeathed to you."

Angel locked eyes on her father and mother.

Merek shot Angel a discomfited look. Gussalen smiled weakly in a vain attempt to hide her guilt. Merek cleared his throat and said to the baron, "Um, when does the prince wish council?"

Baron Cleves smiled. "After the wedding, of course."

Merek once more glanced at Angel. Her jaw tightened with understanding and disgust. Merek lowered his gaze and said meekly, "His desire is my command."

"I told him you would answer such." Baron Cleves again kissed Gussalen's hand. He reached for Angel's.

She yanked it back, "Not in a million fortnights," and stomped off.

Merek smiled embarrassingly at Cleves. "As delighted as she is, it's still a bit overwhelming. She will come around." He looked at Gussalen. "Isn't that right, my sweet?"

Gussalen replied in a flat tone, "Yes, I'm sure she will."

Baron Cleves squeezed the handle of his walking stick. "To that end, I harbor little doubt." He half-bowed to Merek and turned to his driver. "Come, Speer." Speer left the shadows and followed Cleves.

Angry and eyes reddened with the last of her tears, Angel wandered the garden as if sleepwalking. As she passed a fig tree, a man reached out from the other side. He grabbed her from behind with one hand and with the other tightened it around her mouth. The frightened girl screamed, but the hand covering her mouth stifled the sound.

Eddie took a miserable breath and looked around the musty-odored, dingy washroom he was in. He wiped sweat from his brow and picked up a chemise lying on a clothes pile next to the splintered stool he sat on. Eddie swished the garment around the inside of a tub filled with soapy water. Charles stood next to him, humming a tune and writing.

A brawny, hard-faced woman entered. She picked up rags lying next to a fireplace and used them to protect her hands as she lifted a pot of boiling water hanging over the fire. She carted the pot to Eddie's tub and dumped the water in it. "Hey, that burns!" Eddie said.

The woman scowled and left.

"What I wouldn't give for a washer and dryer," Eddie muttered. Charles smiled, but kept humming. Eddie plunged the clothing in and out of the tub and found that he was falling in with the shuffle rhythm of Charles' tune. It reminded him of something the Stray Cats might have played, but it was getting monotonous. Charles had hummed it over and over with little variations since early morning. Finally, Eddie said, "No offense, Chuck, but a change of pace would be nice."

"Sorry. I got carried away. I've been trying to get the bridge right for over forty-five years. It's still a little shaky, don't you think?"

Eddie stopped scrubbing and looked at him. "Forty-five years? How old are you?"

Charles thought a moment. "That's hard to answer. Technically it's 1485, which means I haven't been born yet, but in actuality I've been dead longer than I've been alive. Of course, you don't age the same way when you're dead, that is if you can even call it aging."

Eddie thought about what the Jesses had told him about the difficulty of measuring time. "Yeah, yeah, I know. It's complicated." He went back to scrubbing.

Charles continued to write, but this time in silence.

Eddie thought about Angel and her predicament. That Cleves guy was bad news, but what could he do about it? The only things he knew about the medieval age came from a few movies and a beer-filled afternoon at the Renaissance Festival. What stuck in his mind from the event were axe-tossing tournaments, buxom maidens with lousy English accents frolicking about the grounds, and the so-called King and Queen who performed faux marriages. He remembered the last one because he wanted to go for it, but Carly thought it was sacrilegious—and it cost thirty-five dollars. A thought crossed his mind. "Charles, how many wives are you allowed in Merry Old England in 1485?"

"One, as far as I know. Why?"

"And divorce?"

"I don't think there is any."

Eddie dropped the garment in the tub, sprang up from his stool and said, "Come on!" As they left the washroom, the brawny servant entered, looked at Eddie and grimaced.

Angel dug her elbows into the man who had captured her. He gripped her from behind. She kicked the back of her shoe into his shin.

"Shhh, keep quiet." The man's voice was strained from the effort to hold her. Angel tried to recognize who it was, but she couldn't. She dug her elbows into him again. "By God's blood!" The man released her. Angel spun around with raised fists. She started to swing them but instead cried and hugged him. The man was Falk.

"Forgive me," Falk said. "I didn't mean to frighten you, but I didn't want you to scream and bring others to us." He lifted her head and kissed her.

She continued to sob.

"I didn't wish to make you cry. I'm sorry." Falk handed her a cloth from his satchel.

She wiped her eyes and blew her nose into it. "It was nothing you did. It's because my parents are forcing me to wed Baron Cleves."

Falk held her at arm's length and stared into her eyes to make sense of what she had said. "No," he at last replied. "Cleves is a brute."

"And cousin to the prince who controls my father's spice market," Angel added. "Are you, by chance, kin to the prince? If so, our marriage would allow Father to keep his trade."

There was a rustling sound: footsteps approached. Slipping a knife from the sheath roped to his waist, Falk put himself between Angel and the noise. Eddie and Charles broke through a shrub. Eddie saw the knife and touched the spot on his forehead where Falk had beaned him with the pebble. "I'm with her, remember? The terrace?" Falk nodded and put his knife away.

Angel repeated her question to Falk, "Are you related to the prince?"

Falk glanced at Eddie and her. "If the truth be known, the Falk family and yours are not on the best of terms. My uncle is in debtor's prison over a dispute with your father."

Angel lowered her head and clutched her elbows. "Then all is truly lost." Falk took her in his arms. They clung to each other as if they were about to be burned at the stake.

"I might have a solution," Eddie said. Charles removed his notepad from his pocket and readied his pen. "What if you already had a husband before the scheduled wedding to Baron Cleves?"

"Then it would be too late for him!" Falk again held Angel at arm's length, smiled and stared into her eyes. "What do you say, love?"

Angel looked sheepishly at him. "I...I don't know. It's my parents' will, and there is the oubliette ..."

Falk's smile flattened. "I understand. It was a fool's notion."

Angel looked at Eddie. Her face pleaded for advice.

Eddie shrugged. "Of course I can only speak for myself. But from my experience parents always want what's best for their children."

Angel looked at Falk. "Our marriage could destroy their livelihood."

"She's right," Falk said. "Let us not speak of it further."

"Hold on," Eddie replied to Angel. "No one wants your parents to lose their business, but can you trust this Baron Cleves? What's to say that once you and he are married he won't take it all for himself anyway?"

"It's true. He can't be trusted," Falk said.

"Father has an agreement with the King. Once he returns from the war, the prince would no longer have control over the spice market and it would be restored to my parents."

"The war is going well," Falk said. "It won't be long before we are victorious."

"There you go," Eddie said. "Your parents would still have their business, but you'd be stuck with Cleves forever." Eddie smiled, but behind it was a layer of shame. Though he hadn't lied, he had told Angel what she wanted to hear—what would help him win the bet. He had manipulated the odds and felt like garbage for doing it.

"I'd rather die than live my life with Baron Cleves," Angel said.

"Then live your life with me." Falk lifted Angel's chin and looked into her eyes. "I love you."

She stared at him for a moment, then glanced at Eddie. His smile was gone. He was holding his breath.

Angel locked eyes with Falk and answered with a long, hard kiss.

Relief swept through Eddie. The joy on Angel's face convinced him that he had done the right thing. He smiled at Charles. Charles gave no response. Eddie turned his attention back to the kissing couple and waited for them to stop. Finally, he cleared his throat. Embarrassed, Angel and Falk separated.

"Now then. Who can we get to perform the ceremony?" Eddie asked. "There's a procedure, right?"

"Father Quinn is a friend of mine," Falk replied. "He's the monk who loaned me his tunic and scapula for the masquerade ball. I'm sure I can persuade him to marry us." They heard footsteps approach. Their eyes darted in the direction of the sound. Falk reached for his blade.

Eddie waved his palm at him. "We don't want any trouble."

Falk nodded. "I will go to Father Quinn and make the arrangements. He resides in a small monastery outside of Ceswican. Be there as tomorrow's sun reaches its zenith."

The footsteps were nearly upon them.

"Come, Edward," Angel said. "We have much work to do before then." Falk and Angel quickly kissed. The group rushed away in the opposite direction of the footsteps.

The source of the noise—Baron Cleves and Speer—arrived in

time to catch a glimpse of the trio as they rounded a bend. Cleves pointed to Falk. "Follow that one. I distrust him."

Speer continued on. Baron Cleves remained. He picked a pink carnation from a nearby bush. He sniffed the flower and twirled it back and forth between his fingers. Then he dropped it and crushed it with the heel of his walking stick.

Eddie and Charles watched the two young boys with amusement. One of them raised a wooden stick to the sky and shouted, "With this sword I slay the dragon, Gragoloon!" The boy who declared this was dressed in rags. He—along with Eddie, Charles, and a second boy in rags—stood outside the open gates of a humble monastery. The first boy thrust the stick toward the other boy's chest.

The second boy leaped to the side, snatched the stick from the first boy and tossed it on the ground. He roared and proclaimed, "Gragoloon smites you with his fire!" He leaped on the first boy and blew air over his face. The two tumbled to the ground. Eddie looked at Charles and laughed. The doors of the monastery flung open. The boys stopped wrestling.

Falk and Angel emerged. Father Quinn strolled behind them. He was a smiling, bald man with a tight, gray beard. Eddie removed a pouch of rice roped around his waist and readied it.

"Give 'er a kiss, m'lord!" one of the boys yelled.

"Kiss 'er!" the other one echoed.

Falk and Angel laughed. He lifted her veil and kissed her. The boys cheered. Eddie smiled at Charles.

"May this union bring much happiness." Father Quinn led them through the gates.

"Our eternal gratitude, Father. Our first-born will bear the name of Quinn," Falk declared.

"Or Jacquelyn!" Angel countered.

The couple embraced and shared a long, passionate kiss. Eddie put his hands over Charles' eyes. The boys whooped.

Father Quinn said, "Please, my children, express yourselves in a more secluded setting."

Angel said, "Husband, shall we go to your chamber?"

"Pardon me," Eddie said. "But maybe it'd be wiser to break the news to my lady's parents with a feather instead of a brick?"

"What does that mean?" Falk asked.

"Instead of word leaking back to them, I think it would benefit you both if they were the first to know."

Angel glimpsed at Falk and said to Eddie, "What do you propose?"

"How about you and I go back to your parents' manor and you—we—sit them down and gently explain everything. Give them time to absorb it." Her parents were going to be pissed enough as it was, but this way, Eddie reasoned, maybe it would prevent them from going ballistic and turning completely against her.

"It's a mistake. It'll only feed the fire," Falk said.

"No," Angel replied. "His words bear truth."

Though he didn't want his emotions to gum up the works, Eddie genuinely liked the couple. They reminded him of the exuberance of life with an entire future in front of them. He wanted these two to have what he screwed up with Carly and Ben.

"Given the opportunity, I am sure that they will accept you." Father Quinn clapped Falk on the back.

"Yes, how can it not be so?" Angel removed her wedding band and handed it to Falk.

"What are you doing?" Falk asked.

"She's doing right," Father Quinn said. "If Lord and Lady De Bromwell see it on her finger, the game is lost before it begins."

Falk looked at Eddie. "I don't like this."

"Do you have a better idea?"

"I've already spoken it. We leave now and let the winds blow as they may."

Eddie glanced at Angel. He could see by the uncertainty in her eyes that she was wavering. He said to Falk, "That's easy for you to say, my lord, because they're not your parents, but what about her?"

Falk's cheeks reddened. Eddie thought it was with rage. He back-stepped, afraid that Falk was going to take a swing at him. But Falk took a deep breath, hugged Angel and said, "Forgive me. I wasn't thinking."

"Perhaps you're right," Angel said. "It's best to leave now. Together."

Eddie squeezed his chin twice, hoping they'd make the right decision—the one that would keep her happy and make it a cinch for him to win his bet.

"Your manservant's correct." Falk shot a look at Eddie. "If you can keep in good stead with your parents, you will be happier. That's all I truly want."

Angel kissed his hand.

Eddie smiled at Charles. His face remained flat, but something behind it made Eddie feel unsettled.

Falk slipped her ring inside his satchel. "After today, it must never leave your finger. Promise me."

"By God's salvation, I swear it." They kissed.

The two boys hooted. Eddie tossed a handful of rice at the newlyweds and scooted the boys away. They scrambled off in different directions. One of the boys turned a corner and banged into a bulky man with a crooked nose. The man—Speer—had a sword strapped to his waist. The boy fell on his behind. Speer smiled with tightened lips at the boy, helped him up, then entered a dark alley and waited.

Falk fingered Angel's wedding ring from the outside of his satchel as he and Father Quinn watched her coach depart.

"You'll see. With God's resolve, it will all work out." Father Quinn shook Falk's hand and entered the monastery.

Falk departed down a narrow, stone road lined with stone buildings. A few yards in front of him sat a woman with a bundle. On the other side of the street the lead horse of a parked carriage was urinating. Theirs was the only activity. Falk nodded to the woman as he passed. Speer emerged from the shadows of a side alley and knocked against him. "Watch where you step, young fool."

"I beg your pardon." Falk studied Speer a moment. "Do I know you, sir?"

"Did you call me a cur?" Speer crossed his arms over his chest.

"I begged your pardon, only." Falk raised his palms to show he meant no trouble.

"Now the odious paynim calls me a liar!" Speer grabbed the front of Falk's shirt and pulled him in. "Ah, it's clear, you are a Falk." He shoved Falk back. "Death to the cowardly snakes who crawl from that house of debtors." Speer drew his sword. Falk reached for his knife. The woman with the bundle scurried away.

"Now I recognize you," Falk said. "You're the dog who answers to Baron Cleves."

Speer took a swipe at Falk with his blade. Falk jumped back. The blade whisked by his chest. Falk bolted forward and shoved his knife at Speer. The tip sliced Speer's forearm. Speer lunged his sword forward. Falk sidestepped. The blade grazed his arm. He again rushed Speer. Speer turned sideways and stuck his leg out. Falk caught it on the ankle and tumbled on his back. His knife flew from his hand. Speer pressed his boot on Falk's chest. He brought the tip of his sword to Falk's neck.

"Sir, can you spare a moment for God?" This came from a deep, sonorous voice that echoed down the street and alley like a thunderclap.

Speer glanced toward the sound. Falk used the distraction to shove Speer's foot to the side. Speer stumbled back. Falk grabbed his knife off the ground and at the same time shot a look in the direction of the sound. It was Father Quinn. Falk leapt to his feet as Speer regained his balance. Speer thrust his sword at Falk's stomach. Falk pushed the flat of the blade away with his left wrist. He buried his knife with his right hand into Speer's eye. Speer staggered. He tried to utter something, collapsed and fell motionless. A horde of footsteps racing toward them reverberated in the distance.

Father Quinn ran to Falk. "Quickly, you must depart."

"I won't. It was no fault of mine. He attacked me first."

"'It'll do no good. He's servant to the prince's cousin. That's all the proof needed of your guilt."

"But my wife? I'm to meet her this very eve."

"I'll explain all to her." Father Quinn glanced in the direction of the footsteps, which grew louder. "Go to Hexham Way, ask for James, cousin of Quinn. He'll shelter you until this dies down."

Falk licked his lips with indecision. Soldiers rushed around the corner from the end of the street.

"Go!" Father Quinn said. "Or die."

Falk took off down the alley. Moments later the guards approached. Father Quinn held out his hands to them. "I assure you, it was a rightful death."

The door of the carriage tethered to the horse that had urinated, opened. Baron Cleves stepped from it. He rushed to Father Quinn and pointed his walking stick at him. "The only rightful death is that of this murderer who hides behind the cloth of God." He knelt by Speer's body. "I, the prince's cousin, lost a good and loyal servant today."

"He knows not what he says." Father Quinn motioned to Speer. "This man tried to kill my friend, and I—"

Baron Cleves sprang to his feet. "And you jumped upon Speer's back and held him while young Falk plunged a knife in his eye."

Father Quinn's face reddened. "How *dare* you!"

"I saw it all from my coach," Baron Cleves said to the head guard. "I demand you arrest this man."

The head guard studied Cleves, Quinn, the carriage and Speer's corpse. He said to Cleves, "Father Quinn *is* a man of God."

Cleves raised his nose. "And I'm first cousin of the prince."

The guard tapped his cheek several times and stared at the blood oozing from Speer's eye onto the road's flattened stones. He shrugged and said to the other guards, "Take the Father."

Baron Cleves strolled back to his carriage. "Baron Cleves is lying," Father Quinn said as they dragged him away. "Surely you see that?"

"Surely you see that?" Angel nibbled the tip of her thumb and paced her chamber. She glanced at Eddie, who was packing her belongings in the wood chest near the toiletry table. "Yes, that's what I'll tell my parents, that surely they could see the only way to avoid marrying that troll, Cleves, was to marry another." She stopped pacing and rubbed her elbows. "Then I'll introduce them to their son-in-law, who I know they'll love."

Eddie cleared his throat. "Perhaps you might want to think this over a little more," Eddie said. "You know, slow down and give it deeper thought."

Angel looked worriedly at him. "Do you think so?"

"It couldn't hurt."

Angel stared at the wall for several moments. She took a deep breath. "No, Edward. This is the moment. I fear my courage will depart and never return."

Eddie studied the young girl. He thought of Ben and hoped that one day his son would possess the same kind of strength.

"In that case, Angel, if it works for you, it works for me." Eddie nodded to Charles, who stood in the corner, taking notes. Charles glanced at Angel, frowned, and resumed writing.

The main hall buzzed with activity. Merek directed six servants where to hang on the wall an enormous embroidered blue cloth. Maids placed goblets and small cakes on a large, long table. Gussalen presided over a trio of servants as she regarded the placement of flowers around the room. Angel entered. Eddie followed her. Charles followed him. Gussalen smiled at Angel and pointed to a bouquet of blue flowers near the fireplace. "What do you think? The color matches your wedding dress."

Angel nervously rubbed her hands.

"Well?" her mother repeated.

"Mother, surely you can see, that is…I…"

Eddie whispered to her, "You can do this, my lady."

Angel glanced at him and nodded. "Mother, I'd rather die than marry Baron Cleves."

Merek, who was now sampling a cake, nearly choked. He came over to her. "You *are* marrying the baron."

"Merek." Gussalen motioned toward the servants.

Merek ordered them to leave. Eddie started to follow, but Angel raised her hand for him to remain. Merek frowned, but kept silent.

When the others had cleared the area, Gussalen said to Angel, "What is this all about?"

"I don't love the man."

"Is that all?" Merek whisked his hand. "I thought it was something grave."

Gussalen wrapped her arm around Angel's shoulder. "Dearest, given time the heart can adapt to anything." She shot a weary smile at Merek.

"No. I will never accept Baron Cleves."

"Enough nonsense," Merek said. "We have a room to prepare for tomorrow's celebration."

Angel's eyes watered. Gussalen looked at Merek. "Give her time. She'll do as you wish."

"Time will change nothing," Angel replied. "Because I'm already married."

Gussalen gasped and stepped away from her.

Merek pressed his fists against his hips. "Speak, daughter. Now!"

Angel glimpsed at Eddie. He nodded encouragement. "My most precious parents, I mean you no harm. But I—we—are deeply in love. We married this very morn." Angel waited for their reply, but all they did was stare at her. "My husband is, is—" once again she looked at Eddie, he winked at her, she took a deep breath, "—the son of Falk, he is—"

"Falk?" Merek looked at Gussalen.

"Yes. He is—"

The two burst out laughing.

Angel stared at them incredulously as they howled incessantly. "Is my happiness so amusing?"

Gussalen grabbed Angel's empty finger and turned it toward Merek. "Look, my lord, at the lovely ring. Does it not make you jealous?" They laughed again.

Angel whipped her hand back. She looked at Eddie, who—clueless—shrugged and shook his head. He looked to Charles. Charles raised a brow, but continued writing.

Angel stamped her foot. "I speak the truth!"

Merek wiped tears from his eyes and said to Gussalen, "As if she had no idea the scullion fled after murdering Speer."

"Or that his accomplice, the 'blessed' Father Quinn was thrown in the dungeon," Gussalen replied.

"Daughter," Merek said to Angel, "to pretend to marry that scoundrel is inspired." He kissed her forehead. "You've truly inherited the De Bromwell's sense of humor."

"A natural jester," Gussalen agreed. "Oh, how she loves to tease her poor parents."

Merek yelled for the servants to re-enter. Gussalen raced to the fireplace and re-arranged the flower bouquet. The servants trooped in. Stunned, Angel rushed off. Just as stunned, Eddie trailed her. Charles looked upwards beyond the ceiling to the heavens, raised a brow and followed Eddie.

Falk swallowed the last of his cheese and barley bread. He said to James and his wife, Emily, who was sewing, "I thank you both for your hospitality these past few days, but I must go back. I've done no wrong and I..." He stared into the fireplace of the modest, stone house. "I miss my bride."

James placed a hand upon Falk's shoulder. "I urge you restraint. It's dangerous."

"Caution be damned. Can you spare me a fresh horse? I fear mine's still bruised at the ankle."

James looked at Emily. She kept her eyes on her sewing. He said, "Sleep on it, lad. Your love'll survive the night."

Falk shook his head. "Without her, I have nothing but night." He stood. "Thank you again for your hospitality." Falk gathered his things.

"Without a horse, it's folly," James said.

"It's folly for me to have left. I must get back." Falk strung his satchel across his shoulder.

James looked at Emily. She kept her eyes on her sewing.

"I beseech you. Stay but two days longer," James said. "The only thing that awaits you now is trouble."

Falk walked to the door, stopped and turned back. "Thank you, James. You've treated me kindly, but your family makes me miserable."

"I beg your pardon?" James replied.

Emily stopped sewing and narrowed her eyes at Falk.

"Oh, no!" Falk replied to them. "Forgive my clumsiness." He returned to James. "Your family's so wonderful that it makes me long for the same." Falk knelt in front of Emily. "Watching you two gladdens my heart, but at the same time saddens it because it reminds me of what I'm missing." He kissed her hand and once more headed to the door.

James raised a brow at Emily. She nodded to him and went back to sewing. James went to the side window. He yelled to a boy sweeping the inside of a small stable behind the house. "Ho, John. Mount up Lennox. Make haste."

"Yes, Father!" John answered.

James said to Falk, "And you, hurry along before I come to my senses."

Father Quinn sat on a rock and stared at the dungeon floor. It looked like he felt: cold, lonely, and battered. He heard two sets of footsteps echoing toward him. He prayed to God that it was someone who was going to set him free—or at least give him something to eat. Keys rattled. Father Quinn stood. The iron door swung open. A guard motioned for Angel to enter. She rushed in, Eddie behind her, Charles behind him.

The guard said, "Time is of the essence," and closed the door.

Angel said, "Please, Father, the truth."

"I swear by God our Savior that young Falk wasn't to blame."

"Why, then, did he leave?"

"On my advice. He fled to Hexham Way. I sensed a rat in the pie."

"Cleves?" Eddie asked.

"Aye," Father Quinn said. "He made it appear as if Speer was murdered with intent—" he clutched Angel's wrist "—by your husband."

Angel stared at the dungeon's stone wall to gather her thoughts. She took a heavy breath and said to Eddie, "All is lost."

"No, no, my lady. We'll think of something." He glanced at Charles. "Right?"

Charles was silent. Somber.

"I pray so," Angel replied, once again in the belief that Eddie had spoken to her.

Eddie looked at Father Quinn. "Right?" Father Quinn smiled weakly.

Angel sat on the rock that Father Quinn had previously occupied. She cupped her forehead in her hands and stared at her feet.

Eddie kneeled beside her. He was struck how the strain dampened the hazel in her eyes and dulled the glow of her flaxen hair. "How about we go to Hexham Way?"

"My parents will pursue us and force me to return. Baron Cleves will see to that. You'll be hanged."

Before Eddie could process the last sentence, Father Quinn said, "Cleves again?"

"Her pre-arranged husband to be. You didn't know?" Eddie replied.

Father Quinn shook his head.

Of course not, Eddie thought, why would Falk mention anything that might prevent Quinn from performing the wedding ceremony?

"But now it's clear why Cleves acted as he did," Father Quinn said.

"I'm better off dead," Angel said.

"Never say that," Eddie replied. "Life's precious. It's a gift from God. Right, Father?"

Father Quinn rubbed his hands together and breathed twice before answering. "Perhaps death is a better alternative."

"What?" Eddie bolted to his feet. "Are you out of your gourd?"

Father Quinn raised his hands in protest. "Suppose the baron's bride to be did die. Then what?"

Angel studied Father Quinn. Charles, who had pen and pad in hand, cocked his head with curiosity at the monk.

"I don't like where this is going," Eddie said.

"She doesn't really die," Father Quinn said. "We only make it appear so."

"Then they'd leave me alone and I could live without reprisal!" Angel replied.

"Great plan, Father," Eddie said. "There's only one problem. How're you going to make it seem as if she died?"

"On the shelf of my study there's a glass vial containing a green liquid. It's for the treatment of lepers. One swallow drives anxiety from the body. Two swallows bring on a night of impenetrable sleep. With three swallows the body stiffens and loses heat. Breathing is silenced beyond perception. The body remains like this until the sun rises and again sets."

Eddie said, "I guess the Lord does work in mysterious ways."

"That and my brother is an apothecary," Father Quinn replied.

Eddie smiled at Charles. "That and his brother is an apothecary." Charles glanced at him, flipped a page in his notepad and scrawled in it.

"Edward," Angel said. "You must ride to Hexham Way and give word of our plan."

Eddie clapped his hands. "As if my soul depends upon it."

Outside the cell door, footsteps approached. The guard opened the door. "My lady, you must leave now."

As Angel rose from the rock she was sitting on, Eddie slipped an apple from his pocket and handed it to Father Quinn. "You look like you could use this."

On their way out Angel placed three gold coins into the guard's palm. "Please, for the health of Father Quinn."

"When the time's ripe," the guard said, "the good father will escape. Now hurry." The door slammed shut.

Father Quinn sat on his rock, thanked God for the apple and bit into it.

Shit, Eddie thought, it's a lot more fun betting on horses than riding on them. He was in his fourth hour of bobbing up and down. His butt was numb and his lower back was on fire. He envied Charles, who stood beside him a yard above the ground, gliding smoothly forward as if he were on a moving walkway. They were traveling down a hard dirt road surrounded by underbrush. The sun was nearly overhead. The day was bright and hot. As he had done six times previously, Eddie repeated the directions Angel had given him. "At the fork in the road bear west of the shadows if they fall east. Perchance the shadows fall west, bear to the east of them. Though both roads lead to Hexham Way, this be the shortest." He added, "Where is Google Maps when you need it?"

Charles looked at him. "You ride pretty well."

"Tell that to my nuts," Eddie replied while he concentrated on the road ahead.

Charles smiled. "I prefer motorcycles."

"Motorcycles? Where're you from, the Midwest?"

"No. Texas."

"A Texan who fancies motorcycles over horses." Eddie glanced at his shadow. It leaned in no particular direction.

Charles shrugged. "There are a few of us."

Eddie said nothing. He opted instead to listen to the sound of his horse's hoofs clomping in the dirt. A short while later he asked, "Chuck, why are you here?"

"The Jesses assigned me to keep your bet with them on the up and up."

"No, I mean why are you with the Jesses? You're not one of them are you?"

Charles thought a moment. "I'm not, but my life was kinda... cut short. I didn't want to leave behind my connection with the living until I knew if my life was worth anything."

"You're allowed to do that kind of thing?"

"It's up to the Jesses. They decide."

"Figures," Eddie said. "It seems like they determine everything else around here, so why not that?"

"You shouldn't be too hard on them. They have a difficult job."

"I suppose." They continued a few yards. Eddie added, "Can't they just tell you whether your life was worth it or not?"

"The Jesses have the power to, but for me to possess that knowledge is part of a gray area. It's a form of vanity on my part to want to know, and vanity is a privilege not a right."

"So you have to earn it like I have to earn it."

Charles nodded.

Eddie hesitated, not sure if he should ask the question or not, but he decided to, anyway. "How did you die?"

Charles looked at Eddie. "I don't think the Jesses want me to talk about it."

Eddie pondered that as they journeyed along. A notion entered Eddie's thoughts and he was staggered by it. "Did you commit suicide, Chuck?"

"No. Never. I loved living."

A wave of relief swept through Eddie. "That's good to hear."

"Why? What difference does it make?"

Eddie thought hard about the question as he watched his horse's head dip up and down to its steady clippity-clop rhythm. "It's because we only get one shot at life and we—I—took it for granted." He turned to Charles. "Man, what I'd give to have the chance to be with my family again, even for a second. To tell them how stupid I was, how much I love—" His throat caught and his eyes watered. He turned away in embarrassment.

Charles reached out to place his hand on Eddie's shoulder, but stopped and looked up as if someone—or a group of someone's—had told him not to. Instead, Charles hummed the gospel tune, "I'll Be Alright."

Eddie recognized the bittersweet song from when he was a kid and his parents had dragged him and Frank to church. He took a deep breath, thought again about Carly and Ben and himself, and wondered if they would ever be all right.

Chapter Six

The lobby of First Coast Bank was like it always was on late Friday afternoons, crowded. Five tellers meticulously counted out cash, accepted deposit tickets and rushed between computers, inputting figures. A long, weaving line of mostly Latin customers waited fairly patiently between the roped-off guideposts. Carly stepped from an office located in the lobby on the opposite side of the tellers. *Operations Manager* was sketched on her glass door.

Teller four glanced anxiously at Carly as she made her way over. When Carly arrived, the teller said, "Oh, thank you. I really need to pee."

"Go, Lauren, I've got you covered. Take your time."

Five months pregnant, Lauren pressed her belly and smiled gratefully at Carly, before hastily retreating to the bathroom.

Carly called the next customer over. She thought of when she was pregnant with Ben and how Eddie had fussed over her to the point of making her crazy. She stopped her thoughts. She didn't want to think of him. She'd already shed so many tears and lost so much sleep that she was afraid she'd have to take a leave of absence. She would never admit it to anyone here, but she struggled to concentrate, which was the kiss of death for a bank exec. She couldn't afford to lose her job. Not with the stack of bills they had, the bills Eddie had left them with. Her mind went back to him and it filled her with anger. How dare he do that to her and Ben? How *dare* he? Her eyes welled.

"Señora?"

"Oh, I'm so sorry." Carly forced a smile. She took the woman's check and deposit slip, notated it in the computer, and promptly counted out the requested cash.

Stay focused. Carly motioned a tall, slim, tattooed man forward.

The man came to her window and said, "Just the person I was looking for."

"Pardon me?"

"I'm Jonah, an old friend of Ed's. I was gonna talk to the teller about seeing you, but here you are."

"What can I do for you, Mr...?" She studied the angels and devils on the man's arms and wondered what kind of friends Eddie had been keeping.

"Jonah. Just Jonah. You see, I was at the track with Eddie the day he...fell." Jonah moved in closer and lowered his voice. "Between you and me? I think he had a gambling problem." He continued on in a regular voice. "Anyway, he asked me for a few bucks to buy your kid a birthday gift. Teared up and everything. I felt bad and spotted him eighty cash. The next thing I know, he blows most of it on a horse."

Carly showed no reaction but she thought, sounds like Eddie.

"Well, the horse pays off, sixty-bucks, no big deal, but I can use the cash. I figure it was my money, my ticket. Am I right?"

"I suppose," Carly said. "Can I mail you a check?"

Jonah puffed a cheek. "I wouldn't think of taking money from you. Especially with what you've been through. I just want the ticket."

"I've been through his things," Carly said. "There is no ticket."

"He tucked it in his sport coat pocket, front right side."

"There was nothing in any of his coat pockets except his notepad and a racing form."

Jonah again leaned in. "You're lying and that ain't healthy."

"Look, mister. I think you better leave." Carly reached beneath the counter.

Jonah's face tightened. "I wouldn't press that button if I were you."

"Leave the lady alone. *Now.*" This was Vernon Batton's voice. He was camped behind Jonah's right shoulder.

Jonah smiled menacingly at Vernon, then turned back to Carly.

"This ain't over. Not by a long shot." He pushed past Vernon and exited the bank.

"What the hell was that about?" Vernon asked.

Carly shuddered. "I don't know, but he frightened me."

"Are you okay? Should I call security?"

Carly glanced around at the lines of customers. "The last thing we need is a commotion. I'll be fine."

Vernon studied her a moment. "He won't bother you again. I'll see to that."

Carly nodded. Lauren returned. Vernon started to hand her some checks and a deposit slip, when someone yelled, "Hey that man jumped in front of us."

"Oh, sorry," Vernon said to Lauren. "I saw Carly, Ms. Coyne, and I thought she might be," he glanced at Carly. "That is, I wanted to say hello."

Carly motioned to Vernon. "Follow me." She led him to her office as Lauren motioned the next person forward.

Carly took her place behind the small desk. Vernon glanced around as he took a seat facing her. Not a spacious room by any means, still it was more than a cubicle. He nodded. "Nice digs."

"I'm glad it meets your approval."

Vernon smiled and handed her the checks and deposit slip. Their fingers touched and lingered. Their eyes locked. Carly blushed and broke eye contact. She raised the lid of the laptop lying on her desk and punched information into it.

Vernon rubbed the skin between his nose and lips several times and said, "Look, this may not be the most appropriate time or place."

She stopped typing and folded the laptop screen. "Please, Vernon. Don't."

"Why not?" He took a deep breath. "I'm sorry. That was an insensitive response."

She stared at the folded laptop, then at him. "You've been

wonderful. Without you I…I don't know what I would've done."

He leaned forward. "But?"

"This thing with Eddie has happened so quickly. I can't keep my mind straight." She forced herself not to cry.

"Oh, God, Carly. Forgive me. The last thing I want to do is pressure you."

"It's not you, Vernon. It's me." She reached for his hand, which he eagerly accepted. "I need time to sort things out."

"I understand. I really do. The only thing I ask is that when you do—and if you'll let me—I'd like to be a part of both your and Ben's future." Vernon kissed her wrist. "Will you promise me you'll think about that?"

She sucked her lower lip a moment, then nodded at him.

He leaned forward. "I mean it, Carly. You know how I feel about you."

She hadn't planned to, but Carly leaned in, too. They kissed. She hadn't intended for it to feel good, but it did. When their mouths parted, she studied Vernon. It was easy to see the joy in his smile. She wondered if he saw the guilt and uncertainty that she felt.

"Thank you," Vernon said. "That was nice."

Embarrassed, Carly lifted the laptop screen and went back to typing. "I shouldn't have done that. It wasn't—that's funny."

"Are my kisses that humorous?"

"Oh, no, it's not you, Vernon. It's your account. It's below the free services level."

"Is that all?" Vernon tapped his neck a few times. "The funds are a little low because I just bought out the old Northview strip mall, or as I like to think of it, the Vernon Batton luxury condos." He leaned back and cupped his hands. "Pretty soon we really will be the Platinum Pair."

Carly flinched and went back to punching in numbers on the keyboard.

Vernon frowned. "God, I did it again. That was a stupid comment. Forgive me?"

She stopped typing and studied him as if she were picturing their future together. She nodded and went back to work.

"She still loves you, you know." Charles plucked a berry from one of the hedges lining the dirt road. He bit it, scrunched his nose and tossed it. "Sour."

Eddie barely heard the words. He was groggy, as if he had sleepwalked through a fog. He turned to Charles, who glided beside him. "What are you talking about?"

"Carly. She likes Vernon. But she loves you."

"How do you know about that?"

Charles shrugged. "The same way you do. The knowing."

"The only thing I know is that I feel punch-drunk, and I have no clue what the knowing is."

"You feel punch-drunk because you're not used to the knowing," Charles said. "As for what it is—for some reason we know certain things. Not everything, just certain things."

"Do we both know the same things?" Eddie wiped cold sweat from his face.

"Not always, but sometimes. For instance, I know Vernon's putting the make on Carly. I also know that you know."

"Yes," Eddie said. "But I wasn't sure if whatever it was—"

"The knowing."

"Right. The knowing." Eddie tried to make sense of the knowing, but like everything else that had happened to him since his fall down the escalator, it was impossible to come to terms with, so he just went with it. "So this knowing told you that Carly still loves me?" Even though Eddie knew it wouldn't do him any good, his heart raced at the notion.

"No," Charles said. "That part was my gut speaking."

"Oh." The disappointment in Eddie's voice was easy to discern.

"If she didn't love you, do you think she'd have stuck with you this long? Vernon's doing everything he can to win her over."

"But she kissed him." Eddie couldn't help the jealous tone that crept in his words.

"She's lonely and scared. Can you blame her?"

Eddie sighed. "No, I guess not. She's better off with him. He's got beaucoup bucks. He's even a good baseball coach. Bennie'll love that."

"Eddie, they'd take you over him in a minute."

"That'll be the day."

Charles looked at him curiously. "What'd you say?"

Eddie ignored the question. "Maybe they'd take the old Eddie, the one that didn't care about handicaps and trifectas, but not the guy who had to prove himself by pushing away everyone who gave a shit about him. Even worse, using their love as a tool to manipulate them. Maybe I deserve to rot in hell."

"You're wallowing in self-pity," Charles said. "Not a good thing."

Eddie forced his mind from the dark corner it had traveled to. "You're right, Chuck. Self-pity's a loser's game." He concentrated on lighter, better times that he had spent with Carly and Ben. Little things crossed his mind: sipping coffee at Denny's on Sunday morning while he watched Ben gobble down chocolate chip pancakes, lying in bed and feeling Carly's hand come to rest on his ribs, cradling Ben as he and Carly strolled from booth to booth at the art festival looking for a painting to brighten up their first home.

He rode in silence until they came to the fork in the road. He mentally reviewed Angel's instructions on how to find the shortest road—bear west of the shadows if they fell east, or bear east of the shadows if they fell west. He studied the shadow he was making on the back of his horse. It was non-existent. He glanced up. The sun beamed straight down. He looked at Charles. "Great, no shadows."

Charles shrugged.

Eddie again studied the shadowless ground. "Call it, Chuck. Left or right?"

"Eddie, I...it's not my decision."

Eddie saw a solemnity in Charles' eyes and in the tightened corners of his mouth that aged his boyish features. Eddie contemplated the fork in the road. "You know something, don't you?"

Charles lowered his gaze.

"Come on. Tell me." Eddie waited. Nothing. "Fuck you." Eddie nudged his horse to the left and trotted down that road. Charles lifted his hand and started to speak. He looked up to the heavens and stopped. Instead, he followed silently behind.

A few minutes later, Falk emerged from the right side of the fork, his horse galloping in the opposite direction of Eddie's.

Chapter Seven

Angel twirled the small glass vial between her thumb and fingers. She raised it to the moonlight seeping onto her veranda and studied the green elixir as if it were a diamond. She was nervous, scared. *What if something goes wrong and I truly die, or what if no one comes and I am entombed alive?* No, she thought. This was her path to happiness. *And truly, to marry Baron Cleves is worse than death.* She removed the cork and sniffed the liquid. There was a faint scent of peach and something else. Almonds? She pictured Falk and whispered, "My dear husband, with all my heart I do this." Her heart pounded so intensely the blood thumped in her ears. She brought the vial to her lips and pulled it back. Her hand shook. Her eyes moistened with fear. She took a deep breath, closed her eyes and swallowed once. Nothing. She stared at the black outline of the garden below. Then insouciance fell over her like a sun shower. Her worries drifted on a wave and were swept away. Two more swallows and you sleep, she thought. Light-footed, Angel entered her chamber and sat on the bed. She again envisioned Falk and tried to reach out to him. Yes, she thought, it's a much better fate to chance death as your wife than to live without you. She took the second swallow, then quickly the third. She mumbled something to her parents and fell back on the bed…

Merek and Gussalen stood on the cemetery grounds and stared at the De Bromwell family mausoleum where their daughter's body was housed. The cemetery was in a large meadow located behind a churchyard. The graveyard was dotted with trees, stone markers and crypts. Gussalen broke down. Merek wrapped his arm around her and let his own tears fall. In the distance, caravans of mourners who had attended the funeral ceremony had nearly disappeared from sight. Five servants stood a few feet away from the grieving De Bromwells. Their heads were bowed. Two of the servants—women—wiped tears from their eyes. Despite the blue sky the day felt black, cold. Merek motioned for two of the servants. They came and assisted him and Gussalen into their waiting carriage. The coach slowly made its way home.

When it disappeared from view, Falk's friend, Devin, stepped out from behind a large tree several yards away. He walked to the mausoleum. Poor girl, he thought. But who can blame her? "Rest well, maiden." Devin walked away, but stopped when a horse carrying a rider galloped toward him. "Why, it's Falk!" Devin exclaimed as the stallion neared.

Falk leapt off the horse and ran to the mausoleum. He stared at it for several seconds and said to Devin, "How can this be? We...She had so much to live for. Why?"

"She was to wed the wretched Baron Cleves." Devin grinned. "Is that not reason enough for anyone to kill themselves?"

Furious, Falk punched him in the face and withdrew his knife. "Draw your weapon."

Devin took a step back. "Ho, Falk. What madness is this?"

Falk breathed heavy clumps of air. He looked at Devin as if he didn't know him. "Leave me." Devin stared wide-eyed. "I said leave." Falk stiffened his knife-wielding arm. Devin held up his palm to signal he got the message. He trotted away. Falk's cheeks turned from angry red to ashen white. He lowered his knife, staggered to the mausoleum and pulled back the oak door. It creaked open. He looked around to see if anyone had noticed. There was no one. He entered and shut the door behind him.

Eddie and Charles approached the De Bromwell's manor. It was dark. Silent. Eddie spotted the grouchy laundry woman who had dumped hot water in his washtub. She was wiping her eyes with her apron. He dismounted his horse and approached her. "Where have they taken her?"

The woman looked up. She was sobbing. She saw it was Eddie and walked away. He raced to her and grabbed her by the shoulders. "Damn it, where have they taken her? Tell me."

The woman looked at him as if she were in a trance.

Eddie shook her. "Tell me!"

"The churchyard. She's sleeping in the family crypt."

Lady, Eddie thought. You don't know how right you are. "Where's the churchyard?" The woman pointed easterly. Eddie released her, mounted his horse and raced off, Charles gliding alongside him.

The interior of the mausoleum was as bleak as Falk imagined it would be. Two lit torches secured in sconces cast long, dreary shadows along the small entranceway. The fumes smelled of dead, burnt wood. The walls were as cool and sterile as the stones they were built from. Most biting was the silence. It was deep, grim and smothering. It drew from Falk and left nothing. In the center of the chamber was a marble pedestal with Angel's stone casket upon it. Leaning against the casket was the lid. *De Bromwell* was etched on it. Falk's eyes welled. He thought of the last time he kissed her and used the memory to gather strength to approach her corpse. He took two steps forward—the outside door creaked open. He stopped. Deciding caution was best served; Falk raced to a shadow-filled corner of the chamber and blended into it.

Baron Cleves entered the room, walking stick in one hand, rose in the other. He casually looked about and approached the casket. He studied the contents for three breath's span and said, "Ah, sweetness, we would have made a glorious couple: the cousin of the royal kingdom and the daughter of the spice kingdom." He sniffed the rose and sighed. "If only you knew how much effort I spent convincing the prince to take over your father's business." Cleves plucked a petal from the flower and watched it drift downward into the casket. "Not to mention having to rid myself of that foul lover of yours. And then there is poor, poor Speer." He bent over the casket and whispered, "I'm sure you will agree, the least I deserve for my efforts is a kiss." Cleves leaned in, squeezed her breast and pressed his mouth to her lips.

"You filthy pig. Never again will your stench desecrate her!" Falk rushed at him with his knife in tow.

Eddie guided his galloping horse to Devin, who walked along a dirt road just beyond the churchyard. "Where's the De Bromwell vault?"

"To the east," Devin said, "near the large tree."

Eddie raced his horse toward it as Charles continued beside him.

Devin glanced bewilderedly at Eddie and muttered, "Perhaps it's something in the water," before continuing on.

Baron Cleves avoided Falk's blade with a last second step sideways. As Falk's momentum carried him past Cleves, the baron spun and kicked him from behind. Falk stumbled, banged his head against the casket lid, went woozy and fell flat on his back. Cleves slipped out a sword housed inside his walking stick, straddled Falk and raised the tip of the blade over his heart. "We'll see whose stench will desecrate this tomb." He drove the blade into Falk's chest, let it sit for a second and removed it. Falk groaned. Cleves smiled smugly and spit in Falk's face. Falk kneed Cleves between the legs with everything he had. Cleves howled and doubled over on the ground. Falk crawled to him, plunged his knife into Cleves' neck and twisted the blade. Cleves eyed him with astonishment. His mouth opened and shut several times, but made no comprehensible sound. Cleves took a quick gulp of air and went limp. Falk staggered to Angel's casket and gently touched her cheek. "Why? We were to live our lives together." He removed her wedding band from his finger and placed it on hers. He kissed her, slumped beside the casket and listened to the silence until his heart stopped and he could breathe no more.

Eddie tied his horse to the tree. Charles and he sprinted toward the mausoleum. Eddie pushed the partially open door all the way. As Eddie was about to enter, Charles reached for him but was overcome with pain. Charles grabbed his stomach, moaned and collapsed. Eddie propped him to a sitting position and said, "Shit, you're pale as a ghost. What's wrong?"

Charles looked beyond the clouds, then back at Eddie.

"The Jesses?"

Charles nodded. "I…I wasn't doing my job."

"Maybe you should wait out here while I go in."

"No," Charles said. "No." His voice was firm.

Eddie studied him. There was gloom on Charles' face that he'd never seen before. "What aren't you telling me?"

Charles shook his head and gripped his stomach.

"Come on, Chuck, give me a hint."

Charles turned away.

"Fine, you and the Jesses play whatever games you want, but I haven't got time for it." He entered the vault. Charles struggled to his feet. He looked upward and his eyes darkened with anger. He followed Eddie inside.

They made their way to the end of the short hall. Eddie stopped. His stomach wrenched—blood pooled on the floor in two overlapping puddles. He didn't care about Cleves, but when he saw Falk vomit rose to his throat. "Chuck, is Falk…?" Eddie knelt beside the slumped body. Charles said nothing, but he didn't have to. Eddie saw the bloody hole in Falk's chest, felt his clammy skin and examined his lifeless eyes. He raced to Angel, leaned his ear to her nose and pressed his fingertips against her carotid artery. He nodded at Charles and said, "Thank God." Eddie lifted her from the casket and carried her outside. Charles followed.

Eddie sat Angel against the side of the mausoleum and tapped her cheek several times. She didn't respond. "Angel, wake up. Come on, wake up!" Nothing. He removed one of her slippers and tickled the bottom of her foot. Her toes wiggled. He removed the other slipper and tickled both feet.

She giggled, opened her eyes and said, "Stop it, Mother!" and coughed several times. Eddie leaned her forward and patted her back. When the coughing jag ceased, she looked at him with a dazed look. "Edward? How goes it?"

"Fine, my lady. Just fine."

"The plan? All is well?"

He averted her eyes. "Sort of…"

"What does that mean?"

"Well, um…" Eddie glanced at Charles, who was taking notes. "Young Falk has been delayed."

Angel squeezed her fingers together as she scrutinized his words. Eddie felt her apprehension as if it were a hand clamped around his throat. Then she abruptly stopped. She stared at the ring on her finger and back at Eddie. He felt himself plummet. It was her wedding band—the band that Falk had been holding for her while he was away. She broke down. Eddie hugged her and said, "It'll be all right. Baron Cleves is gone. Falk took care of that, so you could live." The same crappy feeling came over him that he had had when he raised his hand to Ben, when he stole from the household savings, when he cheated on his English Lit exams, and every other goddamned thing he ever did wrong. He was lying to this poor girl to save his own skin. What a piece of shit he was, but still he went on. "Look around, Angel, at the squirrels, the birds and even my horse and the tree that he's tied to. They're all part of life, and life is precious. You must never forget that. Never."

She continued to sob.

"You can't give up. Falk wouldn't want that. He fought so you can live your life—for the both of you."

Her sobbing slowed. "Do you truly believe that?"

He thought about it a moment. Despite his own motives, he wanted this girl to live. She deserved a future, a chance to marry and have children of her own. Just like Ben deserved it, like he and Carly deserved it. She had been dealt a horrible hand, but she was young. She could get over it. He glanced at Charles. He had stopped writing and was studying Eddie. "Look, Angel, the important thing is Falk thought so. That's why he got rid of Baron Cleves. He wanted you to have the chance at a happy life."

"That will never happen without him," she said.

"When God is willing you'll be together again."

She thought about this for several seconds. "Is this the truth?"

Eddie again shot a look at Charles, who was again writing. "Believe me, there's life after death."

She wiped her eyes and nose on her sleeve, stared into the mid-distance and pondered. Eddie watched her. He squeezed his chin twice and waited. This was it. He had no better argument to make. He pictured the Jesses and spoke to them in his mind. *This is a sweet girl who deserves to live. Give her a break.*

As if in answer to his plea, Angel said, "Gather the horse, Edward, so we may depart home."

"Do you mean it?"

She nodded, put her slippers back on and stood. "Your words are full of wisdom. They give me hope, and hope is what will carry me forward." Her tone was melancholy, but determined.

Still not convinced, Eddie studied her face. Her eyes were grief stricken, but her raised chin and clenched jaw were wrapped in resolve. A bucket of relief washed over him. Okay, he thought, it's now or never. "Angel, what do you say before we leave that we make a pledge?"

Charles looked up from his writing.

"A pledge?"

"A vow—a pact so to speak. We clasp hands and express our resolve to carry on by saying the words, 'I accept life.'"

Angel cocked her head. "Does that not seem odd?"

"Maybe, but it's a statement. A blow against Baron Cleves

and a—" He stopped himself. He was going to say a memorial to Falk, but that was too much, even for Eddie. Instead he said, "—and a way to remember." Eddie held out his hand. "What do you say?"

She looked at it, then at him with skepticism.

Eddie smiled the same way he had when he'd manipulated Frank into swiping a couple of bucks from their mother's purse.

Angel's eyes bounced from his smile to his outstretched palm. She stuck her hand out, brought it to his, but pulled it back before they touched. "This pledge is important?"

"It is," Eddie said. "Extremely."

"Then I must have a moment to cleanse my palm." She held it up for him to see. It was dirty and sticky from mucus and tears. "You may gather the horse as I do so."

Eddie glanced at the horse, which was about fifty feet away. "Your hand is fine."

"If this vow is as important as you say it is, my hand should be pure, or isn't the pact that important?"

"Well, I suppose…" He looked at Charles for help, but he gave no sign of response. "Okay, Angel, clean yourself up. I'll be back in a second." He and Charles headed toward the tree where the horse was tied up. Several yards away, Eddie glanced back. Angel was swiping her hands through the grass.

Charles clasped Eddie's elbow. "Eddie…"

"What?"

Charles hesitated, glanced up at the sky and then shook his head. "Forget it. It was nothing."

Upon their arrival at the tree, Eddie started to untie the horse's reins but stopped and turned to Charles. "Look, Chuck, I have no hard feelings with you or with the Jesses. They did Angel and me a favor. I really like the girl. She reminds me of Ben. The truth is I'm glad she's alive, you know?" Charles nodded. Eddie untied the horse and glanced back at Angel. She was gone. Eddie looked at Charles. Charles said nothing.

Eddie jumped on the horse and sped to the mausoleum. Charles followed. Eddie hopped off, and they rushed inside. Eddie ran through the entranceway and into the center chamber.

He stopped. This time he did vomit. He felt like he was heaving up his guts. He wiped the garbage from his lips and stumbled to Angel, who was lying next to Falk. His knife was buried in her heart. "Why, goddamn it?" Eddie knelt in the blood and cradled her. "You didn't have to do this, Angel. You could have made it." He whispered the last sentence to her three more times, then removed the bloody instrument.

As he lifted her body into the casket a rock fell from her hand. Puzzled, he placed Angel in the coffin and looked around for the stone. He glanced at Charles, who was intently eyeing him between his scribbling.

Eddie found the rock. Bending down to retrieve it, he noticed the casket lid, which was lying close by. He went cold. Angel had used the rock to scratch out *De Bromwell* and to replace it with *Romeo and Juliet Falk*. Eddie's cheeks reddened. He leapt at Charles and slugged him in the mouth. Charles stumbled back. His glasses went cock-eyed but managed to remain on. "You knew all along where this was going!" He looked toward the sky. "You all knew!" Eddie raised his fists upward and screamed the words again.

"Stop, Eddie. You're hurting your case."

"Fuck the case." Eddie sprang at Charles and took another swipe at his face. Charles ducked. Eddie took another swing. Before his fist could connect, Charles vanished. Eddie pummeled his fists against the wall. "She didn't have to die, damn it. She didn't have to!" He continued to pound until tears filled his eyes and his arms grew heavy. He lowered his fists and whispered, "She didn't have to die..."

He glanced around the silent, dark chamber. Eddie felt an overwhelming desire to enter daylight, breathe clean air and attempt to make sense of what was going on. He took a step toward the exit and staggered. His head went light. His ears hummed and his heart raced. He felt as if he were plummeting into a black, bottomless hollow. He leaned back against the wall for support, but before he could steady himself, he disappeared.

Chapter Eight

The Lockheed Electra 10E jostled in the sky like a drunken silver seagull. A slim, goggled woman wearing a neck scarf, a leather bomber jacket and flight cap wrestled with the yoke. The twin-engine plane screamed, rocked and rattled. She yelled, "Hold on. We're almost there!" to her navigator, who was seated next to her.

Panicked, Eddie gripped the back of their seats with everything he had. He was seated behind them in a small, cramped space. Something bumped him in the chest several times. He glanced down. It was a large, vintage camera strapped around his neck.

"Easy…easy," the navigator said.

The woman didn't hear. Her mind was on controlling the plane as it wobbled downward in the white-hot sun toward the landing strip below.

Eddie's heart pounded against his chest like an elephant stampede. The airstrip was practically in his face. He squeezed. His knuckles popped a bright red. He muttered, "Oh, shit," and pulled back.

The Lockheed landed with an earth-shaking thump that caused a rear widow to break. The aircraft skidded several yards. A screech like a two-ton fingernail scratching against a Brobdingnagian chalkboard sounded from beneath the plane's belly. When it came to a halt, the woman removed her goggles and aviation cap. She laughed. "I certainly smacked it down that time, didn't I, boys?"

Eddie opened his eyes and gasped. The boyish-looking woman

with short-cropped hair, freckles and a gap tooth could only be one person—Amelia Earhart. Before he had time to make sense of anything, a slew of automobiles that could have come out of *Bonnie and Clyde* and *Chinatown* raced toward the plane. Crowds of people surged behind the vehicles. The men wore fedoras and boater hats. Women were dressed in ankle-length dresses with butterfly sleeves. Amelia Earhart and her navigator removed their seat restraints. Eddie realized he was strapped in, too, and did the same.

A long, sleek, black Cadillac Fleetwood the size of a tank stopped a few yards from the airplane. A middle-age man with rimless glasses, a firm jaw and a tailored, double-breasted suit stepped from the driver's side. The man propped his hands akimbo, raised his head and frowned at the plane. A man in his early twenties stepped out of the passenger side. He was dressed in oily overalls. He had white-blonde hair, a good-natured expression and a greasy rag in his hand. The man with white-blonde hair circled the craft, sometimes stooping, sometimes standing on his tiptoes to examine the plane's twin tails. Amelia, her navigator, and Eddie jumped out of the cockpit. The man in the double-breasted suit walked up to Amelia and said, "Damn it, Meelie, this is going to set us back at least eight grand."

Amelia said, "We're okay, G.P., thank you very much."

Embarrassed, G.P. wrapped her in his arms and said, "I'm so sorry, dear. I didn't mean it like that. Forgive me?" Amelia smiled lightly. He kissed her.

While they were doing this, Eddie saw Amelia's navigator slip a flask from his flight jacket, take two slugs and slide it back in as the kiss came to an end. When it did, G.P. said to Eddie, "Snap a pic before the newshounds barrel over."

"What?"

"Quit foolin' around. They're almost here."

Eddie glanced at the cars and people behind them. They were less than a minute away. Eddie reached for the camera strapped around his neck. He didn't have to look at the name on the cumbersome thing to know it was a Speed Graphic.

As if he had done it a thousand times before, Eddie deftly

adjusted the shutter speed dial and the aperture ring attached to the front lens. He unlocked the shutter-cocking device, popped open the focus hood in the back of the camera and took a quick look through the glass to confirm it was in focus.

He glanced at the advancing cars. They were barreling down on them.

Eddie removed a 4x5 film holder from a pouch on his belt and inserted it into the back of the camera. He pulled the dark slide—the one blocking the film from exposure—out of the film holder slot and pointed the camera at G.P. and Amelia. He tripped the front shutter button just as the first car stepped on the brakes.

Eddie contemplated the camera in his hands as if it were a newborn baby. *How the hell did I do that?* He decided it must be what Charles called the knowing.

The crowds descended. G.P. clutched Amelia's elbow and rushed her to the sedan's gleaming hood ornament: a silver, spread-winged angel. He helped her onto the hood, then climbed up, too. A group of reporters with notepads and cameras similar to Eddie's surrounded the pair. G.P. wrapped his arm around Amelia's shoulder and smiled big. "Here she is, boys. Lady Lindy!" The cameras snapped. G.P. whispered to her, "Act as if everything's jake." Amelia rolled her eyes.

"What do you think of Miami, Amelia?" one of the men yelled.

"Well, the airstrips are alike, that's for sure." The crowd laughed.

"Seriously, did you miscalculate?" a woman asked. "Is that why you landed at the wrong airport, first?"

Amelia glanced at G.P. His face was locked in his smile. She said, "No...we were testing the landing gear, that's all. Everything went according to our calculations."

"Any truth that you're planning an around the world trip starting right here?"

"We're considering it. But we haven't made a final decision."

"Mr. Putnam," a reporter shouted. "How do you answer your critics that you're using your wife for personal fame and fortune and not scientific progress as you claim?"

"Whoa," G.P. said. "The last thing George Palmer Putnam

needs is anyone's money. Each and every one of you is well aware that I make plenty in the publishing business."

"Sure," the reported answered. "But even you can use a little—"

"That's enough," G.P. said. "Amelia's tired. It's been a long day." There was a collective groan. "She'll talk to you in the morning. I promise." He helped her down and past the mob of reporters and fans and into the Cadillac. Before leaving, G.P. shouted to Eddie and Amelia's navigator, who had remained by the cockpit. "Eddie, you come with us. Fred, stay here. I want a full report on the plane."

"Okay, boss," Amelia's navigator, Fred, yelled back.

"You too, Al," G.P. said.

Al, the young man with white-blonde hair and oily jeans, was examining the broken rear window. Al waved his hand to indicate he got the message.

Eddie pushed his way through the reporters and worked his way into the four-door's back seat. Charles was seated on the other side. Charles smiled tentatively at him. Eddie gave him the middle finger. Despite being pissed at Charles, he wasn't going to make the same mistake as last time. He said to him, "Amelia Earhart?"

Charles nodded. "It's 1937."

At the same time Amelia said, "Yes, Eddie?" in a tired voice.

Eddie cringed. He had forgotten that no one could see or hear Charles except himself. Charles pointed to Eddie's camera. "Um, I was wondering," Eddie said to Amelia, "if I should take a picture."

"In a minute," G.P. answered as he slowly weaved the vehicle through the dispersing crowd. He glanced at Amelia. She was slumped, resting her head in her hands. He said to her, "Didn't I tell you Eddie was the best?" He looked at Eddie in the rearview mirror. "Trust me, Ed, you're gonna make your fortune as the official photographer of America's Angel of the Air."

Eddie had no idea what he was talking about, but he smiled and gave him thumbs up.

"Please, G.P., no more showbiz talk," Amelia said. "I really am exhausted."

"Sure, sweetheart. I understand." He drove a few more yards and added, "I spoke with Paul. We've got *Cosmopolitan* and *Life* lined up. *The Tribune's* going to give you a byline, and get this, only photos approved by me and taken by Coyne, here—" he winked at Eddie through the mirror "—are to be used. And for the coup de grace," he paused for emphasis, "*First Lady of the Sky* goes into film production immediately upon your return."

Amelia rubbed her temples. "It sounds swell, but I need time to rest."

G.P. squeezed her knee. "Of course, baby. Understood." He drove in silence for a few minutes and said, "According to *Popular Aviation*, Amy Johnson is ready to take off any day now." He glanced at her. "But what does that rag know?"

"Okay, okay," Amelia said. "I get it."

"I just don't want you to be the second female to circle the globe. No one remembers second place. Am I right?"

Amelia stared silently out the passenger-side window.

"Baby, I asked you if I'm right."

Amelia said nothing.

G.P. stopped the car. He squeezed the steering wheel a moment and faced her. "I'm working my ass off from sunup to late in the night to promote you. All I get in return is this kind of attitude. I love you, but you're ungrateful."

Amelia's face tightened. "I'm trying to accomplish something serious, and you're making it into a circus. I never asked for the articles and films and interviews."

G.P. grunted. "But you didn't refuse them. And you haven't turned away a penny of the investor money that came from them, either. Now, I'll ask you one last time, do you want to be the first or second woman to make that flight? It's your choice, not mine."

Amelia cupped her forehead in her hands, took a deep, weary breath, and uttered, "The first."

"I didn't hear you."

Eddie was about to tell him that was enough, but Charles

shook his head not to interfere.

Amelia glared at G.P. and said in a stern voice, "The first."

G.P. nodded. "Good." He turned back to Eddie. "Okie dokie, Ed, now you can snap that picture."

Eddie prepped the camera.

G.P. said to Amelia, "Meelie, put your arm around me." She slid over, wrapped her arm around his shoulder, slumped and waited without expression.

"On three," Eddie said. When he got toward the end of the count Amelia straightened her shoulders, smiled radiantly and waited for the snap. When it was over she scooted against the passenger-side door and slouched against it.

G.P. patted her wrist. "I love you, doll. You know that, right?" She wrenched her arm away. He shook his head and drove off.

G.P. drove south down Collins Avenue. Lines of heavily chromed automobiles painted black, green, and red, rumbled in both directions. Each side of the two-lane roadway was lined with hotels. The hotels were an eye-dazzling array of aquas, tans and pinks. The two and three-story structures were adorned with circles, lines, and geometric flora and fauna motifs—art deco at its peak. Eddie stared out of the window in amazement. They passed a hotel built like the bow of a ship, complete with portal windows, and another shaped like a windmill. The hotels had names like the Mermaid, the Centurion, Sunset Tide, and Blue Wave. The low, westerly sun illuminated the buildings, sending lengthy shadows toward the Atlantic.

Behind the hotels on the east side of Collins Avenue, the ocean glittered like a million blue and bluer mirrors. Between the buildings, Eddie caught glimpses of men, women and children in one-piece bathing suits lounging on the sand beneath wood-poled beach umbrellas. He glanced at Charles, who looked as if he had entered Disney's Magic Kingdom for the first time. Eddie knew the feeling, because he felt the same way.

G.P. turned the Fleetwood left and entered the circular driveway of a three-story, white with tropical green trim hotel called the Palm Arms. Immediately, two valets in yellow, button-down shirts and green slacks opened the doors. G.P. handed the keys to one of them. The other valet opened the trunk and blew into a whistle hanging from a lanyard around his neck. He removed several bags of luggage as a bellhop scurried out of the lobby with a cart.

Amelia, Eddie, and Charles stepped from the sedan. Amelia took a deep breath of the salty breeze. She smiled at Eddie. "It smells wonderful."

The men loaded the luggage onto the cart and escorted them inside and to the front desk. The lobby was an ornate room with a large donut-shaped crystal chandelier and, of all things, an unlit fireplace. G.P. checked them in. He tossed Eddie a room key and said to the bellhop, "The small valise is his."

Eddie glanced at the number on his key and went for the bag. The bellhop started to protest, but Eddie said, "I can get it," and grabbed the bag, which he figured was supplied by the Jesses. The bellhop escorted them into the elevator. The elevator attendant shut the cage doors and turned the lever upward. They ascended.

Eddie glanced at Amelia. She was slumped against the wall, staring at the passing floors. Her thin features were beautiful, but on the verge of emaciation. She really was drained, Eddie thought. Her tiredness was like a yawn that blanketed him. He thought, I've been running on adrenalin since my time with Angel...*and my fall down the escalator.* Recollections of his head banging against the steps and the cracking of his bones shocked him. Scared the shit out of him. Panicked him. He looked at Charles, who seemed to sense what was going on. Charles squeezed Eddie's shoulder.

The doors opened.

Eddie knew this was his floor by the key number, but he was afraid to move. He didn't want to be in limbo. He wanted to be back with Carly and Ben in his shoebox of a home. He wanted to give them the life that he had planned on, but never delivered — the one filled with family dinners and flowers from the street vendors, movies and school plays, and growing old together.

"Sir?" The elevator attendant raised a brow. "This is your floor."

"Right." Eddie pinched back tears. "Sorry." He and Charles stepped out.

G.P. said, "Get some grub and a good night's sleep. We'll see you tomorrow." Amelia smiled—a sincere smile—at Eddie. The wire cage shut, and the elevator ascended. Eddie studied it, then trudged down the hall to his room.

The Palm Arm's crowded, oversize pool was painted deep blue. An illustration of a sailfish adorned the bottom. The late morning sun shone bright in the ripples. Most of the lounge chairs were occupied with suntanned men and women in bathing suits. Beach towels were draped over their shoulders. The majority sipped strawed drinks housed in coconut half-shells purchased from the poolside cabana bar.

Amelia sat on the edge of the pool wiggling her feet in the water. She was dressed in a one-piece bathing suit with sunglasses and a wide, floppy sun hat that hid most of her face. Still, someone would occasionally steal a glance her way, or nudge their companion to look in Amelia's direction.

A young woman with a friendly, pretty face was seated on a lounge chair near her. She held a steno pad. The young woman looked to be in her late teens and wore a knee-length dress and a small brim hat that fell over one eye. She read to Amelia from the steno pad. "At four-thirty, councilman Bascom is to escort you and Mr. Putnam to city hall, where the mayor will present you with the key to the city and declare it Amelia Earhart day."

"Well, that doesn't sound too time consuming," Amelia replied. "Thank you, Louise."

"There's more." Louise flipped a page. "At five-forty you are to give a speech to the National Women's Society in the hotel's Gigi room. At six-twenty—"

"We are to have dinner with the very wealthy W. Bruce Mac-Intosh," G.P. interrupted. He approached, carrying three drinks.

"At seven-o-five I will hit him up for an investment in America's Grand Lady of the Clouds as she becomes the first woman aviator to fly around the world." He handed a drink to Amelia and Louise. "Wear that slinky, gold dress tonight, Meelie. The one that, you know," he cupped his free hand to his breast, "shows MacIntosh that we mean business."

Amelia shot him a disgusted look. "I'm not a prostitute."

"Excuse us a minute, Louise," G.P. said.

Louise glanced at Amelia. She nodded. Louise took her drink and found a shady spot by the cabana bar.

"No one's asking you to sell your body," G.P. said when Louise was beyond earshot. "All you're doing is putting him in a good mood to donate to our cause. That's called smart business."

"I told you before, G.P., I want this to be something we can both be proud of."

"I get it, but what's the big deal if he gets a glimpse of your bust line?" He nodded to the swimmers. "Hell, it's less than what most of the women here are showing."

Amelia stood, removed her sunglasses and looked him firmly in the eyes. "I'm an aviatrix, not a poolside beauty queen."

G.P. huffed with frustration. "I'm fed up with this holier-than-thou crap. You want the goddamn glory, but you expect me—Mr. Amelia Earhart-Putnam—to do all the shit shoveling."

Amelia thought about that. "Honestly, I don't." She laid her hand on his shoulder. "But you're letting the money overshadow everything."

"Not true. Look, Amelia, I understand that all you care about is flying."

"No, it's not all about flying. It's also about paving the way for women."

"Understood, but either way flying costs lots of money. So does your crew, that secretary of yours, Coyne and his camera, this hotel and that new Cord Phaeton you have sitting in our summer home."

"Yes," Amelia said, "but there's still something unsavory about the way we're going about it."

"I assume by 'we' you mean me."

Amelia lowered her eyes.

"OK," G.P. said. "I suggest you find someone else whose methods are in tune with yours."

"That's not what I meant."

He continued as if she had said nothing. "There are several top-notch people I can recommend. They're not as good as I am at PR and fundraising, but their ways will be more to your liking. Give me the word and I'll set up the meetings for you."

The two stared at each other.

A bellhop approached and waited. Amelia put on her sunglasses and turned to the pool. G.P. slugged a good portion of his drink.

The bellhop cleared his throat. "Sir, Councilman Bascom has arrived. He apologizes for being early and was wondering—"

"What's it going to be, Meelie?" G.P. asked. "Shall we cancel?"

Amelia glanced at him, but remained silent.

"That is, he would like to come over, he's a big fan of Miss Earhart." The bellhop motioned to a hefty man in a brown suit who stood near the lobby doors leading to the pool area.

Amelia took a deep breath and said to the bellhop, "It's perfectly all right. Ask him to join us."

"Yes, ma'am." The bellhop made his way to the man.

G.P. squeezed Amelia's hand. "This will all work out for the best, baby. I promise." He waved to Bascom.

Amelia removed her sunglasses, put on a bright smile, and held her hand out to the councilman. "You're just in time!"

Chapter Nine

"You're just in time!" Carly yelled as she checked the thermometer imbedded in the turkey. It was roasting in the oven. She heard the front door shut. A moment later Vernon entered the kitchen and went to her.

"It smells delicious." He held an unopened bottle of wine and a bag with a sporting goods label on it.

"Dinner'll be ready in fifteen minutes." Carly removed her oven mitts. "I hope you're hungry."

"Starved." Vernon's eyes caught hers. Carly blushed, but kept her gaze on his. He brought his lips to her mouth.

"Mom," Ben yelled from the living room. "Can I eat in here?"

As if awakened from a spell, Carly pulled back.

Vernon exhaled a deep, frustrated breath.

"No, Bennie," Carly yelled over her shoulder. "We all eat together. You know the rules." She said to Vernon, "The corkscrew and the wine glasses are on the dining room table."

Vernon saluted her good-naturedly. "Yes, ma'am. I'll see that they're full when the fixins arrive." She reached into the refrigerator and removed a large bowl of salad. Carly scooted to the pantry for spices. Vernon watched her a second, half-smiled and entered the dining room.

While he poured the wine Vernon glanced at Ben. He was in front of the TV on his stomach and elbows watching *SpongeBob SquarePants*. Vernon finished up, brought the sporting goods bag with him into the living room and laid it next to Ben. "Here, pal, try this on for size." Ben glanced at the bag, but didn't open it.

Vernon patted his head. "It's okay. I understand."

Carly entered. "Bennie, milk or soda?"

"Soda."

Vernon smiled at Carly. "As if you had to ask. By the way, I hope you have a fifties outfit because I made reservations for the July 18 reunion."

Carly's face tightened. She said with a glint of irritation, "I never said I was going." Ben glanced at them.

"Oh, come on." Vernon walked up to her. "The Hard Rock is a fun place." He clutched her arm and said in a hushed voice, "With everything you've been through, you deserve a break."

Carly welled up. She caught a glimpse of Ben eyeing them and forced herself to smile. "Hey, what's in the bag, Ben?"

"Go ahead," Vernon said to him. "Open it."

Ben reached into it. His eyes widened, he almost removed the item, but didn't.

"What is it?" Carly asked.

"A catcher's mitt," Ben said with little enthusiasm. He laid back on his stomach and faced the TV.

"You shouldn't have," Carly said to Vernon. "Really."

Vernon waved her off. "It's nothing."

She looked at Ben and quietly added, "He's having a really rough time."

"Believe me, I understand. Do you mind if Ben and I have a little alone time together? Man-to-man stuff."

Carly thought about it a moment. She said loud enough for Ben to hear, "Why don't you two men chat while I set the table and bring out the food." She re-entered the kitchen.

Vernon sat on the floor beside Ben and watched Mr. Krabs bounce across the TV screen. He waited a bit and said, "I had a pet hermit crab once when I was your age. He wasn't a perfect pet, but I loved him more than anything in the world. When Harry died I got a new pet, and you know what?"—Ben glanced at him—"It took me a while, but I learned to love him just as much as I loved Harry... Not like Harry, but just as much."

Vernon reached into the bag. "Your mother needs your help, Ben. Your dad's gone and I...I'm only asking for a chance." He handed Ben the glove. "Nothing more."

Ben studied the glove. His eyes watered. "My daddy's not gone."

"He is, pal. He is."

Ben laid the glove on the rug and wiped his tears.

Carly removed a broccoli florets steam bag from the microwave. In the middle of opening it, her cell phone rang. She flinched and gave herself a steam burn. "Shit!" Carly dumped the contents into a bowl, ran to the kitchen counter where the phone was lying and picked it up. "Hello? Hello…? Go to hell!" She ended the call and plunked the phone back down.

Carly carried the broccoli to the dining room table and laid it next to the sweet potatoes. Vernon carved the turkey. Ben sat next to Carly's seat. Vernon said, "Another one of those calls?"

Carly looked at Ben and put on a smile. "Just a man wanting to make me a million dollars in three weeks. I told him I wasn't interested." Her tone was light but edged with anxiety.

"Next time, let me speak to him." Vernon's voice was serious. Not smiling, Carly nodded and took her place next to Ben. Vernon caught her eyes a moment, cleared his throat and said, "All right, who likes white meat and who likes dark?"

Eddie smashed out the last of his cigarette in an ashtray and placed it on the nightstand next to his hotel bed. He had given up smoking in his twenties for health considerations, but figured what the hell does it matter now? He was lying on his back in a muscle T and boxers, staring at the ceiling. Charles was seated at a wall desk, writing in his notepad. He said, "They both love you, Eddie."

Eddie glanced at the wall clock: one forty-five in the morning. He glared angrily at Charles, then resumed looking at the ceiling.

Charles stopped writing. "If I told you about Angel, it would have been over for both of us. You would have lost, period, and so would I."

"I don't care. She didn't deserve to die like…like Romeo and Juliet, for Christ's sake. Neither did Falk."

"I'm sorry. I really am. I liked them, too."

Behind Charles' half-rims, Eddie could see that the kid was sincere. Shit, he thought, here I am blaming everyone else for what happened when it was my fault. If I had picked up on Shakespeare 101, I could've done a thousand things to change the outcome. I could've delayed the marriage, or stopped Angel from taking the sleeping potion, or… He inhaled and let it out with deep exasperation. *No wonder I'm in this mess.* Eddie reached for another cigarette, but stopped. "Vernon's right, you know, they're better off without me."

"No, they aren't."

"The guy doesn't get short with Ben. He handles crank calls and carves a turkey better than me." Eddie propped himself half-recumbent against a pair of pillows. "I miss them."

"They don't love Vernon. They love you, Eddie."

"Even if that's true, there's just one little problem. Isn't there?"

"Eddie, you need to follow —"

The telephone rang. The heavy, black Bakelite object rested on the nightstand, next to the ashtray. Eddie reached for the receiver. "Hello…? Oh, hi G.P…What time? Yeah, sure, OK. I'll be ready…Right." He hung up.

"What's going on?" Charles asked.

"You don't already know?"

"I'm only privy to whatever the Jesses think I need to know. Just like you."

"Yeah, yeah, I remember," Eddie said. "Let me ask you something. Besides giving me glimpses of Carly and Ben, can the Jesses read thoughts?"

"They can do a lot of things, but not that."

Thank goodness, Eddie thought. "G.P. called to say that Amelia's testing the plane this morning. We have to be at the field at five a.m…Sharp! That guy's starting to irritate me."

"You need to follow your gut, Eddie."

"Thanks for the advice, Chuck," Eddie replied in a tone that said, "Thanks for nothing." He rolled on his side. "My gut says I need shut-eye." He pulled the blanket over him. Charles started to say something, but his face grimaced with pain. He clutched his abdomen. A moment later it passed and he released his grip. Charles tugged the desk lamp chain. The room went black.

A rose tint painted the eastern horizon. The Fleetwood pulled onto the airstrip. G.P. was driving; Amelia—in a tan jumpsuit and a white ascot—sat across from him. Eddie was once more in the back clutching his camera. Charles was with him. Three men and a young woman milled around the plane. It was several yards outside of the hangar. Other than the building and the airstrip, there was nothing but brush and cows. G.P. braked near the hangar. They hopped out and approached the foursome. The morning was cool, but Eddie knew in the next few hours that would change.

Charles grabbed Eddie's arm and motioned for him to stop. "The Jesses want me to give you a rundown on these people."

"No tricks," Eddie said.

"No tricks," Charles replied. "It's orientation."

"Hey, Ed, you're invited to this party, too," G.P. yelled. "Let's move."

"Shoe's untied, be there in a sec." He bent down and fondled the lace.

"You already know Fred Noonan, Amelia's navigator," Charles said. "The blonde-haired man with the toolbox—"

"He was in the car with G.P. when Amelia's plane belly flopped. Isn't his name Al?"

"Right," Charles said. "Al Meeyair, her mechanic."

"How come I don't have this through the knowing?"

Charles rubbed his lip a moment. "I suppose it has something to do with the Jesses testing my ability to follow orders."

"I keep forgetting we're both on trial," Eddie said. "Who's the serious-looking guy with the mustache?"

"Kelly Hanson, Amelia's aircraft designer. The young girl with them is her personal secretary, Louise Siskin."

"Come on, Ed." G.P. said. "For God's sake you're holding up production!"

Eddie grimaced and trotted over to the group. He neared and heard Kelly say to Amelia, "You pushed the throttle down too hard. She doesn't like to be jerked. "

"I'll know better next time, Kelly. Promise."

"It's not a matter of knowing, Amelia. It's a matter of doing. You need to become as familiar with it as you are with the back of your wrist. Now, let's take her up so you can practice."

"Louise?" G.P. said to Amelia's secretary.

Louise flipped opened her steno pad. "Miss Earhart has a live radio broadcast in two hours with Eleanor Roosevelt...Friar's at ten, racetrack at one, and Women for Equality fundraiser at eight p.m."

"No, no." Kelly tugged on his mustache. "We have to take the plane up. Can't you reschedule the broadcast?"

"The plane's shocks need adjusting, too," Al said to Louise. "It shouldn't take long, but it has to be done." He laid his toolbox on the ground and opened it. "I also want to double-check the aluminum sheet I replaced that busted rear window with to make sure it's secure."

"The broadcast can't be changed," G.P. said to Kelly. "It's the goddamn wife of the president. You want to tell her?"

"I don't give a damn who it is," Kelly said.

"Don't forget about transmission frequencies," Fred added. "We need to go over them, Amelia. Also, the coordinates for Howland Island still aren't right."

"Everybody shut up," G.P. said. "As far as I'm—"

Eddie snapped a picture. The flash bore down on the group like a cold bucket of water. They all stopped and stared at him. He smiled. "Just pretend I'm not here."

"Son of a bitch," G.P. said. "I ought to fire you right now."

"Enough," Amelia said. "Al, when we're through here, make the final adjustments on the shocks and the window. Fred, we'll discuss the frequencies and coordinates at the track."

"What about taking her up?" Kelly asked.

"We'll make time for Amelia to do that," G.P. said. "You have my word."

Kelly raised an eyebrow at Amelia.

"I know it's important. I'll make the time."

"When?" Kelly asked.

"Soon."

"You're planning a trip around the equator, not to Palm Beach. This is suicide."

Eddie's eyes widened. He frowned at Charles.

G.P. got into Kelly's face. "Who the hell do you think you are saying something like that to Amelia?"

Al ran his fingers through his blonde hair and glanced at Louise. She glanced back, then stared at the ground.

"Whoa, boss." Fred pulled G.P. back. "He didn't mean no harm."

Amelia stepped in front of them, smiled at Kelly and wrapped her arm around his shoulder. "Can you imagine what it would do to your career if word got out that you were afraid to let your own plane fly long distances?"

"That's not what I said and you know it. I stand by—"

She put a finger to Kelly's lips. "Now, who is the press going to believe? You or America's Queen of the Clouds?"

"I'm fighting for you, Amelia. Not for me."

"She appreciates that. She really does," G.P. said.

Eddie rolled his eyes.

"I know you are, Kelly," Amelia said, "and I thank you with all my heart, but I'm a big girl. I can take care of myself." Kelly studied her. "Really," she added.

He frowned and again tugged on his mustache. "I suppose we can hold it off one more day, but no longer."

"No longer," Amelia agreed. "Louise, please contact the hotel and ask them to have my lavender dress ready."

"There's a phone inside the hangar," Al said.

Louise nodded and headed toward the building.

"I'll show her," Al said to Amelia. He followed Louise.

"Eddie," G.P. said, "I want you at the racetrack to snap

pictures for the society column."

"Hialeah racetrack?" Eddie could barely contain his glee.

"Unless you know of another one," G.P. replied.

"I sure don't." Eddie squeezed his chin twice and glanced at Charles. "I sure don't." Amelia and G.P. strolled around the plane with Kelly, who pointed out areas that had been repaired or modified. Eddie and Charles wandered over to the car to wait.

As they passed the hangar, Eddie caught a glimpse of Al and Louise. They were standing just outside of the structure's rear door, which was located on the far end. They were locked in each other's arms, kissing. Eddie nudged Charles. "I guess it's safe to say they're an item."

Charles smiled. "It's so easy to fall in love."

"You're a real philosopher, you know that?" Eddie adjusted his camera and snapped a picture. Startled, the couple looked his way. He winked and said, "For the record." They ran inside. He and Charles grinned at each other as they continued to the car.

Eddie stepped from the cab, looked around and whistled in amazement. As he waited for Charles to exit, Eddie studied the half-mile long, mansionesque clubhouse, trying to believe his eyes. It was the middle of the afternoon—he wasn't even sure what day it was—and Hialeah Racetrack overflowed with elegantly dressed people. Eddie himself wore a brown double-breasted three-piece suit with a soft trilby hat. He had found them and other similar clothes in his valise.

Despite the heat, the other men were dressed in variations of Eddie's garb. The women wore graceful, wide rim hats and bias cut dresses accented with silver, pearl and gold jewelry. The grounds were festooned with red and blue flowers, green plants and vines. A procession of Lincolns, Packards, Cadillacs and Duesenbergs waited in front of the clubhouse for valets. Eddie felt giddy at being a part of the spectacle, but at the same time unsettled, as if he were merely a portrait on the clubhouse wall. He shook the feeling off and paid the cabbie. Like his attire, he supposed the few bills in his wallet had come from the Jesses.

He and Charles walked to the entrance. Eddie purchased a racing form and thumbed through it. "Holy crap. Whole Lot A Hooey is racing in the seventh today."

"Is that good?" Charles asked.

"Good? This is history. It's like seeing Elvis or the Beatles." He made mental notes of the horses' stats that were running in the upcoming race.

"The Beatles?"

"Oh, baby, I *have* died and gone to horse racing heaven." Eddie tucked the program in his coat pocket. "Let's find Amelia and G.P." They entered the building. Making their way to the second floor grandstand, Eddie spotted a lemonade vendor. "Want one? It's on me," he asked Charles as they approached.

"No, thanks."

"Why not, if you're buying," a tall man standing next to Eddie said. Like everyone else, he couldn't see or hear Charles and had assumed Eddie was speaking to him.

Eddie glanced at the man. He was dressed casually in a gray, single-breasted lounge suit and had the same southern drawl as Charles. "Make that two lemonades," Eddie said to the vendor. He looked at the man again. "You look familiar."

The man smiled. "It's the big ears. They look like Clark Gable's. Everybody says so. By the way, I'm Howard."

"Eddie. Eddie Coyne." Eddie reached his hand out.

Howard looked at it and hesitated. Instead of grasping Eddie's hand, he reached for one of the lemonade cups that the vendor had placed on the counter. He took a big swig and said, "Tip-top stuff. Thanks, Eddie."

"No problem, Howard. Anytime."

As he walked away, Howard nodded to the vendor and added, "Give a nice tip to Phil, there. He can use it."

"Thanks, Mr. Hughes." Phil handed Eddie back his change.

"Howard *Hughes*?" Eddie asked as he motioned for Phil to keep the money. Phil nodded. Eddie looked at Charles and widened his eyes.

They walked to the second floor stairs and approached the

area where forty years from now the escalator would be built. Eddie's knees buckled. The memory of tumbling and falling, bones breaking, flesh tearing filled him again. Worse, the hollowness of forever losing Carly and Ben overwhelmed him.

"You okay?" Charles gripped Eddie's arm.

"I messed things up bad, Chuck, and I can't do anything about it."

"Concentrate on your goal. Win your bet."

"Nothing can make amends for the lousy man I was." Eddie pressed his hands on his knees and took deep breaths to try to gather himself.

A cluster of men and women shuffled past him. A woman raised her eyebrows at one of the men. The man raised his hand to his mouth to simulate Eddie drinking too much.

Charles lifted Eddie back up. "You have to stay strong."

Eddie pushed him away. "I don't have to do anything."

"Yes you do, Eddie. You need to follow your gut."

"Fuck my gut. All it's done is leave my wife and boy without a husband and father and gotten a poor girl to commit suicide."

"Don't do that to yourself. That's what they want."

"Who?"

Charles flashed a rapid look upward.

"The Jesses?" A match went off in Eddie's head. "They're toying with me to take me off my game, aren't they?"

Charles said nothing.

Eddie looked up. "Screw every one of you. If you think you're gonna win by cheating, you've got another thing coming!"

"Eddie," Charles said. "Keep your voice down."

Eddie looked around. A man was pointing at him and speaking to a security guard. The guard eyed Eddie. Eddie smiled at the guard and nodded. "Come on, Chuck," he said under his breath. "Let's find Amelia." He ascended the stairs.

Charles started to follow, but stopped. He looked skyward and said, "Yes, I understand. Observe only. Isn't that all I did?" He went pale and fell against the staircase. Charles gripped his abdomen and struggled to take in air. His eyes bulged. His breaths came in sharp, throbbing gulps. Tears of pain wet his eyes. "Please, I wasn't trying to—" he dissolved and returned in a slow wave "—go against you. It won't happen again. I'm sorry." He flickered in and out of physical reality. "I would never say anything to Eddie about *that*." His voice wavered like a punctured accordion. He squeezed the staircase banister and tried to hang on to the corporeal plane. His hand clouded and went transparent. "I'll do the right thing. I promise, I promise, I pro—" he faded completely away…

…And faded back in. Charles stumbled against the railing. He nearly vomited, but forced the sour stench back until, little by little, the pain subsided and his strength returned. He looked up. "You have my word. I won't let you down." Charles staggered upstairs to the second floor.

Chapter Ten

Eddie spotted G.P., Amelia, and Fred in a reserved section of box seats. G.P. had a beer in his hand. He was reviewing the racing form. Fred munched on a bag of popcorn. Amelia looked striking in a peach color jacket with exaggerated shoulders and matching long skirt. She watched the thoroughbreds as they lined up in the starting gate. The gate was at the opposite side of the mile-long circular track.

G.P. caught wind of Eddie and waved him over. "About time you made it. What'd you do, hit the sauce when you got back to the hotel?"

"No." Eddie took a seat and slipped his lemonade underneath it. "I had trouble sleeping last night, so I took a nap. I overslept." He spotted Charles making his way over. Eddie was surprised to see that his hair looked as if it had been blown by a fan and that his face was ashen and sweaty. Eddie gave him a "You okay?" look. Charles nodded and took a nearby seat.

"What do you think, Fred? Is he telling the truth?" G.P. said. "If anyone knows about hitting the booze, it's you."

"George!" Amelia said.

Fred raised his hand. "It's okay. That's all in the past."

"You see?" G.P. said to Amelia. "I told you, he's fine." He turned to Fred. "We were a little worried, but I told Meelie the best navigator in the business wouldn't blow his career on a lousy shot of whatever."

"Never, boss. I really appreciate the chance both of you have given me."

"Forgive us, Fred," Amelia said, "but lately you've looked...a bit under the weather."

Eddie agreed. Fred's eyes were bloodshot, his face was pasty and he had a razor nick on his chin.

Fred sucked his upper lip a moment. "Well, if you must know," he glimpsed around with embarrassment, "I've got diarrhea. All this flying, I guess."

"Hell, you should've said something," G.P. replied. "Tell Louise to pick up some bananas. That'll plug up the old system."

Amelia said, "You're sure that's all it is?"

"Of course. Why? Don't you believe me?" Fred answered in an offended tone.

G.P. patted Fred's shoulder. "Now, now, everyone's a little tense. I'm sure Amelia's more than satisfied. Aren't you, dear?"

Amelia studied Fred. She blew a puff of air and nodded. Despite her affirmation, Eddie saw the reluctance in it.

"Eddie, snap a picture of Amelia, Fred and me."

Eddie readied the camera.

Something caught G.P.'s eye. "Hold on a sec." He hurried to a group of women walking up the aisle.

Eddie reached for the film holder inside his camera case and remembered the manila envelope he had placed there. He pulled it out and said to Amelia, "Give this to your secretary. It's a picture of her and the mechanic."

"I think she has a crush on him." Amelia placed it in her handbag.

"You don't say?" Eddie slid the film holder into the camera and motioned to G.P. that he was ready to take the photo.

G.P. was standing by the women. He blurted out, "Say, isn't that Amelia Earhart?"

"Where?" one of the women asked.

G.P. pointed to her.

Another one said, "Oh, my lord, it is."

The first woman said, "Let's get an autograph."

"No, Viv," a third woman said. "I'm certain she's here to relax."

G.P. nudged Viv. "Here's a pen." He handed it to her. Viv

headed toward Amelia with G.P. and the group of women in tow.

"Oh, Miss Earhart." Viv handed her the pen and a racing form. "You're so brave."

"Your eyes are even bluer in person," another woman said.

"Thank you." Amelia turned to Viv. "To whom shall I sign this?"

Viv grinned. "Vivian."

"Ladies," G.P. said. "All of you hold your programs out for Miss Earhart to sign." The women crowded around her and held them out. "Okay," G.P. said to Eddie. "Snap the picture." Eddie snapped. G.P. said, "I'm sorry, ladies, but Miss Earhart needs to rest up for her next big flight." He retrieved his pen and ushered the group away.

Eddie looked at Amelia. She smiled wearily at G.P. and shook her head. Yeah, Eddie thought, I know what you mean.

G.P. returned, sat back down and revisited his racing form. "Much of a gambling man, Ed?"

He shrugged. "A little."

"What do you think of Celluloid Sandy in the seventh?"

"Whole Lot A Hooey, trust me," Eddie said.

"I don't know. This is Hooey's first race. What do you think, Meelie?"

"Well, I—" Amelia glanced at the tote board "—A Walk In The Park seems to be the favorite.

"Whole Lot A Hooey, trust me," Eddie repeated.

Amelia smiled at Eddie. "Whole Lot A Hooey it is."

"Fred? Are you in?" G.P. asked.

"Not me, boss. I told you, no more vices."

G.P. slapped his back. "Good man." He turned to Amelia and Eddie, "What do you say, twenty bucks to win?" He pulled out two twenties from his wallet.

Eddie searched his pockets. All he had were three ones.

"Don't worry about it." G.P. slipped out another twenty and added it to the others.

Eddie was impressed. "Thanks."

G.P. waved his hand. "I'll deduct it from your paycheck. What do you think, I'm Howard Hughes?"

"Funny you should mention that. I ran into him at the lemonade stand."

G.P.'s brows rose. "Are you pulling my crank?"

"The vendor said it was Hughes, but come to think of it, I'm the one who footed the bill."

"It *was* him," G.P. replied. "Where was that stand?"

"On the first floor, near the stairs."

G.P. handed the money to Fred. "Place the bets while I track him down.

"You got it, boss." Fred tucked the money in his trouser pocket and headed to the betting windows.

G.P. said to Amelia and Eddie, "Man, if we get Hughes on board, baby, our airship will have arrived.

"Really, G.P., he owns his own airline," Amelia said.

"You worry about keeping the suckers happy and I'll worry about collecting the rent."

"Suckers? I don't believe you."

"I didn't mean it like that. I'm sorry." G.P. kissed Amelia's cheek. She pulled back. "What is it with you?" He looked at Eddie for an answer.

Eddie smirked at him.

"Fuck you," G.P. replied to Eddie's gesture.

"That's enough," Amelia said. "I won't stand for that language in public."

G.P. raised his palms to indicate he got the message. He stood and said to Eddie, "As for you, I can find any Tom, Dick or Harry to take a picture."

Eddie snapped the flash in G.P.'s face. "Oops, accident."

G.P. smiled. "Don't mess with me, Ed. You'll come out on the wrong end." He pushed his way past Eddie.

"The guy's a jerk," Eddie said to Charles, who was reviewing his notes.

"It's the pressure. I'm afraid we're all feeling it." Amelia assumed that Eddie had spoken to her. Her eyes watered. "I know it doesn't seem like it, but he used to be quite nice."

Eddie didn't reply, but the disgust in his eyes said, *The guy's an asshole. Plain and simple.* He grabbed his lemonade cup from beneath the seat and studied the racecourse. He had been so caught up in Amelia and G.P.'s relationship that he had forgotten where he was. He settled back and watched in awe as Whole Lot A Hooey exited the crossover tunnel and entered the track, and the layers of people who pressed against the ground railings to get a close-up view of the action.

When the first notes of the bugler's "Call to the Post" rang out Eddie felt as if he'd already won his bet with the Jesses and made it to heaven. The rush of the wager was slowly replaced with a gloominess that drained the joy from his body. The track reminded him of what he was missing. He wanted to feel himself with Carly. Stroke her hair, watch her undress. He wanted to have Ben leap in his arms and hug him. He wanted to be part of them again. He glanced at Charles. Charles scrutinized him with curiosity. Eddie smiled back wearily and sighed.

When the bugler's final note faded, Fred glanced at his wrist-watch. He said to the man behind the second floor betting window, "Three twenties each on Whole Lot A Hooey to win." He handed the man the trio of bills, took the tickets and walked away. He approached a lemonade stand and said to the vendor, "Give me a large one."

The woman behind the counter made the drink and poured it into a cup. "Hot one today, isn't it?"

Fred took the drink. "As hell, my dear, as hell." He walked to a trashcan and dumped the liquid into it.

Eddie studied the tote board. Whole Lot A Hooey hadn't made his reputation yet. Because of that, the odds stood steady at nine to one. That meant they'd each walk away with four hundred dollars. He figured that was nothing to sneeze at in 1937.

"So I gather you're a bit of an expert on horse racing?" Amelia asked.

"Yes." Eddie thought about Amelia. She was pretty, intelligent, ambitious, and brave as hell. Under normal circumstances he would have minded his own business—hell, he had his own problems—but he was sent here for a reason, so he asked, "Why do you put up with G.P.? Is it the attention he brings? The money?"

"I love him."

"That's it?"

"Why not? That's what G.P. thinks. The press seems to think so, too." Amelia leaned toward him. "I'll let you in on a little secret. It's more than love, Eddie. It's also fear."

Eddie's eyes widened.

Amelia raised her hand. "Oh, not physical fear. G.P. can be overbearing at times, but he'd never do anything like that." She took a deep breath. "America's Star of the Stars is afraid of, well, herself."

Eddie shot her a puzzled look. "Are you referring to flying?"

She nodded.

Eddie shrugged. "If you're afraid, then get out. You've made your mark." After he said it he was embarrassed because it was an oversimplification. It was like saying, if you're frightened of war, don't fight; or don't smoke; or stop loving someone; or stop…gambling. Eddie began to apologize to Amelia, but he was cut off by the announcer's voice blaring over the P.A.

"Ladies and gentleman, before our seventh race begins, we request your attention to Flamingo Lake."

Eddie turned to the infield lake in the middle of the track. Two men in white jumpsuits dashed around the shore, swooshing their arms at the flock of flamingoes. The grandstand crowd whooped and hollered. The flamingoes scurried about and took flight.

Along with everyone else who was seated, Eddie and Amelia stood and watched the long-necked, pink birds circle the infield area. They looked majestic against the bright blue sky.

"Have you ever flown?" This was Amelia. Her eyes were on the gliding flamingoes.

"Pilot a plane? No way," Eddie replied.

"There's no greater feeling than watching the world become

so tiny that you think you can hold it in the center of your palm. That far up, it feels like nothing can harm you." She glanced at Eddie. Her cheeks flushed.

Eddie tried to make sense of what she said. He looked at Charles. Charles was keenly observing the both of them.

"Daddy was an inventor, you know," Amelia added. "When I was in high school he came up with a track changer for the railroads. He said we were going to be rich." Amelia's eyes remained locked on the birds, which were circling back to the lake, but Eddie could see she was in the past. "We threw a big party for him. The whole town came out. It was grand..." She glanced at Eddie. "Until he discovered someone had secured the patent a month earlier. My father never recovered from the loss. He drank himself to death." The flamingoes landed. The crowd cheered even louder than when the birds took flight.

"I'm sorry," Eddie said.

"My mother said I was ambitious like him." Amelia and Eddie took their seats. "There is an unwritten rule among us insecure overachievers. Each new triumph compels another greater triumph. Do you understand what I'm saying? Because, God help me, sometimes I don't."

Their eyes locked.

The announcer said, "Post time, ladies and gentleman." A shot rang out. "And they're off!" The crowd standing by the railings pressed forward. Those seated in the grandstand sprang to their feet and cheered.

Eddie and Amelia remained seated, oblivious to the activity. Eddie saw in her eyes the same thing that he imagined was in his eyes after the incident by the staircase when he realized the Jesses were messing with him. It was the desire to prove herself.

Amelia furrowed her brows in surprise. "You do understand. Don't you, Eddie?"

He thought about his gambling and the longing to prove himself by winning at it. "Yes, I suppose I do." That type of yearning made him feel foolish and small. Ashamed, he focused his attention on the charging thoroughbreds, and for the first time, he felt no rush.

Fred entered the Equestrian Lounge. The patrons of the well-stocked bar were cheering on the seventh race through the back wall panoramic window that faced the track. Fred walked up to a vested bartender. "Double vodka and tonic. With lemon."

"Sure thing, mac." He grabbed a glass and nudged his chin toward the others. "Gonna miss the race."

"Racing's a vice I don't indulge in."

The bartender raised a brow and mixed the drink. "That'll be six bits."

Fred reached for his wallet. "Tell you what, let's make 'er to go." He handed the bartender two dollars along with his empty lemonade cup. "Keep the change."

"That works for me." The bartender poured the vodka tonic into the cup and handed it to Fred. "Enjoy your day."

Fred smiled, took a swig and walked out.

The horses kicked up the turf as they rounded the corner and headed for the straight leading to the finish line. Eddie watched the crowd. They were on the edge of their seats. Every man and woman seemed lost in his or her own heart hammering, get-rich-quick world.

The announcer's voice was high-pitched, frantic. "At the stretch it's Good Ship Lollipop, Whole Lot A Hooey, and Bigelow!"

Those standing slapped their programs, bounced and squeezed their wrists in madcap ebullience.

Eddie watched them as if he was the only sober person at a celebration and he hated himself for it. *I should be enjoying this. It's a gambler's wet dream.*

"Whole Lot A Hooey has taken the lead, followed by Bigelow and Good Ship Lollipop!"

Are the Jesses fucking with me again? No, he thought, I'm fucking with myself.

"It's Whole Lot A Hooey by half-a-length! Followed by

Bigelow and Good Ship Lollipop."

The crowd roared and moaned and whooped and grumbled.

"Woo, you do know your horses!" Amelia hugged him.

Eddie smiled weakly and watched Whole Lot A Hooey head to the winner's circle. He tossed his program on the ground.

Fred approached, clutching his drink in one hand and the winning tickets in the other. He grinned. "Looks like Freddy's just in time." He handed a ticket to Eddie. "One for you," and another to Amelia, "And one for you." He took a sip from his cup and said to Amelia, "A.E., I want you to know I've got a swell feeling about our world flight. We're gonna do it!"

Amelia glanced at Eddie. He puckered his lips and shrugged as if to answer, "Beats me."

G.P. exited the stairs, walked over and slapped Eddie on the back. "Ed, you're a goddamn genius!"

"Did you find Hughes?" Eddie asked.

"Aw, he gave me some malarkey about being tied up in a cowboy flick with someone named Russell. Ever hear of him?"

Eddie glanced at Charles, who smiled. "Yeah. He's got a thirty-nine inch bust and his first name is Jane."

Amelia smiled. "Sounds like a real man's man."

"I don't trust Howard," G.P. said. "I think he's planning to circle the globe before us. Let's get out of here."

"Good idea," Amelia said. "I promised Kelly we'd go over the radio frequencies this afternoon. The antenna is—"

"No can do, honey. We have the Tourist Bureau's dinner in an hour, and we still have to polish up your bon voyage speech."

Amelia frowned.

G.P. kissed her. "You'll have tomorrow, I promise. I purposely kept your final day free of outside activities."

"Don't worry, boss. Freddy boy'll help out." Fred finished his drink and dropped the cup on the ground.

"Good man, Fred," G.P. replied.

Eddie shot an eye at Charles. Charles curled his bottom lip.

G.P. motioned for them to leave. Eddie lingered behind. He picked up Fred's cup, sniffed it and held it out to Charles. He smelled it and flinched. Eddie said, "Freddy boy'll help out." He crumpled the cup, tossed it away and departed.

Eddie snapped pictures at the Tourist Bureau dinner. The dinner was just as he thought it would be, boring as hell. His mind was on speaking one-on-one with Amelia. He wanted to feel her out. Was she thinking of committing suicide? He didn't get that impression, but he was sent here purposely. Maybe she wasn't the one. But then, he thought, if not her, who? No, it had to be her. He loathed admitting it, but his gut told him it was.

After dinner and the subsequent press gaggle, he tried to get her alone. It was impossible, though in the car ride back to the hotel he managed to spill the beans about Fred's drinking at the track. Amelia was naturally upset. G.P. told her he'd handle it.

That evening Amelia and G.P. holed themselves up in their room and worked on her farewell speech.

Eddie sat on his bed and smoked. Charles stared out the window and watched the moonlit waves crest and wash along the beach.

"Things are moving too quickly," Eddie said. "Amelia's flying in two-and-a-half days. I need to speak with her alone, but her upcoming schedule's busier than it was today." Eddie took a drag on his cigarette. "I mean, she's gotta be the one I was sent to convince, don't you think?"

Charles kept his eyes on the waves.

"Except that I don't get it," Eddie said. "She's super determined, obsessed with success, in love, and not withstanding her occupation, well grounded. Though her flight is destined to fail, the farthest thing from her mind is dying." He took another drag. "It has to be more trickery on the Jesses' part. After all, how can I prevent someone from committing suicide when they have no intentions of doing it in the first place?" He mashed the cigarette out in his ashtray. "Maybe tomorrow night or the morning of her takeoff her nerves will shatter and she'll have thoughts of killing herself. Maybe that's when I'm supposed to make my pitch. I'm telling you, Chuck, I'm lost. What d'ya think I ought to do?"

Charles took a deep breath, kept his eyes on the waves and said nothing.

Eddie went to him and tapped his shoulder. "Earth to Chuck. Are you listening?"

Charles turned. "Don't you get it? I can't tell you anything. Not one word."

"I'm not asking you to give away secrets. I'm asking for your opinion. Man-to-man."

"It's your bet. Not mine." Charles turned back to the window and the beach outside. "You have to figure it out yourself."

"I hope you rot in fucking hell." Eddie shot a look skyward. "You, too." He grabbed his package of Chesterfield's lying on the nightstand and tried to force a cigarette from it. It snapped in half. Eddie crushed the entire pack in his fist and heaved it against the wall.

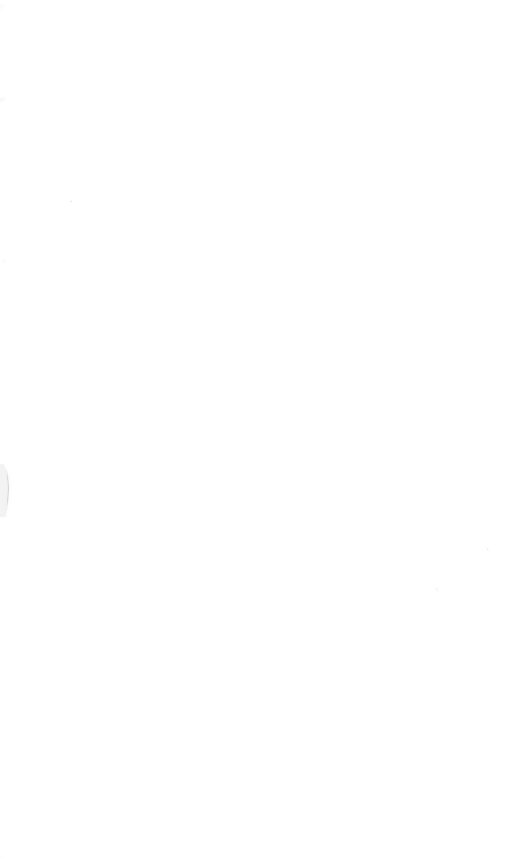

Chapter Eleven

The next day was exactly as Eddie predicted. G.P. had Amelia on a whirlwind tour of Civic Leaders, society clubs, celebrities and politicians. She gave radio interviews and read her farewell speech to a packed crowd at city hall. They arrived back at the hotel after ten that night. Eddie made a last ditch attempt to speak with Amelia, but she barely had enough energy to raise her hand in protest and say, "Good night, Eddie."

The next day—the last before her flight—was as G.P. promised, strictly for Amelia. Other than taking a couple of pictures of her and her team in the morning, Eddie was granted no access. In fact, G.P. gave him the day off with a, "I'll give you a lift back to the hotel. You can drop your gear off and go spend the day at the track."

Eddie's heart raced at the prospect. The old enthusiasm—the gambler's roar—blazed through him, but by the time he had made it back to his hotel room, the sensation had receded. An empty feeling replaced it, one that had nagged him since the other day at the horses when he'd won. *So what if I did win? It didn't bring me back to Carly and Ben. It didn't change the person I am. The only thing it did was prove that I knew which horse was going to win.* He laughed. The insignificance of that achievement hit him like a bad joke.

"You okay?" Charles was seated at the wall desk, dealing himself a game of solitaire with a deck of hotel playing cards.

"Sure," Eddie replied. "I'm gonna take a walk on the beach."

Charles stopped, lowered his half-glasses and eyed Eddie.

"You're not going to the track?"

"No. And yeah, I feel as screwed up as the look you're giving me."

Charles smiled. "I didn't mean anything by it." He slid his glasses back up his nose and went back to dealing cards.

Eddie watched him for a moment. "Let me ask you something."

"Eddie, I can't say—"

"It has nothing to do with the bet."

Charles raised a brow.

"The cards. If you're a ghost, how can you be handling them?"

"I'm not a ghost. More like a displaced angel," Charles replied. "That is, I kind of straddle the spiritual and physical world. There's enough of me in the physical world to grasp objects, but not enough to allow anyone but you to see or hear me."

Eddie scratched at his temple. "I suppose that makes as much sense as everything else that's been going on." He walked to the door, hesitated, and turned back. "You want to go?"

Charles laid down the cards. "Do you want me to?"

Eddie shrugged. "I'm not sure what your role in all of this is, but I know you have to look after your own skin just like I've got to look after mine. I…I can't blame you for that."

"Thanks."

"That doesn't mean I'm not still pissed," Eddie added.

"I know."

"So, you want to go or not? I'll keep the conversation light and away from the bet."

Charles nodded. Eddie wasn't sure why, but he felt relieved.

The sun and salt air drained Eddie's energy. The light conversation, which consisted mainly of Florida humidity and Cuban cuisine, also helped to clear Eddie's mind. By the time he and Charles returned, Eddie had decided his best plan of action was to get back to basics. That meant concentrating on one thing—preventing a suicide.

That led him to wonder if the Jesses had placed him close

to Amelia Earhart as a diversion. He had lost the first time by underestimating them. It wasn't going to happen again. Another thought crossed his mind: *Before I met Amelia's crew, Charles had said that the Jesses wanted him to orientate me to each member of Amelia's team: Fred, Kelly, Al and Louise. What if it's one of them contemplating suicide?* As he settled down to bed, he thought he'd keep his eye out for that, just in case. Feeling like he was starting to regroup, Eddie managed to fall into a decent sleep.

G.P. snuffed out his third cigarette. He sat on the bedroom balcony and tapped his fingers nervously against the concrete balustrade while he watched the dark outline of waves wash upon the shore. The moon was hidden behind a string of clouds. Between the waves crashing he could hear Amelia sleeping: a slight wheeze when she exhaled. The night was chilly. He quietly entered the room and tightened the blanket around her. The phone rang. He flinched and hurried to pick it up. Amelia stirred.

"Front desk, Mr. Putnam," the voice in the receiver said. "Four a.m. wakeup call."

"Thank you." G.P. nudged Amelia to wake up. "Have our bill ready in an hour. We'll be checking out."

"Yes, sir." The desk clerk hung up and pulled from his pocket a business card with a ten-dollar bill wrapped around it. He unwrapped the bill, snapped it tight a couple of times and placed it in his wallet. He dialed the number on the card and said, "Today is definitely the day. They're checking out in an hour, so I would imagine Miss Earhart's flight will be taking off the next hour or so after that. If you get the Pulitzer, I want a byline." The person on the other end hung up. The desk clerk said, "Some reporters have no sense of humor," and placed a wake-up call to Eddie's room.

D ressed in his muscle T and boxers, Eddie watched toothpaste drip from his mouth and toothbrush into the bathroom sink. He heard Charles in the other room singing and yodeling to some bluegrass tune about being blue and being lonesome. Though the kid could sing, being down and alone was the last thing Eddie wanted to be reminded of. He rinsed his mouth and said, "Do you mind? It's four-thirty in the morning."

Charles stopped singing.

"Sorry," Eddie said. "I didn't mean it to sound so harsh." He gargled and waited for a reply. There was none. He felt bad. The more he had thought about being upset with Charles for not telling him about Angel and Falk, or anything for that matter, the more Eddie realized that they each had their own bets to win. Why should either one of them stick his neck out for someone he barely knows? Charles was only doing what he—Eddie—was doing under the same circumstances. Beating the odds had to do with calculations, not emotions. *If anyone knows that, it's me.*

Eddie rinsed his mouth and walked into the bedroom. "Chuck, I want you to know I was wrong to take my anger out on you when I found out about Angel." He extended his hand. "In fact I'm a little embarrassed by it because I thought...well, forget about what I thought."

"No." Charles glanced at Eddie's hand. "What did you think?"

Eddie shook his head. "It was nothing."

"I want to know. Really."

Eddie shrugged. "It's stupid, but I was upset at you because I thought that we were, you know, friends." Eddie felt like an idiot. He had embarrassed himself all over again. He tried to recover. "What I mean to say is that I understand we're here because of happenstance. Nothing more. I expected too much of you." Eddie held out his hand. "I'm sorry."

Charles remained still.

Eddie heard him swallow. "Chuck?"

Charles grabbed Eddie's hand. He shook it, and said, "Expect nothing from either one of us. Right?"

Eddie gave a firm, single nod. "Exactly." He reentered the bathroom.

Eddie nodded in the bedroom mirror at his attire: a short-sleeved maroon V-neck slipover and pleated khaki trousers. He glanced at the wall clock: 4:40. They had twenty minutes before they had to be in the lobby.

He said to Charles, who was leaning against the opposite wall. "I know you aren't gonna answer questions, so I'm just gonna spout off my thoughts. Is that cool?" Charles looked at him, but said nothing. "I'll take that as a yes."

Eddie gathered his camera equipment. "I like Amelia a lot even though I think her priorities are a little screwed up. She's sincere and she's got guts. That counts big time." He glanced at Charles, who was studying his feet as if he were mulling over what he was hearing.

"I'm not sure this around-the-world flight—which we all know the ending to—can be considered suicide." Charles glanced at him. "Amelia doesn't know what's going to happen to her and she's not trying to kill herself on purpose, so how can it be suicide?" Eddie sat on the bed and took a deep breath. "Should I be focusing on someone else? Kelly Hansen, the aircraft designer, is upset about not having the time to work with her and about losing his reputation. Do you think that's enough to make him take his own life?" Eddie shot a look toward Charles. "I don't expect an answer."

"You told Amelia about Fred."

"Of course. You were there."

"It wasn't a question," Charles replied. "She's aware of radio problems and she cut back on her practice time."

"Yeah, and that only puts Hansen in a worse position, right?"

Charles started to say something but stopped. He glanced at the clock. "It's four-fifty-five. You have to be downstairs in five minutes."

Eddie stood. "Right again, Chuck."

Before they left the room, Charles again turned to the clock, but this time his eyes went farther up—to the heavens.

G.P. motored northbound on a quiet, two-lane road. The Cadillac's angel hood ornament reflected the first rays of the sun. The only other occupant was a green pickup truck heading in the opposite direction and carting a bed full of hay bales. Other than an occasional coral rock house, the surrounding land was all brush and pine. G.P. said to Amelia, "I want a full report as soon as you get to San Juan. Is that understood?"

Amelia was dressed in her leather aviator jacket with a scarf tucked around her neck. "Why, Mr. Putnam, I do believe you care." She winked at Eddie and Louise, who were in the back seat. Despite her playful demeanor, Eddie detected nervousness in her voice.

"Look, Amelia, I'm serious."

"I know you are." She glanced at her watch. "How long before we reach the Hialeah airstrip?"

"Any minute now," G.P. said.

"Wonderful. That will allow us a good hour to prep before takeoff."

"I want some nice aviatrix photos," G.P. said to Eddie's reflection in the rearview mirror. "Amelia with oil on her face, going over charts with Fred, that sort of thing."

Eddie glanced at Charles, who sat between him and Louise. Charles stared straight ahead. Eddie cleared his throat. "Look, G.P., we shouldn't interrupt her time with Kelly. They have a lot of last minute arrangements to make."

G.P. snorted. "Since when do you make those decisions?"

"All I'm saying is they can use the time."

"I can spare five minutes for photos," Amelia said.

"I don't think Kelly would agree. Every minute counts."

"Kelly agrees with whatever Amelia and I say," G.P. replied. "And so do you."

Eddie didn't give a shit about what G.P. thought. The only way he was going to win his bet with the Jesses was to make Kelly Hansen happy. "I'm not taking any pictures until Kelly's satisfied they've gone through everything." Louise looked at him and gasped.

G.P. stopped the car and turned back to Eddie. "Are you out of your fuckin' gourd? I'll sue you for every last penny you own."

"Stop it, you two," Amelia said. "I don't need this right now."

G.P. took a hard, long breath, pointed at Eddie and said, "Later." He drove on, then made a right turn down a smaller road. Seconds later they emerged on the airstrip. A loud cheer went up. Spotlights lit and a marching band boomed out Sousa's *Stars and Stripes*.

Amelia glared at G.P. "How could you?"

"I swear. It wasn't me." G.P. raced the Caddy past them. He braked the car near the hangar's rear door as a slew of reporters rushed forward. The high-stepping marching band and throngs of spectators followed them. G.P. and the others raced inside the building. Once inside, G.P. slammed the door shut and locked it.

The building smelled of its contents: engine parts, paint, oil barrels and rags. Standing at a table, Fred reviewed a large map. Al lay on his belly atop of the Lockheed's left wing, tightening a bolt near the propeller. He glanced at Louise, who shot him a quick smile. Kelly, on his knees, inspected the right front tire. When he saw Amelia he stood up and shouted over the marching band music, "We need to discuss radio communication. Why in the hell did you drop the DF and CW transmitters?"

"I'm more familiar with the MCW," Amelia shouted back.

Kelly went over to her. "But those frequencies aren't optimal for direction finding. What if you get lost?"

"We aren't going to get lost, are we Fred?"

"We've got the best charts money can buy," Fred shouted. "And I've never let you down, have I?"

"This is madness," Kelly said to G.P. "She needs backup communication."

"How long would it take to install?"

"Two or three weeks, tops."

Al hopped down from the wing. "I'd also like to double-check the fuel-flow gauge before takeoff."

"Is something wrong with it?" G.P. asked.

Al walked over to them. "No, but I want to be on the safe side. It can get finicky."

"All we're asking for is a little more time to get everything right," Kelly added.

G.P. took a heavy breath and squeezed his hands a couple of times as he thought about it. "Amelia, this is your call."

"Get everything right first," Eddie said to her. He glanced at Kelly and Al, "Can you get it all done in two weeks?" They nodded.

Amelia asked G.P. "Can we afford to wait?"

He shrugged. "Amy Johnson may be in the air before then."

"Fuck Amy Johnson. You're gambling with your life," Eddie said to Amelia.

"Gambling?" G.P smiled. "This is odds manipulation and we've made sure the odds are stacked in Amelia's favor."

Eddie felt like he'd been punched in the face. It was the same logic he threw at Carly every time he headed off to the track.

"It's your call," G.P. repeated to Amelia.

She glanced at G.P., studied the aircraft for two deep breaths and glanced at Eddie. "I don't want to be the second woman to circle the globe. Louise, hand me my flight cap."

G.P. wrapped his arms around her. "Are you sure?"

"Are you?"

He frowned. "No, but I don't think the odds are going to get any better."

Eddie glanced at Kelly, who was rubbing his mustache and shaking his head at the floor.

Amelia kissed G.P. "If you can do something about this damn crowd noise, I'm ready to give it a whirl."

"Give me ten minutes, and I'll have them quieter than Charlie McCarthy sans Edgar Bergen."

Kelly walked away in disgust. Eddie watched him take a stool lying in the corner and sit on it with his head in his hands. Now was the time, he thought, to convince Kelly that he had done his best and that he should move on. *With a little luck I can get him to take my hand and say the winning words and still have enough time to convince Amelia to wait until all the bugs are worked out before she attempts the flight.* Eddie started toward him.

"Where are you going?" G.P. asked.

Eddie nodded toward Kelly.

"Let him sulk. You haven't got time to play cheerleader." G.P. turned to Louise, who was removing Amelia's flight cap from a clothes rack. "Grab Eddie's flight gear, too."

Eddie cocked his head at Charles, who stood beside G.P., taking notes. Charles glimpsed at him but continued to write. Eddie looked at G.P. and Amelia. They stared at him with brows raised. "Wait a minute. I never said anything about going on this flight."

"It's in your contract. You are to accompany and photograph all flights," G.P. said.

Eddie glanced at Kelly Hansen, slumped in the corner of the room. He couldn't afford this time to lose the bet. "Find yourself another monkey. I'm through."

"You little piece of sh—"

Amelia raised her hand at G.P. She approached Eddie and said in a soft voice, "You're part of my team. We need you." She smiled. "Please?"

Eddie felt his throat catch. Damn it, he liked her. Just as he liked Angel and Falk. Just as he liked the life he had, the life he had thrown away, and for what? For a lousy payoff at the track. He looked at Kelly slumped on the stool. *I can't blow it again. I can't. The Jesses may not give me another chance.* "I'm sorry, but I'm not going."

Amelia nodded kindly.

"You know what?" G.P. said. "Fuck you and the train you rolled in on. Anybody can push a shutter button. Al, you ever snap a picture before?"

"Well, sure, a little."

"Give him the camera," G.P. got in Eddie's face. "We can't afford cowards on this trip, anyway."

"No!" Louise rushed to Al. "Miss Earhart...?"

Eddie sought Charles' eyes. This time Charles looked back. He didn't say anything, but there was a solemn expression on his face. Eddie recognized it. It was the same one he had when he had told Eddie to follow his gut.

"Hand over the camera, big shot," G.P. said.

Eddie watched Louise tug Al's arm in an attempt to pull him away. Al stood firm, but his face was tight, and his eyes showed as much worry as Louise's blanched knuckles did. Eddie looked at Kelly. He had lit a cigarette and was blowing smoke rings at his shoes. *Is he the one I'm supposed to save? Amelia and Fred die, but they don't commit suicide. Follow your gut. Her mechanic didn't choose to go on this trip, but if he flies, he dies. That's not suicide, either. Follow your gut.* He looked upward to where he imagined the Jesses were. *Hansen's the one I'm supposed to save, right? Give me a fucking clue. Anything!*

G.P. yanked the camera from Eddie and motioned for Al to take it.

"No!" Louise started to cry. "No!"

"Everything will be fine," Amelia said to Louise. "I promise."

"Al, I'm doubling your salary," G.P. said.

Al said to Louise, "We can use the money," and gently forced her hands off of him.

Eddie raised his brows beseechingly at Charles. *Please, Chuck. Give me something. I don't want this kid to die for nothing.* Charles's face was still as a statue. Except...except Eddie thought he saw his eyes flicker—once—toward Amelia. Eddie grabbed the camera back. "I changed my mind. I can use the money."

"Thank God," Louise uttered between sobs.

G.P. huffed through his nose. "What a surprise. Don't forget your bananas, Ed."

Charles rushed over and grabbed Eddie's arm as he started to take a swing at G.P.

"All right, troops, let's turn this horse crap into horse power." G.P. walked to the hangar's rear door. "I'll handle the crowd. You get the plane outside."

Kelly stamped out his cigarette and headed back to the plane. Al grabbed his toolbox. Louise wiped her eyes, apologized to Amelia, and retrieved Eddie's flight gear.

Eddie studied the twin-engine, forty-foot long silver bird as Amelia and Fred entered it. The small hatch was located midway between the cockpit and the tail. He looked around at the hundreds of people who quietly stared in awe at the aircraft, which Amelia's crew had moved onto the airstrip. He imagined that to the crowd the plane represented the human spirit, but it also represented something else, he thought—hubris and greed. Did his life represent hubris and greed, too? He wasn't certain or even sure that he wanted to know. He took a deep breath. Before entering, he looked back at Charles, who stood behind him. "After you."

Charles shook his head. "Airplanes and I don't get along."

Eddie smiled. "An angel who's afraid of heights? The Jesses must have a field day with that one."

Charles smiled anemically.

"In that case, see you on the other side." Eddie gave him a half-assed salute and started to enter.

Charles grabbed his shoulder. "This is your second chance."

"I know."

"There may not be a third one."

Eddie's heart raced. "Have the Jesses already made a decision?"

"That's all I'm allowed to say."

"Of course," Eddie said sarcastically. "Of *course*."

"Just don't blow this one, okay?"

"More secret info?"

Charles locked eyes with Eddie. "No. That's personal advice."

The seriousness in his voice collapsed Eddie's bravado. "All right. I got it. Thanks." He entered the plane. Soon the engines roared to life. The crowd cheered and waved to Amelia. The marching band picked-up its Sousa march. G.P. waggled his hat at the cockpit window. Kelly, Al, and Louise stood near the hangar and witnessed, along with the hundreds of others, the Electra's taxi and takeoff.

Charles stood on the tarmac and watched the plane ascend into the cloudless, blue sky. When it faded into serene nothingness, he looked higher up and frowned.

Two weeks after their departure, the days were still nothing but fume-scented, vibrating, cramped quarters and one continuous ear-pounding rumble. They landed in the evenings to sleep, refuel, and check the engines. Most times Eddie had no idea where they were: Puerto Rico one night, Dutch Guiana the next. His stomach was upset, and his appetite shot. The profane rumble remained with him throughout the night and upset what little sleep he could muster. He had no idea how Amelia and Fred endured it. He was so miserable Eddie even missed Charles. Worse, he had plenty of time to think about Carly and Ben and the kind of husband and father he should have been for them. He couldn't shake the picture of Vernon seated in the living room next to Ben offering the attention and comfort that he, Eddie, should have been supplying. Eddie peered out of the Lockheed's window and stared at the ocean below. He wished he had never entered a racetrack.

In the first evenings after their takeoff, he had approached Amelia about choosing to save her life by canceling the flight, but even he had to admit that in light of how well the trip was going, the idea seemed ludicrous. He tried different approaches, but each one came across more lunatic sounding than the one before. At long last, Amelia had told him, "I've got enough disturbances to deal with. If you can't shut up, I'm afraid I'll have to continue on without a photographer."

Eddie got the message. His chances were slim as it was, but if she fired him they would be zero. Instead, he decided to take the opposite approach and help her and Fred out as much as he could. There was nothing technical he could do, but he made himself a good gofer and a good open ear. He even had it in the back of his mind that he wouldn't need that third chance after all. Maybe they would make it. Things were going fairly smoothly. Fred didn't show signs of drinking. Who was to say that past events couldn't be altered? After all, he was part of the team and that was a change of history.

By week three they had flown across Malaysia, Indonesia,

and Australia. It was a grueling journey. Each of them had shed several pounds. They were bleary-eyed, pale, and resembled extras from a zombie movie. Still, Eddie had adjusted to the conditions, and the flight proceeded according to schedule.

It was morning. They had spent the evening near a small airfield in Lea, a province in Papua, New Guinea. Amelia and Fred stood near a hangar constructed of wood. The plane had been stored there overnight. Amelia walked toward the aircraft, which had been rolled onto the grass runway strip. Eddie snapped a picture of her. She motioned him over and said, "I want to thank you for sticking it out. This hasn't been easy."

"It's nothing. I need the money."

She raised a brow. "You and I know it's more than that."

He smiled. "You caught me."

"This is the most difficult part of the journey. We'll be flying nearly eighteen hours over the Pacific." Eddie nodded. He didn't need a college degree to figure out that if they were going to die, this would be the time. "I don't expect any trouble," Amelia added, "but if you want to stay behind as a precaution, I understand."

"No. I wouldn't miss it for the world." Strange as it was, Eddie actually meant it. He admired Amelia. She was something he wasn't—courageous. He wanted her to live. She deserved to. Maybe his being on the flight would change history. Maybe, if something bad were about to happen, he could get her to turn back. But what if he couldn't? What would happen to him? *I can't die twice, can I?* A chill ran through him. *Could I end up even worse off than I am?*

"Eddie, are you all right? You look like you've seen a spirit."

Eddie tossed a crooked smile at her. "Sometimes I think that's all I do see."

Amelia nodded and walked toward the right wing. She stopped and turned back. "Why are you sticking it out? I want you to be honest with me."

He wanted to tell her the truth. He wanted to explain whom he really was and how he knew the flight would end tragically. He wanted to say to her, *Sure, I have a bet to win, but now that you*

know you're going to die if you don't end your flight, you can win, too.
He yearned with all of his heart to convey those truths to her.
He even wanted to admit that he wasn't brave like she was. That
he hated himself for being a coward whose main concern was
keeping quiet so he wouldn't break the Jesses' rules and win a
stinking wager in order to save his own hide. Instead, he said,
"You're making history, Amelia. I want to be a part of it."

She tapped her lip thrice and replied, "I still don't believe you,
you know," and walked to the aircraft's wing.

Chapter Twelve

Chief Radioman Leo Bellarts, a young man with a whispery mustache, sat at his desk in the communication room. It was walled with transmitters and receivers. He turned a frequency dial and spoke into a radio transmitter that resembled a candlestick phone. "US Coast Guard Cutter *Itasca* to Amelia Earhart. Requesting location." As he waited for a response, he glanced at the two men who stood to his sides. On his left was Commander Thompson, a dark-haired man who infrequently smiled. On his right, pacing the few steps allowable in the tight room, was G.P. He had a pair of binoculars around his neck. None of the men saw Charles. He stood in a corner, watching and taking notes. "Request location," Bellarts repeated in the receiver. "When do you expect to reach Howland Island? Repeat, when…"

Eddie studied the ocean and studied the ocean and studied the ocean. That was practically all he had seen for the five hours since their takeoff from the New Guinea airstrip. The broken rear window that Al had replaced with an aluminum sheet after their bumpy landing in Miami had partially popped open. The gap caused the insane rumble of the engines to bore relentlessly through his ears like a jackhammer. His nose reeked of oil fumes, which had picked up. Eddie shifted. His ass hurt from the stiff, vibrating seat nearly as much as his back did.

The plane rocked from a rainy wind gust. He was seated in

the front of the cramped hull, near the left propeller. The cockpit was directly in front and a large step above him. That was Amelia and Fred's home. Through their window he could get an overhead view. The sky had been clear earlier, but now it was draped in black clouds. He heard Fred yell to Amelia that the westerly storms had picked up. The radio squawked, "Repeat. When do you expect to reach Howland Island?"

Eddie heard Amelia cough. The fumes were getting to her, too, he thought. She shouted over the engine noise, "Fred, how far are we?"

Fred had a chart spread out in front of him. "Can't tell. The sky's too overcast and the gyroscope won't stop shaking." The plane pitched again from a windblast. Rain whipped against the cockpit.

Amelia tapped the fuel gauge. Eddie stretched his neck to get a look at it. It was hugging empty. She picked up the mic. "Amelia Earhart to *Itasca*, take bearing on us at 3105 kilocycles…"

Inside the *Itasca's* radio room, Bellarts, Commander Thompson, and G.P. huddled around a speaker mounted into the wall above Bellarts' desk and listened. "…bearing on us at 3105 kilocycles. Fuel is running low. Maybe one hour left."

"What did she say?" G.P. asked. "I couldn't hear through the static."

Bellarts said, "Volume is S-2, barely readable."

"I don't give a shit about that." G.P. ran his hand through his hair. "I want to know what she said."

Bellarts glanced at Commander Thompson. He nodded. Bellarts said to Thompson, "Sir, we can't get a good bearing on a frequency of 3105 kilocycles."

"Ask her to send out a signal on five hundred or to take a bearing on us," Commander Thompson said.

"Yes, sir." Bellarts sent out the request.

Amelia turned to Fred. "Did you understand that?" Fred shook his head.

"I think I did," Eddie shouted over the engines. "He wants you to send him something on five hundred. A bearing?"

Amelia gave him thumbs up. "Fred, how are we? Do you have a fix on our location?"

"I'm working on it, damn it, I'm working on it." Fred ruffled the chart. It ripped down a seam. "Fuck," he pushed his way past Eddie to the end of the plane's hull and shuffled through a compartment. Eddie slipped into the cockpit and took Fred's seat. Amelia glanced at him. Even through her goggles and aviator cap he could see she looked as if she'd aged ten years. The skin on her face was grimy and looked as if it had been pulled tight. Her blue eyes had dulled, and her mouth had stretched so thin that he almost saw the gap in her front teeth. Her hands gripped the plane's yoke as if they were welded to it.

Still, she shot Eddie a smile. "After this flight, I think I really will settle down. Raise a family." She looked at the fuel gauge and added, "Isn't it wonderful what the Pacific Ocean and an empty fuel tank will do for your perspective?"

"Amelia, I wish I had half your nerve."

"You do, Eddie, or you wouldn't be here."

Leo Bellarts' voice came through the radio. It was stronger than previously. "*Itasca* to Earhart. Broadcasting on five hundred kilocycles. Acknowledge. Repeat, broad—"

"—Casting signal on 500 kilocycles. Acknowledge." Bellarts waited. Nothing. He looked at G.P. and Commander Thompson. The commander's face was even, but his right thumb and forefinger clamped the side pleat of his trousers. G.P.'s brow beaded with sweat. He was staring at a charging panel. He spun and said to the men, "How can this be? This is bullshit!"

Charles stopped writing and listened.

"Mr. Putnam," Commander Thompson replied. "We're trying everything we can, but I'm afraid Miss Earhart's higher radio frequencies aren't carrying through the stormy weather outside."

"Radio frequencies?" A look of panic crossed G.P.'s face.

"Yes," Thompson said. "Lower frequencies are better suited for location finding under these circumstances. Do you know what kind of transmitters are on her aircraft?"

G.P. stared blankly at the two men. "No, I..." He cupped his mouth in his palm and shook his head.

Thompson clapped his shoulder. "Stay strong. We'll find her." He looked at Bellarts.

"The commander's right, sir," Bellarts said. "I've still got a few tricks up my—"

"Earhart to *Itasca*. Message received, but unable to get bearing." Amelia's words came over the speaker weak, static, and broken up. "No sign of island...fuel running low. We are running north and south." Then there was nothing.

G.P. raced to the radio transmitter and grabbed it from Bellarts' hand. "Meelie, where are you? Come in, for Christ's sake! Please, come in." More silence. G.P. released the transmitter. He kicked a typewriter stand near the desk. Thompson went to him. G.P. pushed him away and wept. Charles went to him and nearly touched his shoulder but stopped and went back to note taking.

Eddie stared out the cockpit window at the rain falling on the Pacific Ocean. They had heard G.P.'s plea. It had brought tears to Amelia. She had responded several times, but there was only static. The Lockheed's left engine sputtered. The radio went silent. Eddie looked at Amelia with scrunched brows.

"That particular motor powers the generator," Amelia said. "No generator, no radio." She stared out the cockpit as they waited quietly beneath the dark sky.

Fred shouted from the back of the airplane, "Looks like we're going down in a blaze of glory!" He took a deep slug from a flask he had pulled from the rear compartment.

Amelia looked at Eddie and smiled.

"It might not have to end this way," Eddie said.

"What is that supposed to mean?"

He took a deep breath. "I'm not exactly sure how all of this works, but if you take my hand and say 'I accept life' things might conclude differently."

She raised her goggles. "You really don't understand, do you? I've already accepted life. That's why I do what I do. I choose to live my life to the fullest, to leave my mark for others to follow. I wouldn't trade that for anything."

"But you're going to die," Eddie said. "I'm trying to save—"

Amelia placed her fingers on his lips. "When I go. *When* I go, I would rather it be in the pursuit of triumph, not on a porch swing contemplating my losses."

"But you told me you wanted to settle down and raise a family."

"Yes, but after this flight. Not before." She smiled. "It makes no sense, does it?"

"No, I get it," Eddie said. "It's about looking back on your life and not having any regrets."

"You understand more than I give you credit for." Amelia lowered her goggles and steadied the plane.

The left engine stopped sputtering and rumbled to full life. The radio transmitted static again. Eddie settled in and thought maybe there was a chance things would end differently. The rain slowed and the sun returned. It glimmered peacefully across the sea in sparkling patches of blue and green. The plane flew along fine, and Amelia was as tranquil as the water. Eddie tapped her shoulder and pointed to a speck of land in the distance. She gave thumbs up, "Howland Island," and guided the aircraft toward it.

He wasn't exactly sure how this was going to play into his bet, but the thought crossed his mind that maybe it wasn't Amelia or Kelly who was supposed to have been his target. He looked back at Fred seated on the floor in a stupor. Fred made more sense. When they landed and Fred sobered up, he would give Fred a pep talk and get him to say what the Jesses wanted, even if he had to bribe him with another bottle.

As they inched closer to Howland Island, Eddie smiled at Amelia. "We're going to make it. You know how I know?"

Amelia glanced at him.

"Because I still owe G.P. for that advance on the horses, and I know he won't let me get away without paying it back."

"That's an excellent point." Amelia laughed, but abruptly stopped. A strange look came over her. She looked at Eddie. "You won't be going with us, will you?"

And then Eddie knew. She was the one, not Fred or Kelly. "I don't know...I guess not." His stomach clenched and felt as if it had dropped.

The left engine propeller stuttered and fell silent. The plane yawed. Amelia clasped the yoke and tried to level the craft while at the same time frantically working the rudder pedals. Fred yelped and tumbled on his side. The right engine stammered.

"I'm begging you. Take my hand," Eddie said as the plane shot downward. "Not for me, Amelia, for you." He didn't have time to question if he really meant the last part because the final thing to fill his head as he vanished was Amelia's voice shouting, "Eddie, where are you? Eddie!"

Chapter Thirteen

"Eddie, where are you? Eddie!"

The Jesses stared at him. They were seated at their table. Eddie was out of breath, and his stomach was upset. He felt as if he were simultaneously somersaulting upward and downward.

"Eddie? We're speaking with you."

Eddie's vision fell into focus. He was dressed in the sport coat and jeans he had worn when he fell down the escalator. He was again standing in the Jesses' chamber. The six of them were dressed in their gray hoods. They were positioned much as they had been the first time they met—hands pressed together, resting on the tabletop. The man and woman seated in the center of the table were speaking, but like before he heard all six voices simultaneously.

Charles stood with his omnipresent notepad. He was at the same spot as before, to the left of the Jesses, near the overflowing trashcan.

"As we were saying," the Jesses said. "We thought you would be more up to the challenge."

There were two differences from the last time he was here, Eddie thought. The first was the addition of three more trashcans, each one spilling over. The second was less subtle, but more ominous. The Jesses had lost the twinkle in their eyes that he had noticed when they first met. Their faces were hard, glum.

"Frankly, we're extremely disappointed and are cancelling the bet." The Jesses clasped their hands together and interlocked eyes with Eddie.

Eddie felt himself descend. A black void ate into his heart and brought him to tears. He was standing at Ben's funeral. It was cold, wet. His son's tiny casket was being lowered into the ground. Eddie welled up. As quickly as the feeling came, it washed away.

"That was a sample of your eternity should we decide against you," the Jesses said. "We felt it was only fair to prepare you."

"But that was worse than what you originally showed me."

"Yes, but you've blown your two opportunities at redemption. The losses add extra weight to the scale."

Eddie was more than scared, but he willed a smile and went with the only thing he had left—a bluff. "You're gonna call the wager off when I was only testing the water? That goes to show how much you know about horse racing. You never bet the thoroughbred unless you're sure of the win."

The Jesses looked at each other. Eddie glanced at Charles. The corners of his mouth tightened. Eddie reasoned that meant Charles knew what he was up to.

The Jesses smirked. "Are you saying you haven't been trying on purpose?"

"No. I've been working my butt off, but there was no clear-cut opportunity. If you want to play fair, you've got to at least throw me a bone. You aren't exactly playing by Jockey Club rules, you know."

"Are you're accusing us of cheating?" Their tone went from skepticism to threatening.

Eddie took a step back. "All I'm saying is that I was getting used to the track, so to speak."

"The wager's off," the Jesses said. "We'll deliberate your case and come back shortly with our decision."

"No! A bet's a bet. I can win this." Eddie didn't trust that he had lived a decent enough life and the thought of spending eternity at a funeral for his six-year-old was more than he could bear. "I'm so sure I can win this thing, I'm ready to up the stakes."

Charles peered over his half-glasses and raised his brows at Eddie as if he were insane.

The Jesses' eyes gleamed. They leaned forward, placed their

elbows on the table, and lifted their hands to their chins. "What do you have in mind?"

Eddie looked around while he tried to think. Charles was still staring at him as if he were nuts, and the Jesses eyed him like pythons about to devour a mouse. His time was running out. He glanced at the trashcans lining the walls, cleared his throat and took a step forward. "You said if I lose that I'm to be immediately sent below here, right?"

"You're wasting our time, Eddie."

"I'll tell you what. If I lose, before I go I'll clean the entire place up. Spic and span. Immaculate." Lame, Eddie thought, but his mind had gone blank.

The Jesses leaned back and smiled widely. Eddie was caught off guard by the response. He looked at Charles. He shook his head and wagged his pen at Eddie as if to tell him to take it back. Eddie crimped his brows in puzzlement.

"The entire place?" the Jesses said.

Eddie thought about it. The front office where what's her name worked was a junk pile, but it was no big deal. "Sure. The reception room. Everything."

"And that's all you want? The third try?" They again stared at Eddie like hungry serpents.

Something didn't make sense. Eddie lowered his head and shaded his eyes with his hand so he could peek at Charles without the Jesses noticing. Charles scribbled something on the page of his notepad. He glanced at the Jesses, who were eyeing Eddie, then turned the page slightly so Eddie could get a glimpse. ASK MORE was written on it.

"Time's up, Eddie," the Jesses said.

"I want more."

The Jesses looked at Charles with narrowed eyes. Charles shook his head as if to say, "It wasn't me." The Jesses turned back to Eddie. "Proceed."

"I want to go back in time to before my accident. Say right after I won the bet, and I want to remember what'll happen to me if I take the escalator."

"If you think for a second you have that much bargaining

power, you're even less deserving of a third chance than we thought. Get serious, or we're through."

"You can't blame me for trying." Eddie smiled at the Jesses, though his head danced as he tried to think of something they'd accept.

"Final chance," the Jesses said. "Speak."

From the corner of his eye Eddie caught Charles tapping his pants pocket with his pen. *Morse code?* If it was, Eddie couldn't read it.

"Time's up." The Jesses clutched their hands and squeezed. Eddie's heart thundered. The weird feeling of *the knowing* enveloped him—the Jesses were rendering their final decision regarding his fate. A bleak darkness crept through him. Still, through the corner of his eye he saw Charles tap, tap taping. Eddie patted his own pocket. Charles nodded ever so slightly and stopped. Eddie reached into his pocket. Inside were the ticket stub and Ben's birthday card. He grasped them and blurted out, "If I win, Carly gets my winning ticket and Ben gets the card I wasn't able to deliver to them."

The Jesses loosened their hands. They looked at each other, nodded and shook their heads. Though their mouths didn't move, Eddie understood they were communicating with each other. He looked at Charles. Charles looked grave. The Jesses turned back to Eddie. "We're not guaranteeing anything. As far as the ticket and card is concerned, you're on your own."

"What does 'I'm on my own' mean?'"

They grinned. "Exactly what it sounds like."

"I don't know. Give me a moment." Eddie didn't like the look on their faces. They were up to something.

"There are no more moments." The Jesses crossed their arms. "Take it or leave it."

Eddie took a deep breath and held it. Something was off-kilter. He looked at Charles for advice, but his face was expressionless. *Really, though, does it matter whether he gives me a sign or not? He knows, the Jesses know, and I know that there's only one choice.* Eddie exhaled. "I'll take it."

"Fabulous!" The Jesses smacked their hands joyfully together.

"By the way, how's your back?"

Eddie tilted his head in bafflement. "I'm no body builder, but I do okay."

"Excellent. Our last sanitary engineer, poor fellow, couldn't handle the strain. He begged us to send him back home."

"I'm not sure I get your drift." They were fucking with him, but he needed to find out why.

The Jesses leaned forward. "We're just saying that the sanitation job can get, well, a little difficult."

Charles lowered his head.

"First off," Eddie said. "I haven't lost the bet. Second, maybe the work's a little strenuous, but I expected that. And third, I can understand why your 'poor fellow' wanted to go back to heaven or nirvana or whatever home is called around here. I'd rather be there, too."

The Jesses barely contained their laughter. Even Charles smiled.

"What's so funny?" Eddie asked.

"I'm afraid you're under the wrong impression," the Jesses said. "Our sanitary engineer—a quiet fellow named Melchor who had an earthly obsession to start fires—didn't reside above. His home was below. Way below." No one smiled now. They stared at Eddie with grim eyes. Charles had a similar look, but his eyes were tinged with sympathy.

Eddie realized that whatever he'd gotten himself into wasn't good.

The Jesses said, "Allow us to give you a tour of our facility."

Before he could ask what that meant, Eddie was swept up in the center of a cyclone, looking down on rows and rows and rows of people. Hundreds, millions of them, waiting—waiting for their turn to be judged. There were mothers toting soil-diapered babies, colostomy-bagged patients in wheelchairs, and boozers hoisting liquor bottles. Soldiers were there, as well as soccer players, Roman gladiators, swimmers, kings, queens, beggars in rags, impeccably suited men and women, dashiki dressed couples, everyday Joes, and teens.

Trash was strewn everywhere—half-eaten burgers, Styrofoam

153

cups, tin cans, earphones, milk bottles, transistor radios, tablets, and smart phones. Scores of outhouses were scattered about, reeking from overuse. The higher Eddie spun over the flat, brown landscape, the more of this foul, gungy mess he saw. The cyclone stopped, and like Dorothy Gale's house, he fell in a heap. Instead of falling on top of the wicked witch of the east, he toppled where he had begun—facing the Jesses.

"You probably want an explanation," they said as Eddie struggled to his feet. "What you witnessed was the neutral ground. The waiting room, if you like. As it implies, it's neither good nor bad, here nor there, rich nor poor. People arrive and wait their time in line."

"But it's a pigsty. That's less than neutral," Eddie said.

"Do you remember standing in that line?" the Jesses asked.

"No."

They shrugged. "And they won't either. All they'll recall is what happens afterward."

"Then why clean it up?"

"Because, as you said, it's less than neutral."

"In this entire place you can't afford a cleanup crew? I don't get it."

"It's not for you to get," the Jesses said. "You are teetering. The only thing for you to get is your final opportunity to save yourself."

Eddie's head spun. The idea of spending his every minute, every second, scrubbing up muck and who knew what else soured his stomach. He forced himself to clear his thoughts of that. The bet was all that mattered. Everything else surrounding it was interference.

"By the way," the Jesses said. "The preview of what it would be like if you lost your wager. Do you remember it?"

Ben's funeral cast a dark shadow over Eddie's eyes. "I'll never forget it."

"Should you lose, that feeling will be with you as you go about your cleaning duties."

Eddie staggered back. His breaths came in quick, panic-filled gulps. It hit him like a thunderstorm that he had gotten himself in over his head. He wanted to cry. He had to run, but where to go? Vomit kicked up inside his throat. His fingers chilled. Blood pounded in his skull like a taiko drummer's war beat.

The Jesses again leaned forward. "Something wrong?"

Eddie nearly fell on his knees and begged them to give him a break. The only thing that stopped him was fear that it would make matters worse. He glanced at Charles, who had stopped taking notes and was studying him. Eddie thought of Carly, how much he missed her, how much he longed to lie in bed with her—to enfold her in his arms and sweep this nightmare away. He thought of Ben: the son they had made together. *They warranted more than a sniveling coward.* Eddie stiffened his will and forced the darkness to pass. Even if Carly and Ben were never going to know it, he was going to be strong for them. He was going to be the man that they deserved. He'd shovel shit and fight back ugly feelings forever and a day if that's what it took. Eddie forced his breathing to even and then affected a smile. He stepped forward. "Let's get this show on the road. The quicker we begin, the quicker I win."

The Jesses grunted skeptically. "You can start immediately." They glanced at Charles and added, "We wish you both luck."

Eddie turned to Charles. He disappeared. Eddie did the same.

Chapter Fourteen

Eddie stood in a place that was cold, dimly lit and smelled of disinfectant. The floor was gold speckled, white linoleum tile. He was dressed in the sport jacket, shirt and pants that he wore with the Jesses. The same ones he had on when he tumbled down the racetrack escalator. Charles' dress was as it always was—a nerdy, tan pullover sweater and jeans. Eddie took notice of the closed blue curtains circling them and instantly knew where they were: a hospital room.

Inside the curtain, Eddie and Charles stood over an elderly woman lying on a bed. Her hair was snowy white. It was sparse, so sparse Eddie could see the liver spots on her scalp. She was hooked up to a pair of IVs. A nasal cannula flowed oxygen into her nostrils. Wires linked to her fingers and chest monitored her vitals. She smelled of betadine solution and copper. Her eyes were closed. Her breaths were shallow, but even. She was little more than a skeleton swaddled in loose, wrinkled skin. Other than a monitor behind her, a bedside stand holding a framed photo that faced the woman, and a water glass and pitcher, the enclosed space was barren.

"Has she shown any signs of consciousness?" This was a man's voice speaking on the outside of the closed curtains.

"None, Doctor."

"It's a shame, Lilly. There's no reason for it that our team can make out."

Bewildered, Eddie raised an eyebrow at Charles, who shook his head in return.

Outside the curtain, the doctor—Doctor Charlock—studied the woman's chart. He and the nurse, Lilly, stood in the space between the bed where Eddie and Charles were, and another bed surrounded by curtains in the semi-private room.

Doctor Charlock looked at Lilly. "Does she have a living will?"

Lilly shook her head.

"Family?"

"There's a grandson listed, but no valid contact information." Lilly, a Jamaican with a kind face, puffed her cheek. "I know it's not my place, but the poor woman seems so sad. As if she's lost her will to carry on."

Dr. Charlock smiled wearily. "Call me if there's any change."

Inside the curtained bed, Eddie heard the doctor and nurse's soft-soled shoes pitter-patter away. He stared at the unconscious woman lying on the bed. She looked forlorn—beyond forlorn. He whispered to Charles, "The nurse is right, she wants death to take her."

Charles glanced at him. Eddie again turned to the woman. Her eyes opened. She said, "Eddie?"

He jumped and swallowed hard. "Yes?"

"Please, Eddie, call me Lu." Her voice was dry, despondent.

Eddie hesitated as he tried to understand what was going on. When he couldn't he said, "Lu, how do you know my name?"

"I just do."

Eddie turned to Charles. "How can that be?"

"I don't know," Lu said.

"It's the Jesses," Charles said to Eddie. "She's in a coma, but she's also awake, sort of. They've tuned in portions of her consciousness to yours and portions of ours to hers. It's difficult to explain."

Eddie ran his fingers through his hair. "Isn't that just great. What next?"

"I was hoping you could answer that," Lu said, "because I'm frightened."

"She can't see or hear me," Charles said. "She thought you were speaking to her."

"I'm so sorry, Lu, I didn't mean to scare you. I was…I was

talking to myself." Eddie studied her pale gray eyes. The skin surrounding her sockets were near translucent and veined in red and blue as if decades of sun-bleached sorrow had faded away the color of life. "How long have you been in here?"

Lu raised her arm and winced in pain.

"Is it bad?"

She nodded.

Charles removed his pen and notepad from his jeans pocket.

Eddie took a deep breath. He knew what his mission was. He knew this was his final chance to win the bet and that time was running out. "Things'll get better, Lu. You'll see. Have faith. You can choose life."

"No. It only gets worse." She dry-hacked and flinched from an ache in her chest.

"Have you spoken with your doctors?"

"I'm in a coma, Eddie. Remember?"

"Yes, but I heard him speak to the nurse. You can come out of it if you choose. I mean, wouldn't you like to see your friends and family again?" Eddie glanced at Charles, who watched and took notes.

"My friends are long gone. I don't have a family anymore. I lost my husband nearly ten years ago." She reached her hand toward the framed picture on the bedside table. Lu took a slow, burdened breath. "I'd give the world to feel his touch again."

"But you have a grandson, yes?"

She looked at Eddie. "Our grandson...we had a falling out years ago. He came to us late in life, when our son had succumbed to a stroke. Two years earlier, our daughter-in-law had died in a skiing mishap." Her eyes teared. "They were so young."

"Oh, God," Eddie said. "I'm sorry." He thought about his parents' horrible death years ago by a drunk driver. At least they had lived a long life.

"My husband and I tried, but I was fifty-nine and Allen was sixty-two."

"How old was your grandson when he came to live with you?"

"Six."

"There was no other family? Someone younger?"

She looked at him with a touch of scorn. "Even if there were, we would have wanted to take him in. He was our grandson. My son's child."

"I'm sorry. I didn't mean it like that."

She nodded. "He had trouble sleeping. He wet the bed. We went to counseling sessions and eventually things calmed down. Maybe my husband and I were naïve, but we truly believed everything was going to be fine. In hindsight, there was so much anger beneath the surface…so much." Her eyes went elsewhere.

Watching Lu, Eddie could practically touch her sorrow, her grandson's sorrow. *How do you lose your parents at six-years-old and not come out unaffected?* His mind naturally went to Ben. As much as it tore him up inside he knew that Ben would be better off with not only Carly, but Vernon, too.

Lu's eyes again focused on him. "By the time he reached his teens, my grandson couldn't contain the storm inside of him, and I…I overcompensated by being too indulgent."

Eddie sized up the sad, little woman who barely made a dent in the mattress. She deserved to rest, to have peace. He clenched his fist to squeeze that thought aside. Her serenity wasn't his concern. He had to win the bet. Period. He felt Ben's card in his pocket. There was too much at stake. "Lu, if you don't mind me asking. What exactly happened?"

She turned her eyes away from him. "I'm ashamed to say."

"Please. It'll help to talk about it." Eddie nodded encouragement. He gave her the same reassuring smile he used on Frank to get him to do his dirty work—the same smile he gave himself when he needed convincing that he only gambled to improve the lives of his family or that losses came with the territory and that he'd make up for the miscalculations in spades with the next wager.

She glanced at him. "Do you really think so?"

"Yes."

Lu studied his face.

He held the smile and felt like scum for doing so.

She nodded. "It started with trouble in school: bullying,

stealing lunch money. Later it turned into cars and electronics. Liquor and drugs. It culminated when he was seventeen with a shouting match between my husband and him. He took a swing and fractured my husband's nose. I broke down. My grandson cried and begged us for forgiveness. My husband hugged him. My grandson drove him to the hospital. The next day he ran away and we never saw him again. That was over twenty years ago."

"Did you and your husband try to find your grandson?"

"He didn't want to be found. We failed him. We let our son and daughter-in-law down." Lu's eyes moistened. Eddie knew exactly how she felt. It was the same thing that was, still is, eating at him. "With my husband I could weather that burden, but when he died, I couldn't—can't—handle it anymore."

"Please don't cry. It'll be fine. You'll see." He wished he really believed that.

"No. We botched everything."

"Lu, that's not true. There comes a time when everyone, even your grandson, has to be responsible for their actions." His own words turned on Eddie and ripped into his conscience like the bite from a rabid dog. *When have I ever taken responsibility for anything?* He had to get this bet over with now and end the misery eating away his soul. He clenched his hands together to firm his mind and to wring out any guilt he felt for what he was about to do. "I can end this for you. Make you feel better."

She stopped crying and looked at him. Her pale gray eyes widened. They darkened into a curious hue that was edged in fear and hope. "Are you the grim reaper?"

Eddie smiled. "No, just the opposite. What I'm offering you is life. An honest to goodness chance to reclaim yourself. To start again."

"Never. I don't want that."

Eddie studied the blips on the monitor screen. If he was going to win this thing it was time to play hardball. He turned back to Lu. "Are you religious?"

"I'm Jewish, if that's what you mean."

"Suicide is considered a sin in Judaism. Right?"

She started to say something, stopped, and uttered, "Are you religious?"

Eddie was taken back. *Am I religious?* There was no doubt that since he met the Jesses he believed in the afterlife, but did he believe in what religion stood for? Did he believe that humankind was cupped in the hand of someone or something that had humanity's best interest at heart? That within each of us there was a yearning to do what was right? That we may never understand why things do and don't occur? As he had done so many times since his spill down the escalator, he thought about his family, of his own stupidity and wasted life, and now of this frail woman before him who yearned to die.

He answered, "Yes, I think I am religious," not because he wanted to do right by Lu, but because he knew those were the words that would save his own pathetic skin. He felt Charles watching him. Eddie glanced over and saw admonishment in his eyes.

"But I'll be so lonely…and the ache in my heart. Please don't make me live with that."

Eddie's throat caught, but there was no choice. Gambling comes with winners and losers, and he couldn't be the loser. Not this time. He held out his hand. "It'll be fine, Lu. You'll see. Take my hand."

She shook her head. "No. I'd rather commit a sin than live like this." Lu shut her eyes.

"Lu?"

She remained motionless.

"Are you still conscious?"

Nothing.

Eddie looked at Charles. He had lowered his glasses and was watching her.

Shit! Of course the Jesse's wouldn't make it that easy. Eddie massaged his temples hard for several seconds until a mosquito—a revelation—buzzed into his head. He leaned toward Lu. "What if I could arrange it so you could see your grandson again? Would that make things better?"

She opened her eyes. "Can you do that? Find him?"

"I have lots of connections." It was evasive, but not a lie. He'd worry about the rest after he got her to utter the words.

"After he left it was like he fell off the planet," Lu replied. "I want to believe you, Eddie, but…"

"What?" Eddie said.

"But it's impossible. We hired a detective. A psychic. No one could find our little Whale."

"Your little what?"

"I'm sorry," Lu replied. "Sometimes I still think of him as a little boy. My husband gave Jonah the nickname as a joke because he was tall and skinny."

Eddie went numb. He wasn't sure what he had just heard. He squeezed his chin twice for luck and said, "Lu, are you saying your grandson's name is Jonah the Whale?"

"That was long ago."

Eddie sucked his lower lip and studied his trembling hands. He was eager to ask the question but also afraid that it was a ruse by the Jesses to give him hope and then to crush it, to crush him. He took a deep breath, clenched his hands together to steady them and said, "Did Jonah have any tattoos?"

"Why do you ask?"

"Just, um, trying to get a picture of him in my mind."

"He had one on his arm of an angel and a devil. We disliked it something awful, but he said he was going to get more anyways."

Eddie cracked a wide, joyful grin. *The goddamn Jesses had overplayed their hand! They couldn't read my thoughts so they weren't aware that I knew Jonah.*

He shot a look toward Charles. He was somber, contemplating Eddie. That sobered Eddie up. *Charles must know that there's more here than meets the eye.* The Jesses had made it too fucking easy for him. He'd been fooled before. He wasn't going to get screwed again. *There had to be a trick, but what was it?* He looked at Lu, who was watching him. Her eyes were heavy, but optimistic. He studied her, then forced himself to turn away. He couldn't afford to feel sorry for her. His best plan of action was to proceed ahead hard-assed and forcefully, but with caution.

He wasn't going to get cocky or complacent like he had done

163

with Angel. Or self-questioning like he had done with Amelia. He was going to be patient, sharp and on full alert. This was the final race and his horse had to win it. "Lu, if I guarantee that I can bring you your grandson, Jonah, would you do as I ask?"

"Is it really possible?"

He smiled. "Yes, it is."

"Bring him to me and I'll do whatever you ask."

"I'll start on it immediate—" He cut himself off with a sudden thought. "Where are we?" Lu looked at him like he was on drugs. "It's a test," Eddie said. "Regulations. I have to make sure you're of sound mind."

Charles rolled his eyes. Eddie winked at him.

"Oh," Lu said. "We're in the hospice ward of West Hialeah Central Hospital."

Eddie could barely contain his astonishment. "West Hialeah *Florida* Central Hospital?

"Yes."

He knew of the small hospital. It was less than five miles from where he lived. He asked her the year. His amazement widened. It was the present. He glanced at his watch: July 18, 5:36 p.m. It was barely four months since his fall. He could have Jonah here in a couple of hours. He started to tell her that, but stopped. He looked at his watch again. July 18—there was something familiar about that date. He popped his lips—*the high school reunion*. This was his chance to slip Carly the winning ticket and Ben's birthday card. "You hang in there," he said to Lu. "I'll have your grandson at your bedside tomorrow."

"Promise?"

Eddie nodded. "I promise."

She nodded and fell back into a coma. Eddie motioned to Charles for them to leave. A chill squirreled through Eddie when he passed the second curtained bed, the one closest to the door. "This place gives me the willies," he whispered to Charles. Charles glanced at the curtained bed and nodded solemnly as he followed Eddie into the hall and toward the elevator.

"Where are we going?" Charles asked.

"You ever been to a sock hop?"

Charles smiled. "A few."

"Good, because we're going to be at one in about two hours." He pressed the elevator call button. "But first we're making a pit stop at Goodwill and Party City." The door opened and they entered.

Chapter Fifteen

The taxicab drove twelve miles north of Hialeah before pulling into the northeast entrance of the Seminole Hard Rock Hotel and Casino. A lengthy, sluggish line of cars and buses greeted it. As the cab crept forward Eddie and Charles, who were seated in the rear seat, surveyed the garish empire. "Ever see anything like it, Chuck?" Eddie asked. The taxi-driver, a thin man, glanced at Eddie in his rearview mirror and said in a Haitian accent, "My name's Reggie, man."

"Same rule applies," Charles said to Eddie. "No one but you sees or hears me."

Eddie silently mouthed, "Oops," turned to Reggie and said, "Sorry, I was talking to myself."

Reggie nodded.

"This is all for gambling?" Charles asked.

Eddie replied quietly with his hand over his lips. "There's also the hotel, restaurants, bars and bands, a music arena, a shopping mall and God knows what else, but it's definitely the house that gambling built. The casino alone is over 140,000 square feet."

"What kind of music do they play?"

Eddie shrugged. "I suppose mostly rock. Some country. Some dance. I think ZZ Top just played at the arena."

The taxi stopped at an open walkway laced with hordes of people coming and going. "This is the quickest way to the Grand Ballroom," Reggie said. Eddie and Charles exited the backseat. Eddie reached into his wallet, which still had the cash in it from when he had fallen down the escalator. He paid Reggie, who added, "Have a good one," before driving off.

They entered the brightly illuminated, glitzy casino. Eddie tried to suck in the bells, the clangs, the clatter of coins tumbling from the slots, the whirl of roulette wheels and the shuffle of chips sliding across the blackjack tables, but it only smelled of cigarettes and desperation.

"I get the idea this isn't your cup of tea," Charles said.

"Is it that obvious?"

Charles shrugged.

"To be honest with you, Chuck, I don't even think the horses could get my top spinning like they used to."

"It's your family, right?"

Eddie nodded. "I blew it with them. For what? A lousy win or two."

"Three hundred and twenty thousand dollars is a lot of money, Eddie."

"I'd give it all back to hold Carly and hug Ben again."

"Play the hand you're dealt. That's all you can—" Charles groaned and fell to his knees.

"Chuck!" Eddie grabbed him. "What's wrong?"

Charles went translucent and faded nearly away.

A pair of elderly couples came over to Eddie, who was half-crouched, seemingly holding nothing. One of them, a woman, said, "Do you need help?"

"No," Eddie sputtered as Charles seeped through his hands. "Sometimes…uh…my back goes out. I'll be fine in a minute."

"Are you sure?"

Eddie watched in amazement as Charles solidified again. "Yes, yes, positive. Thanks for asking."

One of the men said, "He's fine, Trudy. The show starts in ten minutes," and led her away.

Eddie lifted Charles to his feet and whispered, "What just happened?"

Charles wiped his brow. "I overstepped my bounds. That's all I'm allowed to say."

"It's the fucking Jesses."

"Don't use that word with them," Charles said.

"I know, I know. It hurts my case, right?"

Charles said nothing.

Eddie wasn't irritated with Charles for not answering his question. He understood, and it strengthened his resolve to beat the bastards. He patted Charles on the upper arm. "Let's get to the Ballroom."

Eddie snagged a drink tray left near the outside bar and strolled past the woman collecting reunion tickets as if it were another day at the office. Like himself and the other attendees, the servers were dressed in fifties garb.

Eddie smiled to himself as Charles and he entered the banquet room. Thank goodness his stops at Goodwill and Party City netted exactly what he'd been looking for: high-top sneakers, a black T-shirt and jeans, a motorcycle jacket—admittedly pleather not leather, a Brando style motorcycle cap that looked like it came from *The Wild Ones*, a self-adhesive bushy mustache with goatee, and a pair of dark, retro sunglasses.

Eddie had even spent his dwindling bucks on a prepaid cell phone from CVS with the wild notion that he would call Carly right there on the spot and speak with her and Ben. Fortunately, he had talked himself out of it. If they had recognized his voice— or if he'd broken down—everything would have been lost. *Charles was right. I have to be patient. Smart.*

Eddie looked around. The Grand Ballroom was like everything else at the Hard Rock: noisy and wrapped in more glitter than substance. A crystal chandelier hung from the center of the large room. Ceiling and dance lights webbed out from it. The beige carpet was patterned with black floral scroll and leaf.

There were about fifty or sixty table-clothed circular tables, each with half-a-dozen bamboo backed chairs. At each table's center stood a brightly painted acoustic guitar resting upright on a stand. It was still a little early. Only half of the tables were full.

Front and center on a stage flooded in blue and red lights were the band, Harold and the Hot-Rodders. They were decked out in gold lamé jackets and baggy black trousers. Harold and his crew were banging out "Good Golly, Miss Molly."

The walls were decorated in fifties icons: record albums, hoola hoops and framed posters of Elvis, Fats Domino, the Big Bopper, and The Chantels. Near the entrance, which was at the opposite end of where the stage was located, a CD-playing version of a Wurlitzer 1015 jukebox stood in the corner. A placard beside it read, *Proceeds go to Children In Distress*.

Eddie scoured the room. "There they are, Chuck." He nodded toward a table near the side of the dance floor. Eddie ditched his serving tray against the wall and started toward the table.

Charles grabbed his arm. "Eddie, this is dangerous."

"I'm just gonna slip the ticket and Ben's card in her purse and then we're outta here."

"What about Jonah?"

"What about him? He'll be at Lester's Diner tomorrow morning. I'll take care of him then."

"If Carly finds out who you are, the consequences could be devastating."

Eddie looked at him skeptically.

"What?" Charles asked.

"I don't think I believe you."

"Why not?" Charles said.

"Because that has to be stepping over the line of what the Jesses would want me to know and I don't see you doubling over in pain or flickering or anything."

Charles sighed. "I don't know why they do or don't do things. I haven't earned that right. I slipped up earlier and told you what I thought, though I shouldn't have. They let me do it this time. That's all there is to it."

Eddie rubbed his fake goatee and stared at the band as he thought about it. He had to be careful and not fall into the Jesses' trap. Reluctant as he was to admit it, they were cleverer than he was. This could be a trick. *No.* He wasn't going to second-guess himself. That got him in a pile of shit with Amelia. He was going to do what he should have done the first time Charles had told him: *follow your gut.* He said, "Sorry, Chuck, but I've got to do things my way." He started toward Carly and Vernon's table.

"I can stop you. I have the power, and I don't think there will be interference from the Jesses."

"But you don't know for certain?"

"Not for certain," Charles answered. "But if they were going to stop me, I think they would have fired a warning shot before now."

"Why would you risk yourself for me?"

Charles glanced around the room at the memorabilia on the wall. "Because I don't know if my life had any value. It ended before I had the opportunity to reach my goals. Doing this may be a chance to somehow correct that."

"I don't get it," Eddie said.

"I'm not sure I do, either, but…" Charles breathed deeply. "It feels right."

"Look, you talk about your life being worth something. I screwed up everything of importance that I ever had. My job, my relationship with my parents and brother, and my wife and kid." He stared at his hands to hide his humiliation. "The only worthy thing I ever did right was to win that one lousy horse race." Eddie looked across the room at Carly.

"You're wrong, Eddie." Charles flinched and grabbed his side a moment as if he'd been pierced there. He glanced upward to acknowledge to the Jesses that he got the message.

"No." Eddie turned to him. "They're getting the ticket and the birthday card whether you or the Jesses like it or not." He turned up the collar of his motorcycle jacket, patted his faux facial hair in place, removed the sunglasses from an inside pocket, slipped them on and lowered his cap. "Trust me, she'll never recognize me in this getup."

"I hope you're right."

Eddie and Charles made their way to an empty table behind Carly and Vernon's. They took seats directly behind and facing away from them as Harold and the Hot-Rodders vamped the final chord of "Rock Around the Clock."

Harold, the lead singer, said to the slow growing crowd, "See you in a few, cockatoo." He strolled off the stage with the rest of the Hot-Rodders. Dim chatter and the ting of silverware being placed on the tables by the servers filled the ballroom.

Jonah the Whale entered the ballroom and rolled up the short sleeves of his red bowling shirt until the devil and angel tattoos weaved across his forearms and biceps were fully exposed. He slipped a dollar into the *Children In Distress* Wurlitzer standing near the entrance and played the Everly Brothers' "All I Have To Do Is Dream."

While the Everlys crooned, Jonah's eyes roamed the room until they came to what he was seeking: the table where Carly was sitting. He smiled.

Eddie sat with his elbows crooked on the table and his chin resting on his thumbs. He closed his eyes and swore he could smell the sweet, milky-rose of Carly's skin. His heart raced. He turned his chair slightly and looked over his right shoulder. He could see her and it hit him like an avalanche—she was stunning in her fifties garb.

Carly's lips were full and sensual in deep red lipstick. The high cheekbones that he loved to brush his fingers along were highlighted by Carly's jet-black hair, which hung like silk in a pink-scarfed ponytail. Her black velvet off-the-shoulder blouse and pink poodle skirt not only accented her curves, but fit perfectly with her playful, kind nature. The only thing not fifties inspired, Eddie thought, was her evening bag, which was draped across the back of her chair. He watched her stir a lime-colored drink with her straw and smile at Vernon, who had said something to her.

Because the jukebox—which had moved on to "At the Hop" — was playing, Eddie couldn't hear what it was that Vernon had uttered. But seeing Carly smile like that made him hate himself and hate Vernon, too. No. He had no right to hate Vernon. This was all on him—Eddie Coyne. He had fucked things up. Vernon would give her and Ben a better life. His throat clutched with regret. The regret of forgetting how beautiful Carly was, how caring and protective she was of Ben, how she had tolerated his bullshit and how he had taken it all for granted. Charles squeezed Eddie's forearm. Eddie shuddered. He had been so absorbed in his self-pity that he had forgotten Charles was seated next to him, taking notes.

"At the Hop" ended. The room again filled with the muffled sounds of milling about.

"It's time to get this over with," Charles said.

"You're right. I'm torturing myself by being here." He removed the ticket from his jeans pocket. He was within arm's reach of the evening bag. It would be simple to slip the ticket in the opening. After that, he'd go for the birthday card, which was larger and more cumbersome.

He faked a yawn and stretched his hand out to the purse. As he made contact with the leather, Vernon—who was decked-out in a black-and-white barred shirt beneath a black jacket and jeans like Elvis wore in the movie *Jailhouse Rock*—said in his best Presley drawl, "Come on, Mama, give us another smile. For the king."

Eddie jerked his hand back.

Carly smiled briefly and took a sip of her drink.

Eddie turned his chair and corner-eyed them as he pretended to watch Harold and the Hot-Rodders, who had returned to the stage and struck up Sam Cooke's "You Send Me."

Vernon said in his own voice, "I know it's been tough, but you've got to move on."

She studied her glass a moment, glanced at him and said, "You're right, of course, but…it's still too soon. I'm not ready."

"Honey, Eddie would want you to."

"Not yet. Be patient, Vern."

Eddie was torn. In one corner of his heart he was glad that Carly was so grieved over him that she couldn't let go, but in another corner he knew she had to move on—for her and Ben's sake.

"Of course I'll wait," Vernon said. "It's just that, well, I was hoping I meant something, too."

"You do. You know that. What you've done for Bennie and me. I can't begin to thank you."

He took her hand. "Is there hope?"

Carly kissed Vernon's cheek. "Let's dance." She led him to the dance floor.

Eddie watched Carly's hips sway and the swing of her ponytail as it grazed along her shoulder blades. He tried to avoid the dreamy smile on Vernon's face, but in some ways it was the most difficult not to notice. "Is it wrong to want to punch that bastard in the mouth?" Before Charles could react, Eddie answered his own question. "That was a cheap shot. It's not his fault that I screwed things up."

"We have to hurry, Eddie."

"I know. I know," but Eddie couldn't stop himself from gazing at Carly nestled against Vernon. He glanced at the winning ticket resting in his hand and grunted. "I'd give ten of these to tell her how beautiful she is."

"Eddie, please. The song's nearly over. We should go."

Eddie started to slip the ticket in Carly's purse, but stopped. A bleak thought ripped into his heart. He turned to Charles. "Will I ever see her or Ben again?"

Charles studied him intently. "I don't know..."

The final chord of "You Send Me" drifted away. Carly and Vernon made their way back to the table. Eddie looked at Carly one last time and slipped the ticket into her bag.

Charles closed his notebook, removed his glasses and slipped them in his jeans pocket. "It's time, Eddie. We need to go."

"This'll only take a second." He reached into his pocket for Ben's birthday card.

"We don't have a second."

Eddie glanced back. Carly and Vernon were nearly upon them. He whipped the card out, turned to place it in the purse, but stopped. The couple had reached the table. Eddie bit his lip, turned back around and returned the card to his pocket as Carly and Vernon took their seats.

Behind Eddie, Vernon said to Carly, "Admit it. That wasn't nearly as bad as you thought it'd be, was it?"

"Actually, it was quite nice," Carly said. "Eddie wasn't much of a dancer."

Eddie detested it, but he felt like an intruder listening to them.

"We have to leave *now*," Charles said.

Eddie pushed his chair back and stood. He felt worse than an intruder. He felt like a third wheel.

"Carly, you know how much I liked Ed, and I wouldn't normally say anything, but I hate to see you continue to sacrifice yourself. It's not fair to you or Ben."

Eddie glanced back. Vernon's hand was over Carly's wrist.

"Come on, Eddie," Charles said in a grave tone.

Eddie nodded, but continued to listen.

"What are you talking about?" Carly asked.

"I don't know how to tell you this." Vernon's voice was kind, apologetic. "Eddie was seeing someone else."

Eddie's blood roiled and surged upward into his cheeks and temples. He spun around and leapt at Vernon. Charles raced forward, pinned Eddie's arms to his sides with one hand, and clamped his mouth shut with the other. "If you interrupt this conversation either verbally or physically the bet is over. That's direct orders from the Jesses. You got it?" Eddie's eyes were wide, enraged. His breaths came in thick, fiery chunks. Charles sang a soft, melodic tune in his ear. Eddie recognized it.

It was the bittersweet gospel tune he had sung when they were with Angel—"I'll Be Alright." Charles' voice was smooth, beautiful. He played with the melody until the sadness in the song disappeared and was replaced with a calm, assuredness. The song faded and Eddie felt as if someone, or something, had swept through him and whisked away every dark corner of his soul. Before he could catch his breath the feeling was gone and was again replaced with Charles' singing. But that fleeting moment was enough to allow him to regain his senses.

"Are you okay?" Charles asked.

Eddie nodded.

"No sounds or motions, right?"

Eddie nodded again.

Charles released him. Eddie took his seat and remained

motionless. He heard Carly say, "No. Eddie loved us."

"You said it yourself," Vernon replied. "He was always gone. Money disappeared. Did you really think it was all going to the horses?"

Eddie's head whirled. He wanted to kiss Carly and reassure her and at the same time rip Vernon apart. He looked at Charles for support. Charles' face was expressionless, but his eyes were locked on Eddie's.

"Oh, honey, I didn't want to be the one to tell you, but you had to know."

Eddie heard Carly sob and his heart broke. He reached for her. Charles grabbed his arm. Eddie contemplated the hand gripping him. His eyes welled, but he checked himself and remained still. Charles slowly released his hold.

Eddie glanced over his shoulder. He watched Carly reach for her handbag, bring it to the table and fumble inside for a tissue. The ticket fluttered out with it.

Charles again grabbed Eddie's arm. "Time's up, Eddie." Eddie turned to Charles, pulled his arm away and continued to listen.

"What's that?" Vernon asked.

"I don't know," Carly spoke between sobs. She glanced at the stub and slipped it back in her purse. "That stupid ticket."

Vernon's brows arched. "Heavenly Hiccup?"

Eddie again watched them over his shoulder.

"You'll have to excuse me, Vernon." Carly rushed out of the room with her tissue and purse.

"Damn it," Vernon said. "Damn it." He motioned as if he was summoning a waiter.

"We have to go *now*." Charles was gripped by a sharp, stabbing pain. His face crinkled with agony.

Eddie's eyes remained on Vernon. "Just a second," he whispered. "Something's wrong, Chuck. Not just Vernon lying about me cheating. Something else…" He thought about what had just happened. *The cheating. The ticket. Carly leaving upset. The cheating. The ticket. Carly leaving upset. The chea—*"That's it! How did he know I betted on Heavenly Hiccup?" He turned to Charles in triumph, but gasped when he saw him. Charles was ice blue. His nose was bleeding and his breaths came in labored slabs. He flickered like a worn out fluorescent light—gone one second, here again, gone the next.

Eddie pulled Charles to him in an attempt to keep him from receding. "Come on, bud. You can pull out of this. Stay with me. Stay with me." It didn't help. On each return back Charles felt less like substance in Eddie's arms and more like wind. Frantic, Eddie looked up and said, "He has no influence on me if that's what you're punishing him for. I've never paid attention to him and you know it." Eddie glanced around—people stared at him. Eddie lowered his voice and again gazed skyward. "I don't give a shit about anything but winning this bet. You hear me? Charles' opinions have no sway with me. I decide how I'm going to play the game. I decide, so lay off the kid!" Charles blinked in and out so rapidly he looked like he was standing in a strobe light.

No, we decide. The Jesses' words blew into Eddie's brain and nearly knocked him unconscious. *We determine who is playing correctly and who isn't.*

"Okay, but the kid has nothing to do with this." Only Eddie didn't say it. Not verbally. His words—like the Jesses'—were inside him. "He doesn't deserve to suffer because of me."

He is suffering because of him. He made a choice to ignore his instructions.

"What kind of choice?" Nothing. He repeated the question. Nothing. "Fine, all right, I get it. He said something that was intended to affect the outcome of my bet, but like I said, I don't listen to anything Charles says. He's a geek and even if he wasn't, I don't trust him." Eddie released Charles. He flopped forward in his chair and fell face down on the table. "You want him, take him. I don't care," Eddie said indifferently. He hoped that Charles was right when he said the Jesses couldn't read his thoughts. If they could they'd know how badly he was lying.

Charles' blinking slowed. He blurred into a transparent version of himself, one that resembled a glass manikin. Eddie forced himself to maintain his composure though he felt like retching. Charles disappeared completely. Eddie shrugged as if to trivialize the matter. "It's just as well." The words were spoken inside his head. "The kid was screwing me up with all that note taking." Eddie stood. Though his knees were wobbly he compelled himself to take a firm step away from the table. He heard a groan and turned back. Charles had come back. He was again sitting in his chair, bent over the table. His nosebleed was gone, but he was shivering and covered with sweat. Charles reached his hand out to Eddie. Eddie wanted to rush over and help him, but he didn't trust the Jesses so he turned and took another step away.

"Eddie," Charles uttered in barely a whisper. "Help me up. It's okay."

"Who said?"

"They did."

Eddie glanced up, shrugged and turned back. Trying not to attract attention, he assisted Charles to his feet and held him until the color had returned to his face, the tremors had stopped and Charles could stand on his own. Eddie started to walk away, but stopped. Jonah the Whale was approaching him dressed in a bowling shirt, and with a bottle of beer in each hand. As surreal as everything had been since he had tripped down the escalator this felt like it was in a category of its own. Of all people, here comes Jonah with a fucking drink for him? Eddie wasn't sure if he should laugh, run, or crack Jonah over the head and drag him to Lu. He glanced back at Charles and raised a brow. Charles, who was a half step behind Eddie, kept a neutral demeanor as he readied his pen and notepad.

Eddie turned to acknowledge Jonah, but was even more astonished when Jonah walked past him, sat next to Vernon and handed him one of the beers.

The reality of what was happening hit Eddie like a hurricane. He retook his seat and listened. Charles did the same.

"I thought we were keeping our distance," Jonah said.

"New plan," Vernon replied. "She's got the ticket in her purse. I want it. Tonight."

"Sure, no problem. Providing I get my fifty percent."

"You mean forty percent," came Vernon's reply.

"No, I mean just what I said." Eddie heard one of the men

take a slug from his beer, then Jonah say, "I upped it. After all, I do the dirty work while you play the super-hero who flies in, rescues beauty and marries her."

Eddie slammed his fist on the table before he had a chance to check his anger. Charles startled and nearly dropped his notepad. Vernon and Jonah turned around and faced Eddie, who looked over his shoulder at them. Eddie froze for half an instant, then spun back around, hoping they didn't get a good look at him. He sneezed hard and once more slammed his fist on the table as if it was a reaction to the force of the act.

"Gesundheit, brother," Jonah said.

Eddie raised the back of his hand in response. From the peripheral of his sight he caught Charles frowning. Eddie heard Vernon and Jonah shuffle around and face their table again. A moment passed. Vernon said, "Don't fuck with me, Whale. I've still got friends in city hall."

"Really? I hear all that money you threw at your so-called connections has evaporated into bullshit."

"I don't need money to talk to the police about Ed's so-called accident."

Eddie shot Charles a puzzled look. Charles lowered his gaze.

"If I go down for that," Jonah said. "I'll sing like a bird and take you with me."

Eddie understood immediately—*he knew*. His fall on the escalator had been intentional. He squeezed the edge of the table so hard his knuckles hurt.

Vernon grunted. "I had nothing to do with that."

"Tell it to the judge. And while you're at it, you can also tell your partners at Good Buy! Realty about their disappearing bank accounts."

"Are you threatening me?" Vernon said.

"I ought to kill you right now." Jonah's voice was sharp, harsh.

"You do and the police will get a manila envelope in the mail a few days later, detailing the truth about what happened at the racetrack."

Eddie's pulse pounded. His face flushed with the hot infusion of blood, but he remained in place. To do otherwise, he knew, would be too big a risk.

Vernon chuckled. "Look, why are we doing this to each other? You want half? You got it. I can pay off enough bills with my share to hold me over until I marry Carly."

What did marrying Carly have to do with it? Eddie didn't know for sure, but he could guess. It probably had something to do with her position at the bank. *Maybe he was going to try to get her to manipulate his bank accounts.* That seemed the most plausible explanation and he despised Vernon the more for it.

"Good," Jonah said. "Good." Eddie heard their bottles clack together.

He glanced back and saw them stand. Before they left, Jonah patted Eddie's shoulder and said, "Take care of those sinuses."

Eddie with fire in his eyes said to Charles, "I'm gonna kill them both."

"No," was the reply. "You're not that kind of person."

Eddie breathed heavily. As much as he wanted to strangle the life out of them, he knew Charles was right. Though, he thought, as he and Charles left the room, I wouldn't be averse to beating the shit out of them.

Chapter Sixteen

Carly tossed her tissue in the wastebasket and accepted a new one from the bathroom attendant. She looked hard at herself in the mirror and wondered if she could keep going. She wiped her eyes and pushed the thought away. She had worked two jobs in college to pay for her B.B.A. degree and fought her way up the bank to operations manager while dealing with Eddie's addiction and raising Ben. She would get through this, too. She handed the attendant a dollar and left the room.

The restrooms were down a corridor leading into a 1950s exhibit hall set up exclusively for the reunion. The display was deserted except for a couple in rolled-up jeans and white T-shirts, making out near a corner devoted to Buddy Holly. Carly didn't want to go back to Vernon yet. She needed more time to clear her mind. She saw the kissing couple, hesitated, but entered the exhibit anyway.

Carly wandered aimlessly around the dimly lit room. She glanced at a sampling of the illuminated, framed memorabilia hanging on the wall; Jerry Lee Lewis' glittered jacket and Chuck Berry's monogrammed guitar strap, but behind her eyes all she pictured was Eddie lying in a mangled heap on the racetrack floor and Bennie sitting too quietly in front of the TV, staring blank-faced at it. Her stomach was tight. God, it hadn't loosened since Ed's fall. She stopped in front of a strapless gown worn by Ruth Brown and whispered, "Our life could have been so good, Ed."

She put her head in her hand and stared at the carpet. The

kissing couple tiptoed past her. She glanced at them and murmured, "Sorry." The woman looked back and smiled sympathetically as they left.

Eddie stopped the exiting couple as he and Charles made their way past the bathrooms. "Is there a woman wearing a pink poodle skirt in there?" He motioned toward the exhibition hall.

"Yeah," the man said. "But I don't think she wants to be disturbed."

Eddie nodded and continued toward the hall. "Look, Chuck," he said as they approached. "I don't have a clue what's going on between you and the Jesses, but I'm going to speak like it doesn't matter. When I get to something I'm not supposed to know give me a sign and I'll stop. I don't want any harm to come to either of us."

Charles nodded.

"You knew and the Jesses knew about Vernon and Jonah, right?"

Charles nodded.

"Why wasn't I told?"

"Because."

"Because wh—" Eddie stopped himself. "Okay, I get it. I'm not supposed to know."

Charles nodded.

"Why aren't you or the Jesses stopping me from going to Carly?"

"Because."

"Got it again," Eddie said. As they neared the entrance Charles grabbed him by the arm. Eddie stared at Charles' hand holding him back. "What? Are you saying I shouldn't enter?"

Charles nodded.

"Why?"

"Because."

Oh, shit, Eddie thought, another game of charades. "It obviously has to do with me telling Carly about Vernon and Jonah, right?"

Charles remained silent.

"I promise I won't let her know who I am, if that's what the problem is."

"What if she recognizes you?" Charles replied.

"I have to take that chance."

"Why?" Charles asked.

"Because." The irony of Eddie's answer was lost on him. He pulled his arm loose and started to enter.

"Wait. I'm allowed to tell you that if you enter something could happen in there. Something overwhelming."

"Good or bad?"

"I honestly don't know. I don't think the Jesses know either."

Eddie felt like banging his head against the wall. "Let me put it another way. Do the Jesses want me to enter?"

Charles spread his hands in an open question mark.

Eddie's brain swirled. Charles could be fucking with him. The Jesses could be fucking with him. Shit, even God could be in on it. He clamped his hands together so tightly his joints hurt. He felt dizzy, nauseated. He took a deep, deep breath and waited—pleaded—for something inside him to counterbalance the confusion. He glanced at Charles. His brown eyes were calm, placid, but it was easy to sense the churning beneath them. The weight on Eddie increased. *He's got a stake in this, too.* He—Eddie—had messed up enough lives and even now the list was still growing.

"Eddie, time's running out."

Eddie raised his palm. It was too confusing. Things were moving too quickly. Hell, they'd been moving too quickly since he was pushed down the escalator. He couldn't breathe. He couldn't even see straight. He needed a drink and a cigarette. He needed a racing form; he needed to pick a winner. He—*no! That's what the Jesses want. To mix me up. To throw me off my game.* Eddie forced his breathing to even and the heat in his cheeks to cool. *The answer is simple. Charles had reminded me of it when we were with Amelia.* Eddie turned to Charles. "We're going inside the exhibit hall."

"Why?"

"My gut says to."

Charles stared at him a moment and nodded.

They entered.

It took a second to adjust to the low-lit room. Eddie glanced around. It was purposely dimmed to accent the overhead lights directed on the artifacts. He saw Carly. She was on the other side of the hall, approaching the Buddy Holly display. Eddie's mission was simple. He was going to tell Carly about Vernon and Jonah, then hightail it out of there. No problem. He could handle that.

He took a step and stopped. Who was he kidding? He already had an overwhelming desire to kiss her and tell her how much he loved her, how stupid he'd been, how much he wanted her and that he would never cheat on her. He took a deep breath to regain his resolve and noticed that Charles was roaming around the room, staring at the displays like they were bars of gold. He's an even nerdier guy than I realized, Eddie thought as he again walked onward.

Carly faced a roped off wax figure of Buddy Holly. The musician was decked in a jacket and bow tie. He wore his horn-rim glasses. He was strumming a Stratocaster guitar that had been autographed in pen by the real Holly. Eddie noticed little of this because his attention was on Carly. He crept silently forward and took a place in the shadows not far from her.

She held back tears and thought, it may not have been thrilling or perfect, Ed, but we were growing old together. Ben was growing up…that was good.

Eddie gasped—though the words weren't uttered aloud, he heard them in his mind. The Jesses, he thought. They're tuning him into Carly's conscious like they did with Lu's. "Carly, I'm right here," he mentally blurted. "I'm here." There was no response from Carly other than to reach for her purse and open it.

A frown crossed Eddie's face, the Jesses had allowed him to listen only, but not speak with her.

Carly reached into her bag and removed the ticket.

At least there's the ticket, Eddie thought.

She stared at the slip of paper and spoke in her mind, "God, I hope it was worth it, Eddie. I really do." Carly crumpled the ticket, flung it onto the carpet and stared straight ahead at nothing.

Hearing her thoughts, seeing her look so small and knowing it was his fault overwhelmed him. *If the Jesses want to send me to hell or anywhere else for that matter, so be it.* He stepped toward Carly.

"Babe, are you okay?" Vernon approached Carly from out of nowhere.

Eddie hesitated.

"I've been looking all over for you." Vernon wrapped his arm around her. Carly leaned into him.

Eddie stepped back into the shadow. He had nearly forgotten he had to deal with Vernon and Jonah, too. He waited, hoping to get more information on what was going on.

"I've been thinking it over," Carly said. "You're right about what you said earlier. It's time I move on."

"Do you mean it?" Vernon asked.

She nodded. "I pray for a sign—anything—but there's been nothing."

Vernon kissed the top of her head. "You're doing the right thing. You'll see." He led her away. Eddie was more confused than ever. He had no clue what they were talking about. He tried tuning in to Carly's thoughts, but there was nothing. The damn Jesses, Eddie thought. They had removed whatever they'd done. He started to follow the pair, then remembered Carly had left the winning ticket behind. He picked it off the rug, unrumpled it and motioned for Charles that they were leaving. Charles was examining the wax figure of Buddy Holly. He waved Eddie off. Eddie had no time to argue. Vernon and Carly had gained about twenty feet on him. Eddie hurried toward them.

Vernon and Carly approached a life-size cardboard cutout of Elvis Presley in his G.I. uniform. Jonah stepped out from behind it wielding his knife. He jabbed it at them. "Well, well, it's the lovely Mrs. Coyne and her faithful Indian companion."

Vernon stepped in front of Carly, raised his chin and folded his arms across his chest. "I don't know who you are, mister, but you're going to have to go through me first."

Jonah exhaled an indignant puff of air. "You think so, huh?"

"I know so."

"Shut up, fucker, if you want to make it to the next reunion."

Jonah poked the knife at Vernon.

"No!" Carly exclaimed.

Vernon pulled back enough to barely avoid the blade.

Jonah pushed Vernon aside and grabbed Carly's purse. Vernon went for him, but Carly held him back. "Let him have it. *Please.* It's not worth getting killed over."

"Listen to the lady and no one gets hurt." Jonah rifled through the handbag.

Vernon clenched his fists, but remained where he was.

Eddie had kept in the shadows as he quietly made his way to them. He was about to jump Jonah, but stopped when Jonah threw Carly's purse on the floor and glared at Vernon. "What is this? A double cross?"

Vernon glanced at Carly. "What are you talking about?"

"Don't even think about it," Jonah said in a voice that meant business.

"What's going on?" Carly asked.

Eddie squeezed the ticket between his thumb and index finger—he knew exactly what was going on.

"I've had it with both of you cocksuckers." Jonah stiffened his grip on the knife and stepped toward Vernon.

"Hey! Looking for this?" Eddie said in a gruff, whispery voice. He stepped from the darkness and held up the ticket.

Vernon and Jonah said in near unison, "Who the hell are you?"

"Your worst damn nightmare." Eddie kept his voice unrecognizable. He wasn't sure if he looked terrifying or ridiculous in his sunglasses, heavy mustache and goatee, pleather jacket with the lifted collar and his motorcycle cap, but he was glad he had them on. He said to Carly, "Leave—go now."

Carly looked at Vernon. "Vernon?"

Vernon glanced at Jonah, who was eyeing Eddie like a rattler about to strike.

"Tell her to leave, Vern," Eddie said.

"Shut up, you son-of-a-bitch," Jonah said. "I don't know who you are, but we don't take orders from you." Jonah jerked his head forward as if he were going to pounce. Eddie clasped the ticket in both of his hands and held it up as if he were going to rip it. Jonah raised a palm to indicate he would remain in place.

Eddie said to Vernon, "Tell her, Vernon, unless you want me to explain to Mrs. Coyne about bank account manipulations and Heavenly Hiccup."

Vernon's eyes widened. From his reaction, Eddie knew that he had been correct about why he wanted to marry Carly.

"Vernon?" Carly asked. "What's he talking about?"

"Tell her," Eddie said.

Vernon took a deep breath and said softly, "You better go, Carly." He kissed her cheek. "I'll explain everything later."

Carly glanced at Jonah and Eddie, then back at Vernon for several moments. She said in a cold tone, "Don't bother," and started to leave.

Eddie stopped her. He held the ticket out. "This is yours. You dropped it."

She glanced at it and stared into his sunglasses as if she were trying to penetrate them. "Do I know you?"

Eddie lowered his cap and shook his head. "Take it, Mrs. Coyne." He again offered it to her. "It's yours."

"No. It was never mine. It was my husband's, but he's in no position to enjoy it."

"He would want you to have it."

"It's brought nothing but sorrow. I don't want it," Carly replied. "It's bad luck."

Eddie tried to stick it in her hand. "Please. I can't use it."

She waved him off and stepped away.

"Wait. There's one more thing."

She turned back and again stared into his shaded lens.

He studied her for a moment to cement her image in his soul. "Your husband would never cheat on you."

She again asked, "Are you sure I don't know you?"

He lowered his head to hide his identity. "No...no." The short pause between the twin words felt like an eternal chasm to Eddie—one filled with desire, heartache, and so, so much regret.

Maybe Carly sensed that because she replied in a gentle, but firm voice, "I never thought he did."

Eddie's throat caught and his eyes moistened. Before he could recover, Jonah leapt at him. Vernon did the same. Eddie pushed Carly away and yelled, "Run!"

She took off.

Eddie swung hard. He walloped Vernon in the side of the head. Vernon fell to the floor in a semi-conscious daze.

Jonah grabbed Eddie from behind. He brought the edge of his knife blade to the front of Eddie's throat, pressed it into his flesh and said, "You just made a date with the devil, friend."

"It wouldn't be the first time." Eddie glanced down and saw Jonah's hand tighten. He closed his eyes, realizing he was going to learn if a dead man could die again. The answer was cut short by a loud *wang chung*. Eddie popped his eyes open. Jonah crumbled into a heap beside him. Charles stood behind Jonah, breathing heavily and wielding Buddy Holly's guitar by the neck like it was an axe handle.

"Let's get the Strat back to the display," he said to Eddie. "And then let's get out of here."

"Just a second." Eddie opened his fist and examined the ticket lying in his palm. So many dreams, he thought. So many illusions. He started to tear it into shreds and stopped. He said to Charles, "Carly thinks that it's bad luck. What do you think?"

"Only you can answer that question."

"Yeah, I know." Eddie tucked it back in his pocket. "But I can't make up my mind."

Charles squeezed his shoulder. "We really have to go."

Eddie nodded. He inhaled deeply and followed Charles to the Buddy Holly exhibit. As Charles ducked beneath the velvet rope surrounding the wax figure, Eddie pointed to the guitar and said, "Uh, oh, you smeared Buddy's signature." Charles examined the smudged lettering where it had made contact with Jonah and wiped it away with the sleeve of his sweater. He slipped on his half-glasses, pulled out his pen and wrote the signature back into the guitar.

"I don't think that'll work."

"Why not?" Charles slipped the pen back in his pocket.

"Come on, the Hard Rock people hire experts. They'll know a fake when they see one."

"I suppose you're right." He sucked his bottom lip a moment before saying, "What do you know about Buddy Holly?"

"Not much. I saw that movie a few months ago on Netflix starring Gary Busey."

"People still listen to his music?"

"Oh, yeah. They say he influenced a lot of musicians. Even I know some of the words to 'Peggy Sue.'" Eddie warbled a bad rendition of the chorus.

Charles smiled. He replaced the guitar and turned to him. "Did you know his real name was Charles?"

Their eyes locked. Eddie studied the young, nerdy man. For the first time he took a close look at the wax figure wearing the horn-rims. He turned back to Charles, then to the wax figure again. It was grinning as if it had no care in the world other than to make music. Eddie removed the wax figure's glasses. He slipped off Charles' half-glasses, replaced them with the wax figure's horn-rims, and rearranged Charles' hair a bit. "Holy shit," Eddie muttered. "Ho-ly shit."

Charles smiled—nearly the same carefree grin that the wax figure sported.

"Damn, and you were worried if your life had been worth anything?"

Charles returned the horn-rims to the figure. "I believed in what I was doing, but if I hadn't my life may have taken another turn and it might not have ended so early. I had to know if it was worth it. Does that make me selfish?"

"No." Eddie handed him back his half-glasses. "It makes you human." Charles glanced up. Eddie got the impression that Charles was hoping the Jesses saw it that way, too. Charles again turned his attention to Eddie. He started to say something, but Eddie cut him off. "I know. We gotta go, right?" Eddie motioned to Jonah and Vernon, who were a few yards away. Jonah was stirring and Vernon was rubbing the side of his head and looking around half-dazed. Charles nodded. They raced toward the exit.

As they were leaving, Charles said to Eddie, "There's one last thing I have to do." He looked up and said, "Give us another fifteen seconds."

"What was that all about?" Eddie asked.

"Keep moving." They stepped from the room and down the corridor.

"Come on, Chuck. What's goin' on?"

Charles held a finger up: *wait for it.* As they entered the banquet hall, sirens and lights inside the exhibit room went off like fireworks. "That should keep our two friends busy for a while."

"I was wondering about the alarms," Eddie said. "I'm guessing the Jesses had something to do with keeping them at bay?"

Charles smiled.

Eddie saluted upward as security guards raced toward the exhibit.

Chapter Seventeen

Carly gripped Ben's hand like it was the last hope for civilization. They walked along the first floor of West Hialeah Central Hospital's short, cold passageway toward the elevator. She glanced down at him. "You okay, bubba?"

He looked up and nodded, but his round, brown eyes held a soft sadness that was beyond her reach. Her heart ached at the sight. She got it—God, did she get it. To say she hadn't slept well since the incident with Ed was an understatement. Bills were piling up and Bennie was too quiet. He went to school, he played his video games, he participated in his baseball games, he smiled at her jokes and he nibbled at his food. But he was too damn quiet. And now this shit with Vernon and those two other assholes at the reunion. Her head reeled. *I hate you, Eddie.* She teared up.

"Can I see Daddy?" Ben asked as they approached the elevator.

Carly forced her eyes to dry. She had one job, now. Be strong for Ben. "Honey, we've discussed this before. Daddy's... sleeping."

Ben's chin quivered.

"Want to press the button that brings the elevator?" She pointed to it.

He shook his head. "When is he going to wake up?"

Carly pressed the button, bent down and looked him in the eyes. She hugged him and felt wetness against the side of her neck. It took all of her will to keep her composure. She wiped his teardrop with her fingertip. He lowered his head on her shoulder.

She said, "Don't ever be afraid to cry, Bennie. No matter what happens. Promise me that."

He nodded. The elevator door opened. They entered and Carly pressed the third floor button. She wished with all of her being that she could release her own tears, but she had to stay strong—now, today, more than ever.

Eddie and Charles approached the delivery entrance in the rear of West Hialeah Central. It was a three-story, bland building. The city had three other hospitals. Those were multi-storied, modern conglomerates that served the vast majority of the population. West Hialeah Central was a relic from the early 1960s, when the city was a cow town. Eddie pictured the hospital as more of an old folks' home.

Before entering he glanced around for cameras. He didn't see any and exhaled in relief. If they had gone through the front entrance to see Lu he'd have had to show I.D. That was a no-no. The Jesses had specifically said he couldn't reveal who he was or what he was sent here for. If he was going to lose, it wasn't going to be on a technicality.

Eddie pushed open one of the side-by-side metal doors. "Listen, Charles, or is it Buddy?"

Charles smiled. "Chuck has a nice ring to it."

"Okay, Chuck. Listen, I want to thank—" He cut himself off. A janitor holding a mop stared at him from down the hall.

The man said, "¿Puedo ayudarle?"

Eddie cleared his throat. "I'm looking for someone to sign for a delivery of office supplies. Un hombre para el material de oficina."

The janitor studied him a few moments and nodded over his right shoulder.

Eddie waved, "Thanks," and headed with Charles in that direction. When they had cleared the man's sight Eddie searched around until he found an elevator. He pressed the call button. "Listen, Chuck, what I was trying to say back there was...well...I want to thank you for saving me from Jonah. I'm guessing you took a big chance with the Jesses on my behalf."

Charles shrugged it off, but Eddie could tell by the side-glance Charles had given him that he had been in real danger of pissing the Jesses off. If there was one thing Eddie had learned, it was the Jesses had the power to make the afterlife far worse than miserable.

The elevator arrived and the doors spread. They entered. Eddie pressed the second floor button. The elevator rose. Charles said, "Why did you nearly rip the ticket in half?"

"I was going to, but what stopped me was realizing I could use it to lure Jonah to Lu."

"That only explains why you didn't, not why you were going to."

Eddie thought a moment. "I suppose it's like when you saw that wax figure of yourself. You felt your life had meaning, right?"

Charles said nothing.

"I thought that ticket was important. A chance to prove myself. It was what gave meaning to my life." Eddie looked down at his feet for the right words. "Then when I saw Carly standing there, telling me the ticket was nothing but bad luck...and I couldn't even touch her." He locked eyes with Charles. "I recognized that the ticket meant nothing. That my life meant nothing."

The elevator stopped. The door parted. An orderly pushing an elderly man in a wheelchair entered. As Eddie and Charles exited, Charles said, "Eddie, there's more to what's going on than you realize."

"What is that supposed to mean?" Eddie asked.

The orderly said, "Beg your pardon?"

"He said, 'What is that supposed to mean?'" the elderly man replied as the door closed on them.

Eddie stood outside the elevator. He looked at Charles and waited.

"I can't say any more," Charles finally answered. "Other than remember the first rule."

"The first rule? What was that?"

Charles said nothing.

Eddie frowned. "Come on, Chuck, You have to give me more." Charles hesitated, then started to speak but Eddie held his hand up for him to stop. "Forgive me. I was wrong to put you in that position. If you could say anything else I know you would have."

Charles inclined his head. "How do you know that?"

Eddie clapped him on the back. "Because you're my friend." He smiled. "I'll figure it out on my own, don't worry." They headed up the hall toward Lu's room. Eddie was more than worried. He was scared out of his wits. Something didn't feel right. It was the same feeling he had had with Angel and Amelia—the one right before everything fell apart.

Carly and Ben stepped onto West Central Hospital's third floor, where the medical offices were located. They entered room 324. A small plaque screwed to the door read Dr. E. Rivera. The reception room looked exactly how Carly thought of Dr. Rivera: not rich, not poor, overworked and decent. It was pale brown with a coffee-colored rug. One wall was taken up with the door leading to the exam rooms. Next to the door was the opaque sliding glass that opened to Mayra, Dr. Rivera's receptionist. Another wall held a cream-colored magazine rack. The magazines were limp from overuse. Well above the rack was a flat-screen TV with a paper taped to it that said *Out of Order—sorry*. Six vinyl-upholstered chairs lined the other two corner-to-corner walls. The seats were empty. Carly wasn't surprised. She was the last appointment of the day.

Carly pressed the buzzer next to Mayra's glass. The door slid back. "I have a four o'clock appointment?"

"Mrs. Coyne." Mayra smiled and looked at Ben. "How are you, big guy?" She didn't wait for a reply before returning to Carly. "Come in, the doctor's waiting to see you in his office."

Carly said, "Can he stay in the waiting room?"

"Of course. I'll keep an eye on him."

Ben wrapped himself around Carly's hips. "No. I don't want you to go." He started to cry.

"Oh, honey, I'll only be a few minutes. I promise." She looked at Mayra with an expression that was somewhere between apologetic and helplessness.

Mayra left her desk and rushed to them. She gently pulled Ben away from her. "Come on, big guy." She guided him to the magazine rack. "I've got something that I bet you're going to love." She pulled out a magazine. "It's all about racing cars. It's really awesome." She glanced back at Carly, who was crying. Mayra nodded for her to go. Carly hesitated, then entered the door leading to the exam rooms and the doctor's office. The receptionist moved slightly to the right to block Ben's view of Carly in the event that he looked back.

Carly dried her tears as she passed the exam rooms—three total—to the end of the hall, where Doctor Rivera's office was. His door was partially open. Carly heard him plucking on his computer. She tapped on the door. Dr. Rivera immediately rose and swung the door open. He was a tall, slightly overweight man with soft cheeks and softer green eyes. He was dressed in a blue and white stripe chambray sport shirt and black Dockers. He shook Carly's hand with his two and ushered her to the chair facing his desk. "Carly, I can only imagine how difficult this is for you." Dr. Rivera squeezed her shoulder and returned to his seat.

Carly half-smiled. She had readied herself for this moment. Prayed on it. Spoke with her parents about it. Spoke with Frank about it. Repeated the mantras: *Life goes on. Things happen for a reason. Be strong for Ben. This is what Eddie would have wanted.* She had fostered her anger at Eddie for ripping apart their lives, for caring more about himself than for her and Bennie, for not giving a shit about their future, his job, even for not taking out the goddamn garbage. Still, she wasn't prepared.

Dr. Rivera handed her a form printed on yellow legal paper. While she studied it, he said, "Basically, the DNRO or Do Not Resuscitate Order states that no cardiopulmonary resuscitation will be attempted once life support is removed and the heart stops beating."

Carly nodded. It was a simple form. One meant to be understood by whoever signed it. "Do you have something to write with?"

Dr. Rivera slipped a retractable pen from his shirt pocket and handed it to her. Carly tapped the paper a couple of times with it, then looked at Dr. Rivera. He searched her eyes with kindness. "You have the right to rescind the order at any time for any reason."

She took a deep, shuttered breath and dabbed her eyes. "This is harder than I imagined."

Dr. Rivera passed her a box of tissues. "Would you like a moment alone?"

She nodded.

He stood, and before leaving said, "Five minutes?"

"Yes, thank you." After the door shut Carly tried to again harbor her angry feelings, but the spell had been broken. Her mind drifted to where it really wanted to be—the good thoughts. The way Eddie intuitively knew when to speak, listen, or give her space after a crap-filled day at the bank. How he swung Bennie onto his lap and tickled his sides. How he made love—gently, unhurriedly and lovingly. How un-alone he made her feel, even throughout the arguments. She hated the good thoughts because they reminded her that his gambling problem wasn't because he didn't love her or Ben, but because he didn't love something inside of himself. That made her guilty and sad that she couldn't supply whatever it was that he was missing. No, she craved the angry thoughts. They kept her strong. They kept her chin held up. These thoughts—the good ones—broke her and Bennie's hearts. Despite this, she knew in her soul that she wouldn't trade them for anything.

Dr. Rivera knocked lightly. "Okay?"

She firmed herself. "Yes. I'm ready."

Dr. Rivera entered and took his seat. "I want to again assure you that if I thought there was even the slightest odds of any change I wouldn't hesitate to let you know."

Even in this situation, Carly couldn't help but take note of the irony of Dr. Rivera's words. "Eddie played the odds nearly his entire life. I guess this time it's out of his hands."

Dr. Rivera smiled sympathetically.

Carly clicked the pen's push button several times—yes, no, yes, no, yes, no. She held her breath, clicked a final time and signed her name, trying not to think about what she was going to say to Ben.

Eddie and Charles entered Lu's room. The curtain surrounding her bed was still. The only sound inside it was the steady beat of the monitor. At the other bed, the one closest to the door, the closed curtain occasionally ruffled. The voices of two nurses could be heard inside it.

Eddie stopped for a moment to listen.

"So basically once he's moved, we shut the machines down and don't do anything?" one of the nurses said.

"That's it, Joyce," the other one said. "Nature does the rest."

"A shame," Joyce said. "He's too young to go."

Eddie whispered to Charles. "That poor shmo." Charles avoided his eyes.

There was a slight flutter of the curtain, then the unnamed nurse said, "Did you hear that Anna and Ken broke up?"

"No!" Joyce said. "When was this?"

Eddie motioned Charles onward to Lu's bed. Eddie and Charles slid through the curtain separation. Lu hadn't changed. She was unconscious, bone thin, pallid and hooked up to life support. Eddie quietly stepped to the bedside table that held her water pitcher and the framed photo. He studied the frail woman and wondered if he was doing the right thing. Of course I am, he concluded. Life is always better than death. If anyone knows that, it's me.

Eddie grabbed the photo in the hopes that he could use it to convince her to do what needed to be done. He looked at it and startled. Charles scrunched his brows at him. Eddie turned the picture toward Charles. "This is what I think it is, right?"

Charles examined the photo of the young couple leaning against an airplane hangar, kissing. "Yes," he replied. "It's the one you took of the mechanic, Al Meeyair and his secretary,

Louise Siskin, when they worked for Amelia Earhart."

Eddie was numb. "That means Lu is…"

"Louise." Charles took out his pen and notebook. "Time is crucial, Eddie. More than you can imagine."

Eddie held up his hand: he got it. Shit, did he get it. He turned to Lu. "Louise? Lu? It's Eddie."

Lu opened her eyes. Charles opened his pad and readied his pen.

"Is Jonah here?" she asked.

"Is your last name Meeyair?" Eddie said. "Was your husband named Al?"

"Is he here?" she repeated.

"Not yet, but I can have him here within the hour."

Lu raised her head. "How do I know you're telling the truth?"

Eddie could have told her how he had snapped a picture of the winning ticket on the cell phone he had purchased from CVS. How he had sent the image to Jonah. How the bastard immediately demanded to meet up, and how he had told Jonah he'd tell him the time and place when he was ready. But he kept it simple. "I explained to Jonah that there was something that he'd want to see and that I'd let him know where and when to meet us."

Lu contemplated this for a moment. "I trust you. You're one of God's angels, aren't you?"

"We're all God's angels." Eddie glanced at Charles. Charles flashed a smile but at the same time shook his head. He continued to write.

Eddie decided it was best to change the subject. He repeated his question to Lu. "Were you married to Al Meeyair?"

"Yes. Al was my husband."

Louise…Lu Meeyair, Eddie thought. *I'll be damned.*

"I miss him," she said. "I miss Al so much." Eddie looked at her and thought of Angel and of Amelia. He recognized the longing, the sadness in all of their voices. He recognized it in his own voice—in his own being.

"Time," Charles whispered. "It's nearly gone."

The words drifted to his ears like a mist and awakened him.

He had been staring at nothing. Eddie shook it off and said, "Are you ready, Lu?"

Her nostrils flared. "I don't know. I'm afraid."

"Of what?" Though he already knew the answer. She was frightened of living a life filled with pain. A life void of love. Not a life, Eddie thought glumly, a lonely existence.

"I…I don't know," Lu said.

He hated it, but he had to think of himself. This was his last big bet. *The one that counted the most.* He had no choice but to win it. He smiled with reassurance—the same untruthful, manipulative come-on that he had used his entire life. He held out his palm to her. "It's time."

Chapter Eighteen

Carly wiped her eyes and blew her nose. She tossed the tissue in a wastebasket, then squeezed her hands as if they were washrags and she was rinsing them. She stiffened her spine and opened the door leading into Dr. Rivera's waiting room. Mayra was seated with Ben, flipping the pages of a magazine they were looking at. They looked up at the same time. Mayra smiled sympathetically. Ben looked at Carly with probing eyes.

"We were trying to find pictures of horses, weren't we Ben?" Mayra patted his hand. Ben said nothing. His eyes remained on Carly.

Carly said with a forced smile, "Dr. Rivera said that Ben and I could use an exam room to speak together."

"Of course!" Mayra held Ben's hand and led him to Carly. "I have one reserved for special guests." She winked at Ben. "Hay pescados en las paredes. Follow me." She guided them to the second exam room and flipped on the light. Sure enough, as Mayra had said, there were fish on the walls: painted sawfish, snapper, marlin and bonito. As Carly and Ben entered, Mayra squeezed Carly's arm and whispered, "Take all the time you need." She quietly closed the door.

Other than the sea creatures painted on the walls, the exam room was the usual fare: an adjustable examination table, a wall-mounted blood pressure monitor, a shelf with tongue depressors and gauze pads, and a wheel-bottom swivel stool that the doctor usually occupied. Carly lifted Ben on the exam table and then took a seat on the swivel stool and faced him. She inhaled slowly and said, "Bennie, what I'm going to say isn't going to be easy."

His lower lip started to tremble.

God, she thought. *He already knows.* She nearly lost it, but caught herself. No, he knows something's wrong, but not *that.* "You're going to have to be brave." His eyes were so much like Eddie's. Not just the deep brown, but also the soft, curious, sad nature of them. Carly's throat clutched. Her empty heart longed for him and at the same time ached for her and Ben. "Can you be brave for me?"

Ben glanced at the fish on the walls, then at her. He nodded.

She left the stool and sat beside him on the exam table. "You know this is about Daddy, right?"

He nodded again. "Daddy's asleep."

"Yes…" She held his hand to her lap. "But Dr. Rivera and all the other doctors I've spoken with have said that Daddy isn't going to wake up. You see, when he fell and hit his head, it—"

"He's not waking up because he's mad at me," Ben whispered.

"Oh, God, no!" Carly hugged him to her. "Never, Bennie. Daddy loves you." She sat Ben on the swivel chair, kneeled beside him and forced her eyes to remain dry. "God wants Daddy to be in heaven with Him. That's why he's not waking up."

"How do you know?"

"Because I do," Carly replied.

"I want him to wake up."

"So do I, honey, but it's not going to happen."

Ben's eyes watered.

"I'm going to say goodbye to Daddy and wish him wonderful dreams. I know he'd want you to tell him that, too. How about it?"

Ben stared at his feet dangling a few inches above the floor, but said nothing.

Carly feathered his cheek. "What do you say, bubba? Wanna tell Daddy how much we love him and how much we're going to miss him?" Carly's voice trembled. She smiled at Ben even as she welled up.

Ben kept his eyes on his shoes. He nodded.

Carly pressed her cheek to Ben's and felt the warmth of his tears mingle with hers.

Lu inched her hand toward Eddie's. It looked cool, clammy. Devoid of a healthy blood flow, Eddie thought. He shot a look at Charles, who was writing. Eddie looked up and spoke in his head to the Jesses: *Well, I guess little old Eddie Coyne is going to win the bet and beat every one of you. But tell me, what kind of bastards are you? You know that Jonah's a thug who'll only bring Lu nothing but trouble. He'll milk her for whatever she's got and then leave her to rot in the wind.*

People entered the room. Charles stopped writing and looked at Eddie, who continued to stare upward and speak to the Jesses. Charles peeped through the curtain. The two nurses they had earlier heard speaking entered the first curtained bed. They slid the curtains back and wheeled the bed with Eddie's dying body on it out of the room. Charles' eyebrows rose. He started to say something to Eddie, but nearly gagged. He tried to speak again, but nothing came. Charles glanced up and nodded to the Jesses as if to say, I got the message; he's not supposed to know.

Eddie noticed none of this. He was still absorbed in his one-way conversation with the Jesses: *I get it. You're going to try and lay Lu's misfortune on me. No way. You're the house and you make the house rules. I abide by them. I only hope that whoever you answer to takes notice of what you're doing.*

Charles tapped Eddie's shoulder. Eddie turned to him. Charles pointed with his pen to Eddie's wristwatch. A dagger-like pain pierced Charles' hand and he quickly went back to writing. But Eddie had seen and understood—time was running out. He said, "Are you ready, Lu?" as his fingertips touched hers.

Joyce and the nameless nurse gently led Carly and Ben to Eddie. They had moved him to a private room next door to Lu's. He was limp, motionless. He looked as if he had shrunk beneath the sheets. His face was gaunt and his cheeks sallow. Purple rings lined the bottom of his closed eyes. Except for the vital signs monitor that marked Eddie's faint, steady heart rhythm, the rest of the equipment was gone. Even with the beep...beep...beep, it was eerily silent. Carly shivered and squeezed Ben's hand. He was staring at Eddie.

"We won't be long," Carly said to the nurses. She glanced at Ben's homemade Get Well card and the family picture that used to be in Ed's office. Both rested upright on the nightstand at the head of his bed.

"Take all the time you need." Joyce motioned to the other nurse that it was time for them to leave. "If you need anything, press the red button on the remote." They left the door partially open.

Carly said to Ben, "Sweetheart, do you want me to close my ears or wait outside while you speak with Daddy?"

Ben shook his head. Carly released his hand and stepped back. Ben inched forward and wrapped his six-year-old hand around Eddie's index finger. "Daddy, I love you." He glanced at Carly and went on. "I'm sorry for getting you mad. Have sweet dreams and don't let the bed bugs bite." He kissed Eddie's hand. Carly stood behind him, kissed the top of Ben's head and laid her hands on his shoulders. They remained like that for many moments as they watched Eddie. Finally, Ben looked up at her. "Mommy, do you want me to leave while you talk to Daddy?"

"No, baby. We're a family. We stay together." She motioned to the chair near the foot of the bed. "But you can sit down if you want." Ben squeezed her hand and sat in the seat.

Carly stroked Eddie's face. She was glad to see his IV and ventilator had been removed. He looked more restful. Carly thought, as she had done so many times before, *we could have had a marvelous life—we could have grown old together. We could have played with our grandchildren.* She looked at Ben. He was studying her. Carly smiled at him and turned back to Eddie. *I don't put the blame entirely on you, but whatever comfort you received from gambling I hope it was worth it. I really do.*

Eddie's monitor beeps slowed. Carly's heartbeat raced. She glanced at Ben. He didn't seem to notice. She whispered in Eddie's ear, "Sleep. Peace. Know that Bennie and I never stopped loving you." Carly kissed his forehead and added, "Te quiero." She pulled a tissue from a container on the nightstand, wiped her eyes and glanced at the vitals monitor. The beep, beep, beeps continued to slow and the jagged waves accompanying them had nearly levelled. Carly picked up the remote and quietly said to Ben, "I'm going to call the nurses, bubba. It's time for us to leave." She pressed the red button.

Eddie watched Lu's hand slide over his. He could see the anticipation and fear in her eyes, but he tried to ignore the latter. *She wants to see Jonah. He's her grandson, for Christ's sake. She raised him. She deserves to have closure.* He shot a look at Charles. He had one eye on his writing and the other on Eddie and Lu.

"Eddie, I'm frightened," Lu said as their palms touched.

"Just say the words, Lu, and I'll bring Jonah to you. I promise." He gripped her hand and smiled that wonderful smile—the one that got him into and out of so much trouble. The one that he was growing to hate. He looked up and said inside his mind to the Jesses, *I'm saving her soul. I mean suicide's a sin, right? Right?*

"Hurry, Eddie," Charles said.

"Okay," Eddie said with irritation.

"Okay?" Lu replied, unaware of Charles' presence. "Do you want me to say the words now?"

Eddie stared at her. Lu's eyes were wide and bulging. They watched him like a frightened dog would. The same thoughts continued to swirl through his brain like a fan: Jonah would bring nothing but heartache to her, he'd sponge everything that he could, leave her to languish and by the time she died, she would have been robbed of the little peace of mind that she had now.

He studied the picture on her nightstand that he had taken all those decades ago. Al and Lu were nice people. They were—*no.* He wasn't going to go there. They weren't his concern. The Jesses laid out the rules. It was his job to follow them or end up in the gutter, and he wasn't going to do that. He was going to win the bet.

"There're no more chances, Eddie." Charles' voice was firm. "You must do it now if you want to li—" He groaned, dropped his notepad and blinked in and out of reality. "Follow your—" Charles screamed in agony, then he was gone.

Eddie stared at the place where Charles had stood. Fear overcame him. He turned to Lu. "Say the words. Say them!"

She hesitated.

"Come on, Lu. Say 'I accept life' and Jonah will come. I swear to you." Eddie thought, fuck the Jesses, fuck Jonah, fuck Angel and Amelia. *This is about saving my soul. Everyone else had had their own opportunities. I deserve mine.* His eyes watered. He pictured Carly and Ben and how he had let them down. *I should have been a better man for them.* Remorse filled him.

"I trust you," Lu said. "I accept—"

Eddie withdrew his hand before she could finish. He stared at his empty palm in disbelief. From the next room over, the prolonged whine of the vitals monitor crept into Lu's room. Eddie sat on the side of the bed and sobbed. He felt himself sink. He had blown it again. Even worse, he had done it on purpose. He reached into his pocket and rubbed the birthday card he was supposed to give to Ben. He wanted to throw up. He cupped his face in his hands and felt his head fall through them. Shocked, he looked at his hands. They were gone. His feet blinked and disappeared. "Eddie?" Lu said. "What's happening?"

He watched Lu's breathing stop, her eyes dim and go blank— he watched her die. In the back of his mind Eddie heard the patter of nurses racing down the hall. His legs and arms flickered. His senses wavered in and out like a badly tuned radio. He was going to his fate—his hell. He prayed to God that he had the courage to stand it. Before he could finish his petition, he vanished.

Chapter Nineteen

First there was nothing. Then there was the blinking in and out. The poorly tuned radio that was Eddie's senses slowly subsided. He was back with the Jesses in the gray room. The six gray-hooded figures were seated at the table with the empty chair at the end. Their eyes were locked on his. Scattered about the floor were part of his penance, the overflowing trashcans. Eddie looked to the side and his heart fell—Charles was no longer there.

The Jesses stared in silence for a long while. Finally, they said in their singular-multi voice, "It appears you backed out from winning the bet. May we ask why?"

"It's the same question I've been asking myself," Eddie said. "I wish I knew."

"Why?" It was more of a demand than a question.

Eddie started to flash the phony smile he used to manipulate others, but stopped. Instead, he sucked in his lips and rubbed his mouth for several seconds. He thought back on the photo he had taken of Al and Louise in 1937. Even then he could tell that Lu was a good woman, that Al was a good man. Still, it didn't answer the question. *Why?* He glanced at the Jesses. Their faces were zeroed in on him. He remembered that his last thought before pulling his hand away was of Carly and Ben. He had been a lousy husband, a lousy dad. He had blown it with them, but it didn't explain why he did what he did.

"We're waiting," the Jesses said.

Eddie raised his palm and nodded. He stared at nothing and

thought of Charles, who had at least found the answer to his one burning question—that his short life had made a difference. Time was running out and this would be his last statement before entering his own private hell of reliving an endless loop of his son's funeral while at the same time shoveling shit. He wanted to get it right. He dug deep in his heart and searched. Searched so hard that sweat formed on his brow.

"Eddie, the moment has arrived."

Eddie glanced at the Jesses and continued to lose himself in his thoughts. The closest thing he could come to an answer was more like a smear of emotions—longing for his family, wanting to be more than he ever was, shame over those he had lied to and stole from, and sorrow for letting so many people down. Most of all he felt regret for wasting his life. He wanted to express that to the Jesses, but he knew it was too complicated and too muddled.

Eddie turned his mind to the last piece of advice Charles had given him: *follow rule number one.* He wasn't sure then what Charles had meant, but now he had an inkling. Eddie settled his gaze on the Jesses. He cleared his throat. Their heads tilted forward. Eddie took a deep breath, held it a second and said, "I followed my gut."

The Jesses looked at each. They turned back to him. "Exactly what does that mean?"

"Well, I guess you could say that it means...it means that it seemed like the right thing to do. Stupid, I know, but..." He shrugged.

They studied him for a long while without moving. Eddie attempted to read their faces. It wasn't what he expected. There was no glee in their eyes from beating him at his own game. They were sober, dark orbs. *Were they angry?* Eddie didn't think so. *What would they have to be angry about? They won.* No, he thought, their look was more like one of disappointment. *Had he let them down, too?*

The Jesses grunted, leaned back in their chairs and shook their heads at him.

Eddie's stomach pitched. He had screwed up royally. He

trembled at what was coming—an eternity of depression and misery.

The Jesses leaned in once more. They crooked their elbows on the tabletop and clasped their hands below their chins. "Are you sure you don't want to change your reason for losing your bet? Something more...convincing?"

Eddie grinned. *They're giving me another chance!* He nearly blurted out something about pulling his hand back because of an uncertainty in the house rules, but stopped himself. *Why are they doing this?* He furrowed his brow, but they remained poker-faced. He sensed he was standing on the edge of a precipice. Only he was blind and not sure which direction he faced—toward the chasm below or toward the land. He had no choice except to step, but he was scared. The Jesses' faces were focused on his. His knees weakened. He thought again of what Charles had told him: *rule number one.* Eddie concentrated on his breathing to calm himself and to convince himself that for better or worse he had to live with the decision he had made to pull his hand back. He looked the Jesses squarely in the eyes. "All I can tell you is the truth. My gut said it was the right thing to do."

The Jesses slammed their fists on the table.

Eddie flinched. In his mind he was tumbling down a bottomless cliff.

They raised their palms and said, "Apologies."

Eddie was breathing too hard to reply.

The Jesses waited a few moments until the color returned to Eddie's face. "Are you okay?"

Eddie wanted to scream that no, he wasn't okay. He was frightened out of his fuckin' head. "Yes."

The Jesses glanced at each other. "You see, Eddie. We have a dilemma." They took a deep breath. "Technically, you haven't died yet."

Dumfounded, Eddie stared open-mouthed at them as the words sunk in.

"You were scheduled to expire at the same instant the bet ended and nothing should have changed that, but thanks to a

Louis K Lowy

'Buddy' of yours prodding you to hurry along, things took an unexpected direction."

"Chuck? Is he okay?" The words left his mouth as if someone else had spoken them.

They frowned. "Don't worry about him. He's gotten what he deserved."

Eddie felt like he was riding a tilt-a-whirl. Questions spun in his head too quick to catch. Was he really alive? What about Carly and Ben? What about Charles? What about Lu? *Was he alive?*

Reading the thousand questions on his face, the Jesses said, "Not so fast. You're dying like your friend Louise was, or rather, did."

"She's a good woman," Eddie replied. "She doesn't deserve to go to—you know." He motioned toward the ground.

"Not that it's any concern of yours, but—" They squeezed their hands together. A vision filled Eddie's head. Louise was sitting in a kitchen that, from the looks of the appliances, was from the 1940s. She was young—a few years older from the time Eddie had snapped the picture of her and Al kissing. She was cradling a baby. Eddie didn't know how, but he knew it was her son. Al walked in wearing his grimy overalls. He went to the refrigerator, grabbed a beer and a can opener, sat beside them and kissed her and the baby. Louise smiled. It was a radiant, joyful expression. The Jesses loosened their grip. The image vanished. Relieved that she had been promoted, Eddie couldn't help but smile, too.

Then something crossed his mind. "You told me that suicide was a sin."

"For the most part it is, but Louise didn't die of her own hand. She died of natural causes."

"But she wanted to die."

"Correct, but wanting and doing are two separate things."

"You bastards. You fucked with me." The second the words came out of his mouth Eddie realized he had messed up.

The Jesses' eyes hardened. They squeezed their hands together. Eddie felt as if he was being compressed into himself, pinched between the jaws of a bench vise. His breaths were short and painful. His eyes burnt around the sockets, as if they were going to pop from his head. He crumbled to his knees. "Sorry... Sorry..." The Jesses relaxed their grip. The pressure eased.

The Jesses stood over their table in order to get a better view of him. "And no," they said in a single, placid voice, "we didn't screw with you. We merely did what you claim to do—manipulate the odds."

Eddie shuddered, caught again by his own words. "I deserved that." He struggled to his feet.

The Jesses again took their seats. They placed their hands in front of themselves on the tabletop and watched Eddie. He had the impression they were waiting for him to make the next move, so he said, "Am I dead, or not?"

"You're close enough."

Eddie slipped his hand in his pocket to feel the winning ticket and Ben's birthday card. He was afraid to ask the question. He waited a second longer to keep the hopeful feeling inside of him, then swallowed hard. "Is there a chance I could...not die?" He braced himself for the wrong answer.

The Jesses tapped their fingers on the table for several moments. "That may not be up to you. It's simply another matter of letting nature take its course...then there's the issue of the bet."

Eddie groaned. "I want to contest the results."

"Upon what grounds?"

"Upon the grounds that I assumed I was going to die."

"That wasn't an assumption, it was a fact. Had there been no interference it would have remained so."

"But there was. I demand that the results be voided."

Eddie was taken aback. He had expected them to be pissed at his boldness, but they had been clearly pleased—at least for a second. He thought about it. If the bet was cancelled, the Jesses would be in total control again—dictating new terms and making adjustments from what they'd learned about him. Inside his head he heard Charles repeat his mantra: follow your gut. "On second thought," Eddie replied. "I should hear what you have to say about it."

"It's a complicated issue, but..." The Jesses wiggled the corners of their lips in contemplation. "I suppose the newest member of our governing body has the right to be included in this. Ms. Place, please send in Number Seven."

A gray-hooded figure entered through a sudden opening in the rear wall, and stood behind the empty seat. The figure's hands were folded in the front and the person's head was lowered. The figure faced the Jesses. They stood. Number Seven's head bowed. The others nodded and retook their seats. Number Seven took a place at the previously unoccupied chair and along with the other Jesses folded both hands on the tabletop. Number Seven's head remained bowed.

The others kept their eyes on Eddie. No one moved.

Eddie didn't like this. It felt ominous, and ominous couldn't be good for him.

Number Seven raised his head and winked at Eddie. The others rolled their eyes in exasperation.

Eddie grinned. It was Charles. Eddie squeezed his chin twice and gave Charles a double thumbs up. Charles nodded ever so slightly in return and clasped hands with the other Jesses. His features metamorphosed into the timeless, ambiguous, blended skin tones and eye shapes that defined the others. The seven Jesses released hands and huddled together.

Eddie's heart raced. He tried to make sense of what was going on. He fingered Ben's birthday card and prayed that he would have the chance to give it to him and maybe…maybe touch Carly again. At the same time he didn't want to hope too much. The thought of losing them a second time would be more than he could bear.

After what seemed an eternity to Eddie, the Jesses turned to him. "Here's where things stand. You clearly lost the first round of the bet. Ditto for the second part. Regarding the third and final round…" Eddie held his breath. "You lost that one, too, but as one of us pointed out…" Eddie glanced at Number Seven. The slightest of smiles showed on Number Seven's face. "In losing, you chose to put another's needs above your own."

The pulse in Eddie's neck and temples throbbed so hard he was sure his veins were going to burst.

"Because you decided to go against your own self-interest and do, as you put it, 'the right thing' the scale has tipped in your favor, as it did for our newest colleague." The others glanced at Number Seven. "By prodding you along, he also made the choice to put aside a burning desire to know his self-worth. Therefore..." Eddie felt a hot, joyous prickle surge through his cheeks and spine "...you are hereby declared the winner."

Eddie whooped, jumped up and down, and pumped his fists in the air. He kissed the winning ticket and Ben's birthday card, and started the first steps of a victory jig, but stopped. The Jesses—including Number Seven—stared at him somberly. He understood and was embarrassed. This wasn't a horse race. This was something sacred. It was about living and dying. "I'm sorry. That was wrong of me."

The Jesses nodded. They remained silent. Eddie sensed they were again waiting for him to speak. He held his breath for several seconds and gingerly asked, "Do I get my life back?"

"You won your bet with us by going against the house rules."

"But they weren't the real rules, were they?"

"No," the Jesses replied. "The actual rules were a test of your character. We couldn't tell you that because it would defeat the purpose."

Eddie nodded. It sounded unfair, but he knew that it had to have been done that way.

"There's only one actual rule, Eddie: How you choose. That's all it boils down to. Right and wrong choices. Nothing more."

Eddie understood. He had made so many bad decisions in the past. No more. He wasn't going to be perfect, not by a long shot, but if he were given a second opportunity he'd try with all of his soul to be the best man he could.

He repeated his question regarding his life.

The Jesses said, "This one isn't our call." They looked upward, somewhere beyond their chamber ceiling. Eddie tried to read Number Seven's face, but his vision was where the others were. In that infinitely long, short moment Eddie could do nothing but listen to the blood throb in his temples and pray that he would be given a second chance.

The Jesses focused their attention back on Eddie. They took a heavy breath and said with mock regret, "It's a shame that you won't be around to clean up the garbage."

Eddie clenched his fist and whispered, "Yes!" but then something crossed his mind. "What about after effects?"

The Jesses tilted their chins, not understanding the question.

"I took a really bad tumble down the escalator. Broken some bones?"

The Jesses nodded.

"And I've been bedridden, right?"

"Yes, for four months."

"Will my body and mind function like they did before my injuries?"

The Jesses looked at each other as if to decipher their thoughts on the subject before turning back to Eddie. "You're going to need physical therapy, and you'll probably be able to forecast rain by the ache in your lumbar region, but if you're earnest about healing you should be fine. As for your mind, unfortunately for you what you have is what you get." A warm smile crossed the Jesses' lips. Eddie returned it with a nod and his own smile.

Their faces sobered. "Use your gift wisely, Eddie. It won't come again."

"You can bet, I mean, count on it. My betting days are over."

"Time will tell," they said.

He knew they were right. It wasn't going to be easy, but he was going to give it his all—God, was he going to.

The Jesses rapped their right knuckles on the table three times and said, "If there are no objections—" they raised their brows at Eddie. He shook his head. "—then we declare the case of Edward Brian Coyne officially closed...for now." They stood. "Are you ready to return?"

Eddie smiled, then held up a finger. He glanced around the room. "I know you have final say, but I was thinking. If you need someone to clean up the mess outside and around here I have a recommendation."

"We're all ears."

"There are two men I'd like to recommend for the position.

They'd do a whale of a job. I'd be happy to pass along their names."

"We're way ahead of you on that one," the Jesses said. "Isn't that right, Ms. Place?"

"Indeed," came her sharp reply through the wall.

Eddie looked at Number Seven and for an instant he was Charles. The two smiled. Charles faded back into a Jesse. As he glanced around a final time, Eddie disappeared.

Chapter Twenty

The prolonged, high-pitched shrill of the vitals monitor played in Eddie's hospital room like an eternal, sour violin. Joyce and the nameless nurse rushed in. Carly stood next to Eddie, staring numbly at his closed eyelids and the whiskered, thin gray face that surrounded them. Ben tightened his arms around Carly's hips and buried his face in her waist. Joyce went to the machine. The nameless nurse gently grabbed Ben and led him away. He screamed and tried to pull himself back. Carly said in a flat, trembling voice, "Go, Bennie. Go with her. I'll be out in a minute."

"No!" Ben screamed.

Joyce began to power down the monitor, but stopped. "Would you like to go out, too, Mrs. Coyne, while we clean your husband up?"

Carly looked at Joyce as if she were speaking a foreign language. Ben broke the nurse's grip, ran to Carly and again clamped himself to her waist. Joyce shot a desperate look at the nurse, who said, "Mrs. Coyne, let's you and I and Ben walk into the hall."

Carly nodded as if in a daze. Ben cried. She lifted him, tucked his head on her shoulder and followed the nameless nurse to the corridor. Joyce glanced at Eddie and touched the monitor's shutdown button. Before she applied enough pressure to activate it, the eternal wail ended. A single beep replaced it. Joyce winced. Another beep sounded. And then another and another until it was steady. Joyce turned to the nameless nurse and said, "Fabienne?"

Fabienne had stopped at the doorway on the first beep. She stared at Joyce. Carly stood beside Fabienne. Her eyes were locked on Eddie. Ben forced himself from her arms, jumped down and ran to Eddie's bedside. Eddie opened his eyes. Joyce gulped. Fabienne made the sign of the cross. Carly pressed her palm against her chest and continued to stare at him.

Eddie tried to sit up, but fell back. His back, neck and ribs were on fire. His head was foggy and his muscles felt as if they'd been through a meat grinder. He heard someone wailing and had the idea that it was Ben. He thought he saw Carly, and tried to call her, but could only hack. Despite that, Carly took a tentative step forward.

Joyce signaled Fabienne to call the doctor. Fabienne stared a second longer and sped down the hall.

Ben grabbed Eddie's fingers and said through sobs, "Daddy, I'm sorry I was bad. I'll never be bad again. I promise."

Eddie's head started to clear. He squeezed Ben's hand and tried to speak again, but all that came out was a dry croak. He coughed several times, rubbed his throat and said in a barely audible rasp, "I'm to blame, Bennie, not you. Sorry. So sorry."

Carly ran to Eddie. "Is it really you?"

Eddie cried.

She kissed him.

He motioned to Ben and tapped the side of his bed. Carly lifted Ben and placed him next to Eddie. She sat beside them and smiled, and then laughed. Eddie laughed, despite the pain it brought to his chest. Ben nestled himself in Eddie's side and let his tears flow.

Dr. Rivera flipped a page on Eddie's medical chart. He glanced at Eddie and shook his head. Eddie winked at Ben. He was seated on Carly's lap in one of the two chairs in Eddie's hospital room. Eddie's brother, Frank, occupied the other one. "You're one for the books," the doctor said as he tucked the chart beneath his arm.

"When can I go home?" Eddie's voice was scratchy, his bones still ached and his muscles were flabby, but in the month since his miracle—as it was referred to by the staff—he was also clean-shaven, shuffling short distances with the aid of a walker and nearly weaned off of soft foods.

"I'd like to keep you here another week to be on the safe side."

Eddie looked at Carly. She nodded.

"Okay, but if—"

Dr. Rivera cut him off with a lift of his hand. "If nothing pops up out of the ordinary, I'll be the first one to kick you out the door." He patted Ben on the shoulder and said to Carly and Frank before departing. "He's one lucky man."

Eddie thought of Charles, Angel, Amelia and Lu. *Yes, I am a lucky man.* He said to Frank, "I lied to you the day I fell...I went to the track and won big."

Frank glanced at Carly. "I know."

"I'm paying you back with the winnings. I'm also setting up a college fund not only for Ben, but for Liza and Dan."

"You only have to cover what I loaned you."

"No, I don't," Eddie said. "My debt goes a lot deeper than that. I haven't been a very good brother."

"There is no ticket." Carly lowered her eyes. "I...I didn't want it."

"I know," Eddie said. "It was bad luck, but I'm—we're—going to give it another chance and turn it into something good."

"You don't understand," Carly said. "I threw it away."

"If it should return—"

"I wouldn't take it," Carly said. "It'll only bring misery."

"Maybe this is a conversation for another time," Frank said. "When you two are alone and a little more...acclimated."

Carly nodded to Frank. "I'm sorry."

Eddie thought about it. What Carly had said was true. The ticket represented what he was before. Not what he hoped to be. "You're right. The ticket's not good for us—for me." Eddie smiled. "Who knows, maybe a charity that has something to do with music or flying will receive an anonymous envelope in the mail with the ticket inside. Or maybe a teen suicide hotline,"

Eddie added. "To prevent love-sick kids from ending up like Romeo and Juliet."

"Romeo and Juliet? Since when are you into Shakespeare?" Frank raised his brows and glanced at Carly. She was stroking Ben's hair and staring at Eddie with an uncertain look in her eyes.

"I'm okay. Really. I'm just thinking out loud." Besides mailing the ticket to a charity, Eddie knew there was one other thing he had to do. "I'm joining Gamblers Anonymous." He held his hand up to prevent them from speaking. "I know you've both heard it a thousand times. I swear this is different."

"Should I call the doctor?" Frank whispered to Carly.

"I'm fine. Maybe not a hundred percent fine, but I was given a second chance for a reason and I'm going to work my ass off not to blow it." Eddie looked Carly in the eyes. "I mean it, sweetheart."

The corners of Carly's mouth tightened. She pressed her palms to Ben's ears and said, "Bennie and me have suffered through your broken promises too many times. I don't even know if you love us, Eddie," before lowering her hands.

Eddie was stunned. He didn't blame her for not believing he was going to stop gambling, but to question his love? He started to protest, but stopped. He would prove her wrong. Not with words or manipulative smiles, but with choices. If he learned anything, it was that there were only two kinds: right and wrong ones. He was determined to choose the former.

"How about I take Ben for a soda while you two talk?" Frank held out his hand to Ben.

"Hold on. I forgot the most important thing of all." Eddie smiled at Ben. "Open the closet, would you champ?" Ben glanced at Carly. She studied Eddie a moment, then nodded. He slipped down from her lap, walked to the small closet across from the foot of the bed and opened the door. "Reach inside my coat pocket. There's something inside there for you." Eddie smiled at Carly. Her expression remained flat.

Ben dipped his hand inside and pulled out the birthday card. "You didn't forget! Look, Mommy!" He raced to her. "What does it say?" She slipped the card from the envelope. On the cover was a